CONDUCT UNBECOMING

A C.T. FERGUSON CRIME NOVEL

THE C.T. FERGUSON MYSTERIES
BOOK 15

TOM FOWLER

For Lisa and Isabel, who help me make sure my conduct is usually good enough.

And to the memory of my cousin Chuck, who left us way too soon. His love and aptitude for lacrosse led me to make it C.T.'s sport of choice. I wish I'd gotten to have a few more conversations with him in recent years . . . about subjects other than sports played with sticks. May he rest in peace.

CHAPTER 1

SHE WAS KILLING the vibes in the room.

"Bad week?" I asked my secretary after the first sip of coffee she made a few minutes ago. It was shortly after nine on a pleasant Baltimore fall morning—one made even more so by the lingering aroma of fresh java.

"Eh," T.J. replied.

"Uh-oh. A monosyllabic answer. What happened?"

"Nothing." She stared into her mug. T.J. was young, pretty, and tall, and these three attributes—along with the good wage I paid her—should have carried her to a fine weekend.

"I'm a professional detective," I said. "My vast sleuthing powers tell me you're not being honest with me."

She flashed a wan smile. "Don't worry about it."

"I see you more often than my wife most weeks. I kind of have to worry about it."

"You'll think it's silly."

"Are we gossiping about boys? Should I get my nails done first?"

T.J. rolled her eyes, but a real smile played on her lips. "Have you ever even had a manicure?"

"Once or twice," I said, "and you're not getting out of this by turning around and asking me questions."

"Fine, fine." She put up her hands. "What did you do for your twenty-first birthday?"

"Jetted off to Hawaii." I kicked my feet up on my desk. Keeping the surface free of everything except a keyboard and three monitors made this easy. "Where better to sip a mai tai than the beach?"

She frowned. "Seriously?"

"God, no. I went to a bar with some friends. My parents tried to plan some elaborate *soirée*, and I wanted nothing to do with it. A few weeks later, Rich came back for the holidays, so he and my dad took me out for a more sedate round two." My older cousin—then in the army—now toiled away as a Homicide lieutenant with the Baltimore Police. Thanks to the commendations he'd earned from my legwork over the years, I should never have to pay for a drink in Rich's company. A thought hit me—one I probably should have considered several minutes prior. "Wait . . . did you just turn twenty-one?"

"A couple weeks ago, yeah," T.J. said.

"Why didn't you tell me?"

"You sign my paychecks. You should know my birthday."

Like most self-respecting small business owners, I outsourced payroll, but she had me on this point regardless. "Still. I would have gotten you something."

"You took a chance on me and gave me a job. That's enough."

"I'm a good gifter," I said a little defensively.

"You mean Gloria is a good gifter," T.J. said, "and you're smart enough to nod and go along with what she suggests."

"Sometimes. I manage pretty well on my own." My wife had more talent for picking out the presents, however, and did far better when it came to wrapping them. "Anyway, what did you do for the big day?"

T.J. sighed and rested her chin on her fist. "That's just it. Not much."

"So?"

"So I missed out on lots of things over the years." Before coming to work for me about a year ago, T.J. lived a dangerous life as a prostitute starting in her teens. My friend Melinda's foundation plucked her off the streets and got her an education. She'd learned the skills needed to work in an office and recently completed her GED. T.J.'s placement marked the first for Melinda's Nightlight Foundation. "I wanted my twenty-first to be cool, you know?"

"Who went with you?"

"Melinda, Amy, and a couple girls you don't know."

I chuckled. "Let me guess . . . Melinda didn't want to let you drink."

"She did." T.J. affected a schoolmarmish voice. "But not to excess."

"So you didn't get blitzed," I said. "One of the things I learned later in my twenties is how extremely overrated getting drunk is." T.J. didn't say anything. "You may have missed a few milestones along the way, but you celebrated your twenty-first with people who care about you. Not getting hammered means you can remember it. All in all, I'd call it a win."

"I guess."

"Besides, wasn't this a couple weeks ago? Why so glum today?"

"Like I told you, you'll think it's silly."

"As long as I don't need a manicure to hear it," I said, "hit me."

"Fine," T.J. said. "One of the girls I invited just had a birthday. Her twenty-second, I think. She didn't even invite me."

"Rude," I admitted. "I wouldn't read too much into it. She might like you but not count you as an inner-circle friend."

"I guess."

"This is enough self-pity for a Friday. Don't you have some accounts to balance?"

"I might if you'd accepted more than one case last week," T.J. said.

"I was busy contemplating turning thirty-three soon."

"Now who's throwing a pity party? Besides, your birthday isn't until December." Before I could offer a clever retort, she added, "See? I know when yours is."

"You're just angling for a better gift now," I said.

T.J. smiled and remained quiet. My phone vibrated in my pocket. Gloria texted.

> Hey. Want to talk about something tonight.
> Don't worry. I think it'll be a good thing.

> You found your copy of the Kama Sutra?

> Never lost it, stud. ;-) See you tonight.

I felt color in my cheeks as I slipped my phone away. "If she's sexting you," T.J. said, "I *really* don't want to hear about it."

"I wouldn't tell you," I said. "Seems like you've had enough problems for one day."

———

As I walked through the front door of Gloria's Brooklandville house, the smell of cooking Italian food filled my nostrils.

I'd known my wife for almost five years now and found her to be many wonderful things. A cook would never be counted among them.

Being a professional and sometimes well-paid sleuth, I followed my nose to the kitchen. "Honey, I'm home!" I called crossing polished hardwood floors.

"In the kitchen," Gloria answered in a sing-song voice.

I walked through the door. Gloria's home could swallow my Federal Hill rowhouse three times over, and this has always been most apparent in the kitchen. Much of my first floor would fit between its four walls—especially considering the fourth extended into the living area. She enjoyed way more counter space than I did, not to mention a huge island, an oven which could cook Thanksgiving dinner for the whole neighborhood, and stainless steel appliances. In my less proud moments, I would admit to some degree of envy.

Gloria stood near the oven, her chestnut hair pulled back in a ponytail, an unmarred white apron tied around her waist. She gave me a dazzling smile. "I'm making a meal to celebrate."

Before asking the occasion, I wanted to puzzle out how much heavy lifting she assigned the word "making." I scanned the countertops. "No phone or tablet open to TikTok," I said. The trash can was empty. "No ingredients or take-out bags in here. Your apron is as spotless as the granite." I approached my wife who looked amused at my powers of observation. I leaned close to her and made a show of sniffing her face. "You don't smell like you've been cooking." Then, I kissed her cheek and trailed my lips to her neck.

Her fingers nestled in my hair, and she let out a sigh before answering. "Easy, tiger. I need to check the lasagna."

"A dish I've never seen you make." She opened the door and pulled out a metallic tray. Gloria owned a lot of glass cookware, some of which I'd used to bake pasta in the past. This lent the appearance of originating from one of the good Italian restaurants in the area. "I now have a theory."

"Let's hear it." She smelled the lasagna. Sauce bubbled around golden noodles and perfectly browned cheese. This dish looked like a chef made it.

"You went somewhere nearby, bought a very nice lasagna, and disposed of most of the evidence before I got here."

She put up her hands and grinned. "Guilty as charged."

"Another successful case," I said. "People actually pay me to do this stuff."

"Incredible."

"Thanks."

She smirked and added a tray of garlic knots to the stove. "Now that you've solved the mystery of the lasagna's origins, do you want to know the occasion?"

"Absolutely."

"You're not going to walk around like Columbo and try to figure it out?"

"First of all," I said, "I dress way better than he did." I opened the fridge, pulled out an imported beer, and used the bottle opener stuck on the side—one of my few additions to the place—to pop the top. "Second, I'd rather save my showing off for later."

Color came to Gloria's cheeks as she took her phone from the pocket of her form-hugging jeans. "I got an email from Claire Stevenson at the *Baltimore Sun*. She wants to do a profile on me and my company."

"Fantastic!"

Gloria beamed. "It's really a stroke of good luck. We've gotten off to a fast start with almost no press. I hadn't even hired a PR person yet. Now, I may not need to." She walked up to me and wrapped me in a tight hug. "I couldn't have done it without you."

I set the longneck on the counter so I could put both arms around my wife. "This is your accomplishment. Be proud of it."

"I am," she said.

"I'm only glad my occasional advice and years as a walking, talking, selfless inspiration made a difference," I said.

Gloria swatted me on the shoulder. "Maybe you can claim your share of the credit in Claire's story."

"No." I shook my head. "It's your company. Your tale to tell, and your success to trumpet. I'd rather deal with the press on my own terms."

"You don't want to be interviewed?" Gloria asked.

"I don't see why I would need to be. 'Local woman launches successful fundraising company' is a good enough headline. 'Let's meet the handsome and brilliant husband who inspired her' seems like something from thirty years ago."

Gloria flexed her bicep, and her years of tennis training showed. "I guess I should stick to the strong feminist angle."

"Seems like the way for the piece to go," I said. I was happy for Gloria's success, but my PI instincts kicked in. Reporters often didn't color inside the agreed-upon lines. Early in my career, I made a habit of being friendly with the media to drum up new clients. When my business model became more traditional, I stopped. Keeping my picture out of the paper remained my goal in any interaction with the press.

"Great." She took the garlic knots out of the oven, and I smelled their signature spice. "There's a salad in the fridge. Let's eat."

I opened the fridge door and grabbed the plastic tray of salad. It was a bright and colorful blend of ingredients. "I guess we should get used to carrying in once you're famous."

"One of us needs our photo in the paper," Gloria said.

"Might as well be you. You're prettier."

"Must have been hard for you to admit."

"It was," I said.

CHAPTER 2

CLANGS AND WHIRRS from below provided the soundtrack to my Monday morning.

My office took up the second floor above a car repair shop in Fells Point. Thanks to a recent oil spill on the main level, we enjoyed some interesting aromas coming through the boards. The rent has always been reasonable, and Manny the owner allowed me to stay as a tenant when it probably would have been easier to give me the boot and find someone with a less stressful job. Even two shooting incidents in the parking lot didn't dissuade him—though he did make me pay for a new wall to protect cars left outside.

"You must be deep in concentration," T.J. said.

"I'm deep in many ways."

"What are you working on?"

I stared at my three-monitor setup. While much of my hacking knowledge came from experimentation, I actually had a background—and master's degree—in computer science. Artificial intelligence tools promised huge advances in code generation. I tested one such instance. It could certainly write circles around me in terms of speed, but I needed to make sure the quality remained high. "AI code generation," I said. "It's worth looking into."

T.J. nodded. "Coffee's done."

"Thank goodness." I poured myself a fresh cup and returned to my desk. No sooner did I get settled than the door opened and my cousin Rich walked in. He was six years and change older than me, which meant he neared forty. Despite this, Rich remained in good shape. At six feet, he was a couple inches shorter, but he also outweighed me by fifteen pounds or so. His blue suit and white shirt looked like he put them on at the dry cleaner's this morning. "If you didn't have a girlfriend already, I'd say you were trying to make the list of Baltimore's most eligible homicide lieutenants."

"Pretty short list," he said.

"Guarantees you a good spot."

"Coffee fresh?"

"Thanks to me, yes," T.J. said.

"It's the real reason I keep her around," I said. She grinned and flipped me the bird while Rich poured himself a cup.

My cousin dropped onto a guest chair with his paper cup of hot java while T.J. busied herself at her desk. "Ransomware cleanup is more or less done," he said. "Things are back to normal." A few months ago, Baltimore suffered a major malware attack. Against my better judgment, I went undercover in the hacking group responsible and tried to keep the damage to a minimum without exposing my real reasons for being there. In the end, it all more or less worked out, though there was some obvious fallout.

"You're welcome," I offered.

Rich chuckled. "I don't recall thanking you. You did a lot early on, sure, but plenty of other people have gotten us back to a mostly normal state since. I didn't see you working weekends in the data center."

"I was busy doing anything else."

"Sure." He sipped some hot java.

"Is there a reason you stopped by?"

"You know the sludge in our pots. Can't a man just want some good coffee?"

"He can," I said. "Such a man also has about two dozen places to stop and get it between his house and his precinct. My office is outside those criteria."

"Maybe it's because you're so fucking cheery," Rich said. When I didn't say anything, he added, "I haven't seen you in a while is all." He craned his neck to try and get a look at my screens. "What are you working on, anyway?"

"Checking out how well AI can write code."

"Better than you?"

"Faster, certainly," I said. "The jury is still out on quality, though I think I can give it some tweaks to help."

Rich stood and swigged the remaining coffee in his cup, tossing it in the wastebasket near my desk. "I have to get to work. Let's catch up later."

"Sure." He left. T.J. wandered to my desk and sat on its corner.

"Strange," she said.

"Yeah. I wonder if he came in here wanting to talk about something."

"You think he didn't because I was here?"

I shook my head. "Doubt it. He knows how much I don't like getting up early. If the door is unlocked before nine, I'm sure he expects you to be here."

"Mm." She fell silent, though I felt her eyes on me.

"What is it?"

"He's right. You don't seem very chipper this morning."

They were probably on to something. I took a swig of my

now-warm coffee and plastered a fake smile on my face. T.J. rolled her eyes. "Some reporter wants to do a puff piece about Gloria's fundraising company," I said.

"I'm a little surprised it hasn't happened before now," T.J. said. "Besides, isn't this a good thing?"

"Yes. I'm trying not to lose sight of the benefits for her."

"But . . .?"

"But reporters don't always stick to what they say they're going to cover. One detour into her personal life, and suddenly, I become part of the story."

T.J. crossed her arms. "Didn't you tell me you used to deal with the press on the regular?"

"In my previous business model, yes. The key is it was always on my own terms. Gloria and her company should be the story. I don't need to be a part of it, and I don't really want my picture in the paper."

She nodded. "You've had to go undercover twice in the last year."

"Yes. It becomes harder when someone can snap a picture of you, do a reverse image search, and learn you're a PI."

"I wouldn't worry about it," T.J. said. "You called it a puff piece. The focus will probably be Gloria and her company. If the reporter veers into the personal, I'm sure your very intelligent wife can manage the situation."

"She could."

"Whether you get a plug or not, people will figure out the kind of work you do. Lots of them already have. We don't have any trouble attracting clients."

"True." I looked up from my screen. "When did you become so wise?"

"When I turned twenty-one," T.J. said.

———

Someone knocked on the door shortly after we ate lunch.

"You expecting anyone?" I asked T.J.

"No," she said as she stood and walked across the carpeted floor. "No appointments for today." She opened the door. Two women—one in her forties and the other around my secretary's age—stepped inside and looked around. With no major holiday coming up soon, the walls were bare and the office looked pretty spartan. The yawning doorway let in more sounds from the shop below including a few choice words in Spanish. Our guests paid it no mind. "Can we help you?"

"I hope so," the older one said. She was short with dark hair cut to her shoulder. Her eyes looked red and puffy. The younger woman stood several inches taller but otherwise bore a strong resemblance, so I presumed them to be mother and daughter. They both wore black from head to toe. "No one else is."

"Why don't you have a seat?" T.J. directed them to the two guest chairs in front of my desk. They both sat. My secretary grabbed her own and wheeled it to join us, notebook and pen ready in her free hand.

"What can we do for you?" I said.

"Do you watch the news?" the mother asked.

I shrugged. "If it's on, but I generally don't go out of my way to."

"Did you hear about the county councilman found dead?"

"I did." The story earned pretty regular coverage, but I only caught part of a segment about it.

When the mom bowed her head and couldn't continue, her daughter stepped up. "He was Raymond Ellicott," she said.

"My Ray," her mother added in a teary whisper.

"I'm his daughter Paula." The lingering redness in Paula's eyes told me she'd been crying recently, but she managed to hold it together here. "My mother is Susan."

"We're sorry for your loss," I said as T.J. pushed a square box of tissues toward the pair.

They both bobbed their heads before Paula spoke. "Like my mom said, my dad was a councilman in Baltimore County. This was his fourth term. Everyone liked him." She paused, closed her eyes tightly, and covered her mouth with a fist. One person—for whatever reason—hated her father enough to kill him, and Paula realized it when she mentioned everyone liking him. "He wasn't even fifty yet."

T.J. slipped her phone from a pocket in her jeans, typed something, and her eyes widened at the result. She tilted the device toward me so I could see it. The headline *COUN-CILMAN FOUND DEAD AND NAKED WITH MYSTERY WOMAN* leapt off the screen. After my first case dealt with issues of infidelity, I resolved never to work one again. It's cost me business but saved me aggravation. Still, I didn't want to hammer two grieving women with an unwritten agency rule at the moment. "I know this is tough," I said, "but we need to hear what happened from you, not the press."

The ladies spent a couple minutes composing themselves. T.J. and I gave them the time they needed. Eventually, Susan dabbed at her eyes with a fresh tissue and took a slow, deep breath. "I'm certain that you hear all kinds of things about people. I know for a fact my husband wasn't with some woman at a seedy hotel. Well, he was in the end, but . . . he didn't go there to sleep with her or anything. This is all a setup."

"I'm not sure how things are in the county," I said, "but our city council isn't known for being especially productive or contro-versial. It seems like a local rep would need to be on the wrong side of something major to make any enemies at all, let alone the kind who want to kill someone."

Susan inclined her head. "Raymond's job never seemed to

stress him out. The council is technically part-time even though it didn't always feel like it."

"Did he work another job?" T.J. asked.

"Self-employed," his widow said. "The schedule was unpredictable sometimes, so it would have been hard to have something normal. Raymond went to law school, so he did simple things like contract review."

"Any clients you can think of who would want to kill him?"

"No. I don't even think he's done any legal work for a few months. He certainly never represented a criminal or anything. If Raymond ever went to court, it was in his official capacity for the county."

T.J. scribbled notes. "I have to ask," I said, "do you know who the woman in the room was?"

Susan's face pinched, and she turned away. "We do now," Paula said. "We never knew her. I have a hard time believing my dad did, either."

"Why?" T.J. wanted to know. "Was she shady?"

"No. She was a teacher at some fancy private school in another district. My dad wouldn't have been her representative. I don't think they were aware of each other."

"We talked to the widower," Susan added. "Against our lawyer's advice, but we needed to know. He seems as surprised as we are."

If we took this case, I would want to chat with the man, too. We couldn't represent him, but I also didn't want to assume Raymond Ellicott had been the real target of the murder just because he was a politician. It made him more likely to draw someone's ire than a teacher, but assholes killed people for all sorts of ridiculous reasons. "You mentioned no one was helping you. Is the county working the case?"

Susan snorted. "If you call it working. They're investigating. Have been for a week, and they have nothing."

"Homicide investigations can take a fair bit of time," I said.

"So they've told me."

"Do you know who the detective in charge is?"

"Gonzalez," Susan said. "A sergeant, I think. I didn't catch his first name."

"I know him." Gonzalez seemed to catch most of the investigations I worked in the county. Like Rich, he tended to be dubious on my methods until someone handed him a citation for closing a particularly difficult case. "I'll talk to him."

"Are you going to help us?" Paula asked.

"Let me see what's out there," I said. "I want to know what information they have and what they don't before I commit."

"We'd be really grateful for anything you can do," Susan said. Her voice cracked as she fought through a fresh wave of tears. "We buried poor Ray a couple days ago. I wanted to clear his name first, but that didn't happen."

"We'll be in touch," I told them. The Ellicott ladies gave T.J. their relevant information and left.

"We're going to take the case, right?" my secretary asked. "They're devastated."

"I sympathize, but I also want to know what we might be getting ourselves into. Let's see the article you found." T.J. emailed the link to me, and we read it on one of my much larger screens. It must have been from an early edition because the female victim was never identified by name. Raymond Ellicott and an unknown woman were found naked in a bed together, both shot in the head. The hotel seemed like the kind of place which rented rooms by the hour.

A later piece identified the dead lady as teacher Marcy Russell and went on to say there was no DNA or other evidence to suggest the two victims went to the hotel for a tryst. Both write-ups were short on comments from county police. "You gonna talk to Gonzalez?" T.J. said.

"I think I have to."
"Does he like you?"
"At least as much as Rich does," I said.
"You're in trouble, then," she said.

CHAPTER 3

RATHER THAN SURPRISE someone I didn't work with terribly often, I called Gonzalez from the car as I headed toward I-83 North. Background noise told me he was also driving. "I must be in trouble if you're calling," he said.

"I've been trying to reach you concerning your vehicle's extended warranty."

He chuckled. "I get the feeling this is about to be even worse. What can I do for you?"

"The Raymond Ellicott murder," I said.

"What's your interest in it?"

"His widow and daughter came to see me today. They're not happy with the pace of your investigation."

Gonzalez's sigh hissed through the speakers of my Audi S4. "I told them these things take time. Cops on TV can solve a murder in a few days because it's a show. Plenty different in the real world."

"I tried to tell them the same thing," I said as I waited to make a right onto President Street. After a few blocks, it would become I-83, which I could then take to the Baltimore Beltway. Gonzalez's precinct in Towson would be around fifteen minutes away.

"And?"

"I think I stopped them from sullying your good name any further. They're still not happy, though, so they want me to look into it."

"What did you tell them?"

"I wanted to see what you had first," I said. "And what you didn't have."

"This is a red ball," Gonzalez said. "It always is when a councilman gets killed."

"This isn't ancient Rome. I didn't think it would happen very often."

"It's the third in about a decade. Not a pattern or anything, but the county wants to take care of its own."

"I get it. What about the woman?"

"We can't find a connection between them," Gonzalez said. "If there is one, they took care to bury it really well."

"You consider her as the target?" I asked.

Gonzalez snorted. "She's a teacher at some ritzy school. Popular, too. Got some award last year. No one's gunning for her."

"Considering she got shot, it seems someone was in fact gunning for her."

"All right, smartass." I grinned at the annoyance in his voice. "I guess it's possible some parent didn't like a grade she gave their kid, but you don't stage a sex scene in a no-tell hotel and shoot two people over your kid's fucking report card."

"It does seem a bit extreme," I admitted.

"Look, we dug into her, also," Gonzalez said. "She's a murder victim, too, even if being on the council makes Ellicott the more likely target. She's clean. Probably can't work at her fancy school without a regular background check."

"So they're both saints."

"Pretty close."

"Must make for a shallow suspect pool."

"Now, you see the problem we're having," he said. "Victims' families never understand. They just want whoever killed their loved one to get arrested."

"It happens on *Law and Order*," I pointed out.

"You're not exactly helping."

A horn blared through the speakers loud enough to make me wince as I neared the merge onto the Beltway. "It sounds like you're driving."

"Must be why you're a highly paid private investigator," he said.

"You headed back to your office?"

"I'll be there in about fifteen minutes."

"Good. I'm headed your way. See you soon."

"Can't wait," he said before hanging up. I doubted the sincerity of his final words.

———

I knew I would be a few minutes early, so after parking the S4, I ventured down the street for coffee. Like any good cop, Gonzalez consumed more than his share of the stuff, so I walked back with a cup for him, too. As I moved through the sliding glass doors, I smelled the scent of old coffee and felt the weight of institutional apathy. A generation ago, the off-white walls would have been yellowed by cigarette smoke. Several of the men and women milling about were probably leftovers from a bygone era . . . and maybe even kept ashtrays in a desk drawer for those late evening shifts when everyone else had already packed it in.

The desk sergeant barely glanced up from his phone as I entered. Either he remembered me or assessed me as non-threatening. I chose to believe the former. Once in the bullpen, I navigated the maze of desks to Gonzalez's office to find the man sitting behind his desk. It was somewhere in the middle of the spectrum between neat and chaotic. He frowned until I held up the cup. Gonzalez's expression brightened, and he waved me in. I handed him his hot beverage, and he took a first sip without a word of thanks. "You're welcome," I said.

"Thanks. Anything's better than what's in the pots here."

I dropped onto a fabric task chair which could have also served as a chiropractic torture device. "The same is true in the city. What is it about cops and the coffee they brew?"

"We're too consumed by our quest for justice to make a good pot."

I snorted. "Even your marketing people wouldn't spit out such a line."

"Fine." He took another sip. "The family came to see you, huh?"

"They did."

"They figure we shoulda solved the case and arrested someone by now, I'm sure."

"They do."

"We've had this damn thing for a week," Gonzalez said. "Haven't found anything we can take action on."

"Then, I guess you need a fresh pair of eyes," I suggested. "Especially ones connected to a brilliant and incisive brain."

"We got smart people here, too, you know."

"I know." I sipped my coffee to cover the smirk. "Can you email me everything? We're in the twenty-first century, after all."

"Sure. You got a dot-gov email address?"

"I must have left it in the pocket of my jeans," I said.

"Looks like we'll need to do this the old-fashioned way," Gonzalez said with a grin. "Hope you brought a wheelbarrow."

"You really can't just send it to me?"

"New rules on sharing information."

"How many defense lawyers have dot-gov emails?"

"Outside of public defenders, none," Gonzalez said. "The

difference is keeping shit from the defense is illegal. Rules of discovery and all. You're not a lawyer."

"Thank goodness," I said. "Would you believe me if I said I left my J.D. diploma in my jeans, too?"

"Not likely."

I sighed. "This is why people don't like dealing with the government. Even the MVA lets me do things online."

"Handing over notes from a murder investigation is a little more important than renewing your registration."

"I'll be able to tell for certain once I see what you have."

"I'm gonna print what we have. You might as well get comfy."

"In *this* chair?" I asked. Gonzalez snickered and tapped some keys. Somewhere outside his office, a printer whirred to life and began dispensing pages. "Maybe I'll file a complaint with the environmental people. They care about dead trees."

"Yeah, but no one cares about their department," Gonzalez said. "Seriously, this is gonna be a few minutes. We got a new machine out there. Forty pages a minute or some shit, but you'll still be sitting there a while."

"Lucky me." At least I had my coffee. I checked email on my phone, found nothing of interest, and then checked again. I'd already played Wordle. I considered rediscovering my interest in Sudoku. A couple minutes later, I was back to solving number grids.

After four puzzles of increasing difficulty, Gonzalez said, "I think it's done. Someone needed to load more paper. Not sure how the photos turned out."

"Do I really need a wheelbarrow?"

"No, but a box or two might be nice. Don't worry, I had someone fetch a couple from the supply room. When's the last time you bought a ream of paper?"

"Never," I said.

"You're going to owe the good people of Baltimore County one after this."

"Tell them to put it on my tab." I stood and headed for the door. "Thanks for the notes."

"You won't be thanking me in a minute," Gonzalez said. "If anything new crops up, I'll email you a way to access it." I gave a thumbs up, left his office, and found the multifunction copier-printer in an unused cubicle about fifteen feet away. The massive volume of printouts got dumped into two Office Depot boxes. Some were placed vertically like they would be in a file box, and other stacks lay flat. Whoever dumped everything didn't even try to organize all the printouts.

I perched one cardboard container atop the other and made sure to walk by Gonzalez's office on my way toward the door. "You're a prick," I said as I moved past.

"Told you," he called after me.

———

As I drove back toward Baltimore, I called Gloria. "You heading out early?" she asked.

"The opposite, actually. We might be taking a case, and I just got about a million pages of notes from Gonzalez."

"I guess you'll be going over things with T.J. for a while."

"Probably," I said. "We'll order dinner at the office. Come by if you want . . . and if you don't mind cheery talk of a double homicide."

"Tempting as that sounds, I think I'll heat up some of the lasagna I toiled over for hours yesterday."

"Uh-huh. Your loss."

"Did Gonzalez really give you a ton of papers?" Gloria said.

"Yeah. There's some supposed new rule, and he can only

email official documents to defense lawyers and anyone with a dot-gov address. I'm oh for two there."

"And relieved on both counts."

"You know it," I said.

"I think you'll have a very full evening. Try not to work too late."

"I'll do my best. Love you."

"Love you, too," she said and ended the call. As I-83 South terminated at President Street, I dialed T.J.

"You really needed to go in person?" she said.

"I did." I recounted the tale of woe regarding email addresses, vague new rules, and the strength required to heft two boxes of paper back to the car.

"Guess you got your workout for the day. Sure you can make it up the stairs?"

"Keep being a smartass, and I'll make you carry a box," I said.

"He really gave you that much paper?"

"Told me it was all the notes, pictures, and everything. I figured it would be quite a lot, but I didn't expect the BCPD's information sharing policies to date from the 'eighties."

"Were you even alive in the 'eighties?" she asked.

"For a little less than a month, yes." I turned onto Fleet Street. "I'm a few minutes out. Let's get all this up to the office and try to organize it. It might take a while, but it'll save us time later. Then, we'll have a better idea what we're in for."

"You're buying dinner."

"I figured I would be."

"See you in a few, then." T.J. ended the call. I pulled into the lot three minutes later. As expected, I needed to carry both boxes from my trunk up the metal steps to the office. I did it in one trip and flexed my biceps afterward. T.J. rolled her eyes.

CHAPTER 4

"JESUS CHRIST. How do they get any work done?"

I found T.J.'s question quite prescient as we sorted through many types of papers. We'd cleared both our desktops, the small round table off to the side—my first dining space in a college dorm—and the top of the bookcase which normally held the coffee maker. For now, the brew machine sat on the floor. If we damaged it, I vowed to send Gonzalez the bill. He could cry about the taxpayers all he wanted. My caffeine fix paused for no man.

We made separate piles for officers' and detectives' notes, plus medical examiner observations, crime scene photos, forensic reports from the seedy hotel, and a catch-all stack for the rest. The pictures were obviously gruesome, but their color and brutality looked muted via a combination of regular paper and speed-focused printer. Pop music I'd never heard before played from T.J.'s laptop speakers. When I asked her who the singer was, she told me Alex Anne. My expression must have conveyed how unhelpful her response was. "Never heard of her?"

"No," I admitted.

"Feeling old?"

"Starting to."

"Don't you turn thirty-three soon?"

"A couple months."

"Jesus died at thirty-three. I read it in one of my GED books."

I chuckled. "I'll keep an eye out for Roman soldiers."

The process would have gone faster if the contents of the boxes had been in any semblance of order. Instead, T.J. and I had to move around the office and dance past each other with ridiculous regularity just to get pages in the right sequences. "I'm getting hungry," she said at one point when we had about half a cardboard container to go.

"Let's finish the box and order something." I glanced at my watch. It was about quarter to six. If we did this right, it wouldn't even be a super late evening. "We can look at the pictures before the food gets here."

"Yeah." T.J. grinned. "Don't want you getting sick when you see blood."

"I was thinking of your delicate constitution," I told her.

"Not much about me is delicate."

I didn't answer. She was right and didn't need my contributions, confirmations, or barbs. T.J. lived a rough life, and I only knew some of the details of it. She was tall, pretty enough to get someone's attention, and athletic enough to learn to defend herself—for which I knew she spent time practicing. Working for me also dropped her into what can sometimes be a dangerous occupation even when not out in the field. She'd been shot at with me twice already.

There wasn't much room left to be delicate.

I grabbed another stack. This one went a little faster. Through good fortune, a bunch of consecutive pages held notes by detectives. I grouped the remaining few. After another twenty minutes, we'd finished. T.J. chugged water from her stainless steel refillable bottle. "Who knew sorting printouts would make me thirsty?"

"If we got cases like this all the time, I wouldn't need to run so many miles a week," I said.

T.J. picked up the pile of photos. "It's weird. They're naked in bed together, but the family says he didn't know her."

"She was a teacher, so what was she doing there with a man she'd never met?"

"They could have swiped right on each other."

I shrugged. "Both were married. It's possible, I guess, but it doesn't strike me as likely. They would both need to be unhappy, on the same dating or hookup app, match with each other, and then signal interest. It's a lot of steps."

"Happens every day," my secretary said. "Believe me, men who are unhappy in their marriages seek outlets all the time."

"I'm sure they do." I tapped one picture which focused on the female victim. Her eyes were closed, though I wouldn't describe her expression in death as peaceful. "It sounds like you're presuming he was the target."

"He was a politician."

I snorted. "A county councilman. I'm sure he did a good job, but let's not pretend he's a committee chair in the United States Senate. His gig isn't even full time."

"He could still have pissed the wrong person off," T.J. said. "More easily than a teacher could. Even if some parent wanted to kill her because she gave their kid an F, what's Ellicott have to do with that?"

"Nothing." I kept looking at the picture. One family wanted to hire us, but there were two victims here. "I guess I have trouble buying this woman as a random piece of collateral damage. Was she in the wrong place at the wrong time and got snatched up by the hit squad who shot Ellicott? It doesn't seem anymore likely than the hookup app scenario." I shook my head. "Both are too coincidental."

"We need to eat." T.J. rubbed the stomach area of her light-weight sweater. "I'm hungry, and you're not making sense."

"Great. What's the number for Don't Presume He Was the Sole Target Pizza?"

"I think it's one-eight hundred-go-to-hell."

"Call them, then," I said with a chuckle. "Make sure you get pepperoni."

———

We instead got two pies and a salad from Brick Oven Pizza a few minutes away on Broadway. Despite the walkable distance, I drove to maximize the odds of keeping them hot. Parking near the restaurant was easy on a random Monday evening in October. The manager waved as I left. T.J. and I probably ordered from here twice a week. Back at the office, I shook the salad to mix its ingredients and portioned it out into two paper bowls.

After we ate our greens under the pretense of being healthy, my assistant and I started in on the pizzas. T.J. grabbed two slices of the mushroom and onion, and I took one veggie and one pepperoni. We ate at her desk. A space to the side almost exactly the size of my plate served as my dining area. T.J. went back and forth between eating, typing, and wiping her fingers. "This woman was a teacher at some ritzy school," T.J. said.

"What's the school?"

"The Sterner Academy?" She shrugged. "Never heard of it. Sounds like the kind of place dedicated to cranking out the future assholes of America."

"Not everyone who gets a private education is an asshole," I pointed out.

She put on an artificially sweet smile. "Present company excepted."

"Thanks."

"You heard of the place?"

"Yeah," I said. "I think it covers kindergarten through high school . . . or it did years ago when my parents were looking at it."

"Still does." She turned her screen so I could see it better. The school's homepage practically screamed at us. *THE STERNER ACADEMY. Fostering Futures, Crafting Leaders.* The marketing budget continued on other pages whose titles included *Where Brilliance Begins, A Legacy of Excellence, The Gold Standard in Learning,* and my personal favorite . . . *Bespoke Education for Future Elites.* Whoever devised these knew their target market.

"I didn't go anywhere quite so full of itself," I said. "Still, I learned from quite a few good teachers. We can't draw meaningful conclusions about people because they work in a private school versus public."

"I guess." T.J. pivoted her laptop back, wiped her hands again, and typed some more. "Huh," she said a moment later. "Our victim won an award recently. Maryland Private Educator of the Year."

"Impressive."

"It is. I think it also means someone was unlikely to target her. Not only was she a teacher, but she was a very good one."

"It may not be all she was," I said. "Only one family has reached out to us, so we owe them our best work. They're obviously going to focus on their dead relative, but it doesn't mean we need to. All avenues have to be on the table, and this includes the one where the councilman wasn't the sole target."

"Her husband teaches there, too," T.J. said a few seconds later. "He does high school. She worked in elementary." She looked at me. "Did you always go to private school?"

"No. I went public for a while."

"What happened."

"Someone bullied me in fifth grade. My parents did two

things. My mother insisted I go private, and my father enrolled me in my first martial arts class."

"Seems like one was more effective," T.J. said. "You can't impress goons with your education."

"I wouldn't trade either one. I ended up getting a really good education. Besides, if things unfolded differently back then, I might not be sitting here today."

T.J. shuddered. "I wouldn't want to work for a graduate of the Sterner Academy."

"Thankfully, you don't have to," I said. "Let's get the Ellicott family to sign a contract. We're going to keep investigating both victims, though. Wherever it goes."

"Wherever it goes," my assistant agreed.

CHAPTER 5

T.J. WALKED INTO HER APARTMENT. Her stomach was full of pizza and salad, and her head was packed with the images from the hotel crime scene. She'd spent way too much time in seedy motels, much of it with men she'd meet only once. The places would rent rooms by the hour and had wink-wink arrangements with local pimps. Sometimes, they even kept a block of rooms available. There was more money in a series of short rentals than one for a single night.

She shook her head to clear those memories. They would always be a part of her, and she wished they stayed dormant. Cases like this tended to dredge them up. T.J. loved her job. Working for C.T. and getting justice for people were great, and they were worth the occasional uncomfortable recollection bubbling to the surface.

Before leaving the office, T.J. emailed a standard contract to the Ellicott family. She'd done most of the work of its development . . . with a little input from her boss. It amazed her how C.T. survived without these basic things before she walked through the door. The family could send the document back in the morning, and then, the investigation would be fully underway. This evening's prep was billable, of course. Someone needed to foot the bill for sifting through thousands of pages of poorly organized documents.

T.J. kept coming back to the pictures. The lack of photo paper made them look a little dull, but they still told the story. Someone wanted police to believe Raymond Ellicott and Marcy Russell knew each other. Intimately. Forensic and DNA tests would conclude they didn't have sex despite being found naked in bed together. The medical examiner's report suggested both people were stripped and staged post-mortem. By then of course, the headlines, articles, and opinion pieces had already been written, and local TV news ran the "were they lovers?" angle into the ground. National outlets even picked up on the story and emphasized the lascivious angle.

The real story wouldn't be front-page news.

T.J. opened the fridge and freezer looking for some dessert. She found a new carton of vanilla ice cream. When her hand settled on it, she got an image of one of the photos. Marcy Russell, one arm draped across the naked body of Raymond Ellicott, lay in the bed with a portion of her skull missing. T.J. grimaced, took her hand off the carton, and closed the door. She walked back into the living room and dropped onto her couch.

The apartment was small but suited her. It had two major things going for it: she could afford it, and the place was pretty nice. She lived in a building called The 501. Many of her fellow tenants were students at the nearby University of Baltimore—their rent probably covered by their parents at least in part. Several she met were surprised she wasn't in college and that she worked for a private investigator. The one-bedroom unit fit her needs perfectly. There was even enough room to hang a heavy bag. Upgrading some of her furniture would be the next step.

"What were you doing there?" she wondered aloud. She thought of Marcy Russell and shook her head. C.T. insisting the councilman might not have been the only target rubbed off on her. It made sense. The odds of Marcy Russell being a random victim in something like this were small. The woman was a decorated teacher in a fancy private school—a job she shared with her husband. Ritzy places like the Sterner Academy were part of C.T.'s world. They might as well not have existed in T.J.'s.

She took out her phone and conducted a little research on the place. The Sterner Academy charged eye-watering prices even for kindergarten, but they also had a waiting list for prospective students. Baltimore County lagged well behind Howard and Montgomery for wealth in Maryland, but clearly, many families were doing well. Some of them even sent their kids to places like the Sterner Academy.

Was the school involved somehow? Any place which billed tens of thousands of dollars for learning to count and read couldn't be considered wholesome. "What are you hiding?" she whispered to a picture of the school's main hall. This was the kind of place C.T. would understand and be able to move around in. Gloria, too . . . and Melinda. She grew up in a privileged household before her life went off the rails.

Maybe she could offer a little insight.

––––––––

"The Sterner Academy?" Melinda chuckled. "Wow. I dated a boy from there when I was fifteen."

"I'd never even heard of the place," T.J. said. "This . . . isn't my world, Melinda. I don't know it. I've never moved in these circles."

"It's overrated. Lots of assholes and people who are really impressed with themselves. Usually for the wrong reasons. Believe me, you haven't missed much."

T.J. felt like she'd missed plenty. Not about moving in rich circles but involving life in general. Her home life had never been great, and it cratered when she was fifteen. Not long after that, she ran away from home and ended up working for some very shady people doing things she now regretted. "I can hear you overthinking this," Melinda said when T.J. fell silent. "Don't. Treat this like any other case. Now, what's going on with it apart from some fancy school?"

"Well, the teacher from there and a councilman were found together dead in a hotel bed. Both shot. There's no indication they knew each other."

"Good grief. Sometimes, I wish you didn't get to see man's inhumanity to man as a regular part of the job."

"It's all right," T.J. said. "We're doing valuable work. It's just . . . the seedy venue, getting found with a stranger. It's the kind of shit I used to have nightmares about."

"I think we all did," Melinda said, her voice taking on a soothing tone. Her job running a foundation rescuing girls from the streets forced her to wear various hats—counselor often among them. While most shrinks only talked from theory and whatever they'd learned, Melinda spent years walking the streets before she got her life back in order. Girls trusted her because of this. The cred certainly helped when she approached T.J. two years ago.

"Let's talk about something different," T.J. said. "How's Amy doing?"

"Really well, actually." Amy and T.J. worked together for a pimp named Weasel Boy. When T.J. got out, Amy—operating under her street name of Velvet—stayed in the life. The two had run into each other a couple months ago. Amy got mixed up with the wrong people, and T.J. recommended her to Melinda. "We've got her studying social media management. She has a little experience there, so I think she'll be a natural, and it's certainly something small businesses could use. Like you, she's also studying for her GED. She should take the test soon."

"Good. I'll give her some pointers if she needs them." T.J. sighed. She remembered passing the exam. Her prep work made it easy, but the feeling of accomplishment when she held the certificate in her hand stuck with her. Despite a spotty and incomplete school history, T.J. actually liked learning, and she enjoyed a job that allowed her to indulge her natural curiosity. "Thanks, Melinda. I know I get a little bit in my own head sometimes."

"It's fine," Melinda said. "There's a whirlwind going on in your head. I'm happy to talk things out with you. Just remember . . . you're a part of C.T.'s team now. He was a lone wolf for a while, but now he's gotten used to having you around. You told me you're starting to feel more like an assistant than a secretary, right?"

"Yeah," T.J. said.

"That means he's integrating you into what he does. You're a part of the process now. I'm sure he still does a great deal on his own, but he'll need you before this case is over. You good to go?"

"I think so. Maybe I'm making too much of the ritzy school. Just not my world, you know?"

"There's only one world, T.J.," Melinda said. "You're as much a part of it as anyone else."

T.J. smiled. Talking to Melinda always made her feel better. "Thanks. I'm ready to take down a bunch of snobby assholes now."

"That's my girl," Melinda said.

———

T.J.'s plans to eat dessert kept getting foiled by her recalling the crime scene photos of the councilman and teacher. She ended up falling asleep a little hungry. Her phone played a random song from one of her playlists to wake her up at seven the next morning. A few minutes later, she changed into workout clothes, dragged the heavy bag from the closet, and hung it from the exposed beam in her bedroom.

After slipping in a pair of earbuds and choosing a workout playlist, T.J. felt ready to go. She stretched for a few minutes and then strapped on a new pair of MMA gloves. The old ones wore out in about six months. Maybe these would do better. T.J. tapped them together, took a fighting stance, and got busy.

She'd been taking kickboxing classes at the YWCA for a while and watching videos to supplement what she learned in person. T.J. spent years as a victim. Since working for C.T., she'd been in danger a few times and probably would be again. He knew how to defend himself and encouraged her to do the same. In addition to learning much better punching and kicking techniques, the kickboxing lessons and her own practice improved her cardio.

Her gloves slammed into the bag. She opened with a series of alternating jabs. Often, T.J. visualized Weasel Boy's slender face. Today, she pictured whoever corralled Raymond Ellicott and Marcy Russell into that hotel room, shot them in the backs of their heads, and posed them like lovers. T.J. didn't really care what people did in their spare time. If two consenting adults wanted to meet for a tryst in a motel room, it was their business. The executions and subsequent staging made a mockery of intimacy.

Next, she mixed in crosses and hooks, falling into a steady jab-cross-hook rhythm. T.J. wondered who could have harbored a deep grudge against two people working very different jobs. The lives of a county councilman and private school teacher would rarely intersect. In this case, they did, if only for one horrible moment. C.T. was annoying about not presuming the killer targeted the councilman, but he had a point. Marcy Russell made for an unlikely random victim. Initial research confirmed her home and job weren't near the hotel.

"Who wanted you dead, then?" T.J. wondered aloud as she paused for a thirty-second rest. "You and a complete stranger." Raymond Ellicott also made a poor random victim for the same reasons. Someone specifically wanted him dead, as well. Two people whose lives never intersected saw them cross for a single moment before a pair of bullets ended them both. T.J. tapped her gloves together again and started a series of front snap kicks. Her pink-laced tennis shoes slammed into the bag, and it swayed back into position for the next strike.

She wondered about the school. Expensive. Elite. Steeped in tradition. Those things could compel someone to kill. But why would someone at the Sterner Academy murder a teacher who recently won a major award? "It doesn't make sense," T.J. muttered as she moved on to side kicks. "None of it does." She and C.T. still needed to pore over some notes and come up with a theory or two.

T.J. hoped they would do better putting their heads together.

AFTER A ROUND of coffee and a brief comparison of notes, T.J. and I headed out.

She arranged for a few other members of the Baltimore County Council to meet us. I folded myself into her Mustang, and she drove us to Towson. The building ended up a short drive from Gonzalez's precinct. I considered stopping by and giving him a thorough critique of his organization system—and how much heavy lifting it required the word "system" to do—but refrained. He deserved it, but we would need to work with him again before this mess was over. I could bust his balls during the celebratory beers portion of the case.

T.J. parked in a free lot nearby, and we walked a block into the council building. A receptionist directed us through a set of double doors. Straight ahead was the main chamber where the council conducted its business. Down the hall and to the left, a series of doors led to individual members' offices. Around a corner to the right, four people sat on the same side of the table in a small meeting room. We walked in and closed the door.

A slender black woman with professorial glasses sat in the head chair. To her left were a large man with a bald head and unkempt red beard, a trim and professional man who adjusted his

Oxford-knotted tie as we sat down, and a woman in a polo and jeans who chewed gum at an annoying volume. "Thanks for coming," the lady at the end of the table said.

"We appreciate you inviting us under these circumstances," I said.

She inclined her head as if meeting with us were simply a part of her *noblesse oblige*. "I'm Linda Davis." A bony hand pointed to each of her colleagues in turn. "With me are Jerry McGee, Aaron White, and Helen Brown." All inclined their heads toward T.J. and me. We were the only ones on the other side. Two staring down four. No one said anything for a few seconds, and then a few fissures appeared in Aaron White's professional demeanor.

"Raymond was my friend," he said, his voice cracking. "He had one more term than me, so he showed me the ropes when I first got elected. Our districts were right next to each other, too, so it worked out well."

"Did you all get along with him?" I asked. Each bobbed a head.

"We're awfully shaken," Linda Davis said. "Some of us just hold it in well. This is quite different than something like a Congressman getting shot at a baseball practice. We don't know if Raymond was targeted because of his job or not. Still, it reminds us not everyone is going to like the work we do. At best, we might make sixty percent of people in our districts happy."

"Have any of you gotten threats?" T.J. said.

Helen Brown snorted. "We probably all have." When she didn't speak, she continued to chew gum like she practiced for a competition.

"Anything credible?" I added.

"Usually, it's just some crank. We forward them to the cops and let them take care of any investigation."

"I've never been physically threatened, no," White said. "I

think Helen is right . . . we've all gotten emails and letters we needed to pass along. They never turn into anything."

"Did Raymond Ellicott mention someone harassing him?" I said.

"Not to me." The other three shook their heads in unison.

"Miss Davis, you mentioned you didn't know if someone targeted your former colleague for the work he did here." Her head moved a fraction of an inch in acknowledgement. "It leads me to a few natural follow-up questions. This generally isn't a full-time job, right?"

"Correct," she said.

"Mister Ellicott's other work seemed to be in what we might call small-stakes law. He wasn't going to court and representing tycoons or murderers. It seems unlikely someone who hired him to file their paperwork correctly would turn around and murder him."

"Is that a question?"

"Sure," I said. "We're not on *Jeopardy!*"

"I think you're right so far."

"What was he involved in for the council?"

"No one's involved in just one thing," she said. "The nature of what we do means we take on a variety of projects and topics. I don't think Raymond took on anything someone would hate him over."

"Education was his pet cause," Gary McGee said. "Always had been. He'd never been a teacher, but he fought for them. Wanted to make things better for students across the county. He took a big stand against some new voucher program." Helen Brown rolled her eyes at this but continued sitting in silence—or as silent as she could be while giving her jaw a workout. "If something involved students . . . or schools . . . or curriculum, Ray was going to be involved somehow."

"I was happy to let him," Davis added. "Dealing with school

boards has become a lot harder these last few years." She shrugged as Helen Brown again indicated what she thought of the current conversation. "It has, Helen. Ray stuck it out, and I think it practically makes him a saint."

"Oh, please," Brown said. "None of you can handle a little conflict. Some parents are vocal about what they want for their children. How is that a bad thing?"

"It depends who's feeding them their information, doesn't it?" Aaron White said. "If people want to have honest disagreements, I don't think anyone here objects. But when a bunch of crackpots start circulating crap—"

"Everyone has the right to their own opinions."

"But not their own facts."

Helen Brown sighed and jerked her chin at me. "What do you think?"

"I think this is yet another reason I'm glad not to have children," I said. She rolled her eyes again, and I ignored her to press the issue. "I know public education has become something of a hot-button topic. Do you think someone was particularly aggressive toward Mister Ellicott because of his work there?"

"I doubt it," McGee said. "More than a few crazies come to school board meetings, but they're harmless enough. They just like to yell and gin everyone up. Nothing ever comes of it."

"Do you ever share information about the people who make threats?"

McGee shrugged. "Maybe here and there. Especially if it's funny. Some of these people are just *nuts*, you know? One guy wrote me a three-page letter about how he was going to tie me upside-down, cut my balls off, and a bunch of other shit. I passed it on, but you have to laugh at it, too."

"You know of anyone who made a credible threat against Ellicott?" I said. "Maybe one he mentioned which sticks with you now?"

"No," McGee said, and the others also chimed in with the negative. "I wish I did."

"Where does someone go after the county council?" T.J. wanted to know, opening a new and important line of questioning.

"In reality, to a paid consulting or lobbying position," Davis said. "Maybe a state-level appointment if they've gotten their name in the paper enough. Raymond had his eyes on county executive, though. I think he would've been a good one."

"He'd been here four terms," White said. "Plenty of accomplishments to run on. If he won, who knows where he could have been in a few more years?"

"Was his ambition well known?" I said.

White shrugged while McGee answered. "In here, yeah. Outside, it was catching on. I know he recently set up a website and hired a campaign manager."

"You think someone could've killed him to keep him from reaching a higher office?" Brown said.

"People get murdered for worse reasons all the time," I offered. It didn't seem to placate anyone.

———

As we left the council building, T.J. called Marcy Russell's widower. She walked ahead and talked to him, and I lagged behind in case anyone ran out to share one more nugget of information away from a colleague's prying eyes and ears. None did. "He'll meet us," my assistant said as she rejoined me. "Told me we can head there now. What's taking you so long?"

"I'm busy looking for Roman soldiers," I said. "No gleaming breastplates around here."

T.J. chuckled. "Thank goodness." We headed to her car. She keyed the address into her phone, and Android Auto displayed the route and directions on her Mustang's screen. Based on the ZIP code and what I could see of the destination, I presumed we were heading toward Middle River. Sure enough, we were. The town sat near White Marsh and Essex and was perhaps best known for a small airport and major drive-in movie theater.

The Russell house was a modest two-story Cape Cod on a street full of similar homes. This one was white—though they were all some shade of it—with blue shutters and a matching door. None of the houses had attached garages, though a few we passed featured freestanding ones behind the main structures. A Camry of recent vintage sat at the curb in front. T.J. stopped her Mustang behind it, and we got out.

A short chain-link fence marked the boundary of the front yard. Even a small dog could have leapt it with a running start, and a tall burglar could simply bypass it without breaking stride, so I failed to see the purpose. We opened the gate, followed a short walkway to the steps, and waited after knocking. The man who answered the door a moment later looked like he hadn't slept in days.

Gray showed at the roots of his disheveled black hair. Several days of beard and mustache growth lent age to his face and still held a few food crumbs. Dark circles under his eyes were the biggest tell. "You're the detectives who called?"

"Yes." I showed him my ID, and he gave it a perfunctory glance. I could have displayed a toy badge from a claw machine and gotten the same reaction. "We're sorry for your loss."

"Come on in." He opened wider, and we entered the house. The living room looked and smelled better than its occupant. I tried not to be too judgy—if someone murdered Gloria, I'd be a combination of desperate for revenge and falling apart. A few used paper plates littered the coffee table, along with an empty soda can and two mugs which once held coffee. The carpet was new but needed to be cleaned, and the furniture managed to stay in good repair. A large TV mounted on the wall played national news on mute. "Don't mind the mess."

"It's understandable," T.J. said.

"I'm Edgar Russell." He shook our hands in turn, and his grip lacked strength. "Marcy's husband. Widower now, I guess." He took a deep breath and ended it in a mirthless chuckle. "I think I'm all cried out over the past few days plus this morning."

"I would be, too, in your place," I offered. When my older sister died sixteen years ago, I struggled for a while, and there were times the memories still felt like a gut punch all this time later. Losing my wife simply didn't compute. "The councilman's family hired us, but we don't want to presume what happened was because of him and . . . whatever status he might have."

Edgar Russell nodded. He sank onto a recliner, and T.J. and I took spots on the sofa. "It makes sense. I'm not even sure what to think about anything."

"Do you mind if we ask you some questions?"

"Go ahead." He paused, frowned, and turned his head. "Marcy would tell me I'm being rude. Do you want coffee?"

"I'll never turn a cup down," I said.

"Sounds great," T.J. added.

"I'll be back in a few." Edgar got up and headed out of the living room. I could see about half the dining area from my seat. The kitchen must have been past it to the right. A moment later, the aroma of brewing java made its way to the couch. I inhaled a deep breath. Edgar returned with a pair of matching mugs a couple minutes later. "I forgot to ask how you take it, so I put a little sugar and milk in."

"It's fine," I said. I'd gotten past putting anything sweet in my coffee, but I wasn't about to ask a grieving man to dump the cup out and make me a fresh one. A little more milk would have masked the sugar better, but on the whole, it proved an adequate caffeine delivery system. Once we were all seated and ready, I started with the questions. "As far as I can tell, your wife and Councilman Ellicott didn't know each other."

"I don't think they did," Edgar confirmed. "He's not even our representative. I've read he gets really involved in education, but as far as I know, they never crossed paths." He paused to sip coffee. "I was as surprised as anyone with how they were found."

"We know your wife won an award recently, and she seemed popular. Do you know if anyone had it in for her?"

"I can't imagine. Everyone loved Marcy." As with the Ellicott family, I refrained from pointing out the obvious. "My son and I have been wracking our brains." He shook his head. "Nothing."

"Is your son here?" T.J. asked.

"Not at the moment," Edgar said. "He moved back home a few years ago for grad school and hasn't really left." He snorted. "He's at some kind of meeting. Gerald fancies himself as a budding entrepreneur."

"With two parents as teachers," I said, "I guess I figured he'd go into education."

Edgar frowned, and his lips curled into a scowl. "He doesn't have any parents in education now."

T.J. leaned forward. "What do you mean?"

"I found out yesterday . . . The Sterner Academy fired me. 'Conduct unbecoming a teacher,' they said. Never mind *I* didn't do a damn thing. My wife gets killed . . . and I know the scene looked bad, but they knew her . . . but somehow, I'm responsible."

"That's terrible," T.J. said.

"Awful," I added. At some point, we would need to visit the school. I hoped the principal's office was on the top floor so I could throw him out the window. If he survived, I could drag him back up the stairs and try again.

Edgar waved a hand. "Thank you. It is, but I can't deal with it right now. One of these weeks, I'll get our attorney involved. For now, I'm simply trying to string the minutes together to make it through the day."

"We're going to look into all aspects of what happened," I said. "Do you want us to keep you in the loop?"

He sighed. "If it's something significant, yes."

"We also might want to talk to your son."

"When he's not out setting up a big business deal, sure." Edgar added an eye roll for good measure.

"You mentioned everyone liked your wife," I said. "Did she tell you about any threats?"

"Who would threaten her?" Our host took another swig of coffee. "She was a private school teacher."

"I imagine you must have encountered some difficult parents," T.J. said.

"Sure, but they threaten you with lawsuits or bringing you up before the board. Not with violence. Imagine parents at a Little League game where every family has to pay fifty grand to get on the team."

"I played lacrosse for years," I said. "Pretty much the same there."

"You any good?"

"National champions in twenty-twelve."

"Loyola?" he said.

"Yep."

"Good for you." Edgar sighed again. Based on how weary he looked when we arrived, I was surprised he'd indulged us this long. "I need to keep making arrangements for my wife." He stood. "Please let me know if you find anything important."

"We will," I said. "If you can let us know when your son is here and available, we'd appreciate it." T.J. and I left. Edgar closed and locked the door before we even started down the steps.

"That poor man," she whispered as we headed to the car. "Everything he's already been through, and the school fires him."

"Terrible," I said.

"You think there's something shady there?"

I shrugged. "Probably a bunch of parents complaining about the optics. Some rich asshole thinks his kid will struggle to get into Yale because a teacher got killed a few years before."

"Should we go to the school?"

"We should. You might need to restrain me, though. I think I want to kick the principal's ass."

T.J. chuckled. "Why would I stop you?"

CHAPTER 7

POWERING UP THE LONG, winding driveway leading to The Sterner Academy, I couldn't help but roll my eyes. Another immaculately manicured private school. This one sat in northern Baltimore County. The campus sprawled before us with vast green lawns, walking paths, and not one but three baseball diamonds. Landscapers made sure the hedges were trimmed with nary a speck of green out of place. Leaves changing color and falling from trees spoiled the color palette, and no amount of tuition could stop it. At the heart of it all stood the main building —a grand stone edifice resembling a castle more than a school.

T.J. parked the Mustang in a spot labeled for visitors. "I don't like this place," she said, frowning at the administrative building. I almost expected a drawbridge to lower so someone could ride out on horseback to meet us.

"I have an idea, then, but I'm not sure you're going to like it."

"What?"

"Why don't you stay in the car?" I suggested.

"But I—"

"It's hard to go into places like this without a lot of knowledge. We haven't really done a deep dive into the school. Stay here, see what you can find out, and text me the juicy bits. I'll check them on my watch."

T.J. nodded. "All right. What do you want to know first?"

"Start with the principal and work from there." I climbed out and headed toward the faux castle. Inside the main entrance, the reception area looked like the lobby of a Fortune 500 company with polished floors, leather chairs, and artwork probably costing more than my car—and my car wasn't cheap. Down the hall, the strains of students learning instruments greeted me in a discordant dirge. I felt glad I didn't need to attend some alleged concert where they displayed their lack of expertise.

Large windows dominated the opposite wall, allowing me to see much of the campus. The three other buildings—one each for the elementary, middle, and high schools—stood in a triangular pattern, with a dedicated and marked door leading to each. Heaven forbid the students and staff of The Sterner Academy get drizzled on when moving to and from the administrative wing. To the far left, a stadium with permanent bleachers pulled double duty as both the soccer pitch and football field. To the far right was a squat building the right size to house a gym and basketball court.

"May I help you, sir?" a receptionist asked, poking her head out of the office. She looked like a recent college grad and wore an official school polo above her professional slacks.

"Does the lacrosse team use the same field in the spring?"

"Yes, sir."

"How much is tuition here?" She told me, and I somehow stifled a coughing fit. "And there's still no separate facility?"

"Sir?"

"Sorry. I need to speak with the principal." I glanced at my watch. T.J. helpfully provided me his name. Not his title, however, so I made a guess as to his academic bona fides. "Doctor Hinson."

"Do you have an appointment?"

I told her I didn't, showed her my ID, and explained the reason for my visit. I left out the part about throwing her boss out the window for firing a grieving widower. A place like this probably used glass you couldn't easily toss people through, and I didn't want to deal with the embarrassment of bouncing a middle-aged asshole off it a few times. We all have our limits.

"I'm sure he'll be happy to make time for you," she said, and the smile she pasted onto her face suggested Doctor Hinson may in fact be less than overjoyed. While she picked up the phone, I checked my assistant's text on my watch.

Sounds like a real peach. What I've found suggests people don't really like working for him, but he's good at the job. Big on education and putting the right curriculum in place. Lots of pictures with donors and the like. Got a PhD a few years back in leadership of all things. I'll keep looking.

"Sir?" the young secretary said as she hung up the receiver. "Doctor Hinson will see you now. If you go upstairs, you'll find his office right above this one."

"Thanks," I said, and I headed for the steps. The second level looked much the same as the first. The principal's sanctorum covered the same square footage as the area below but was laid out differently. Another young woman served as gatekeeper. She wore an identical shirt to the lady toiling away on the first floor and may have been plucked from the same university graduation. She swept a slender arm toward the door behind her checkpoint.

"Doctor Hinson is ready for you, Mister Ferguson."

I figured he was not, but I didn't want to let him know.

———

The room must have been eight hundred square feet. T.J.'s apartment might not have been as large. Shelves filled with books lined three of the walls, and the man himself sat behind a desk large enough for a team of four to work comfortably, but much of his domain was empty space. Anthony Hinson was in his early fifties and actually let his hair go gray at the edges instead of dyeing it. When he stood, I could tell he was about my height but with a classic runner's physique accentuated by a slim-fit suit. "Mister Ferguson." He smiled, but it didn't reach his eyes. We shook hands and then both sat on the appropriate sides of his desk.

"I got called to the principal's office a few times in my school days," I said. "It never looked like this."

"We're very lucky here at The Sterner Academy."

"When you charge forty grand a head for admission, I figure you can afford to make your own luck."

Another fake smile. "We've never hidden from our mission to provide an excellent education. It's not cheap . . . but then again, what is anymore?"

"This seems like a lot of work for one person. Thirteen grades counting kindergarten."

"We have vice principals and assistants," he said. "They do much of the day-to-day administration of each level. My role is more like a CEO."

His phony facial expressions and the content of his answers did little to my urge to expel him through the nearest large pane of glass. Instead, I took a slow breath and got down to business. "I'm sure you know why I'm here."

"Yes," he said, and Hinson's face twisted into an expression which was probably supposed to be sympathetic and instead made him appear constipated. "We all loved Marcia. Especially her students. I've ensured there's a grief counselor available should anyone require it."

Of course he would call her Marcia. "Councilman Ellicott's family hired me, but I think it would be foolish to presume someone targeted him, and Ms. Russell was simply a random and unfortunate victim."

Hinson's head bobbed a fraction. "A sensible approach, but like I said, everyone loved Marcia. She recently won a major award. Her colleagues thought she was great. Students always raved about her. Teaching is a hard job, and I think there's an impression it's easier at a private school. I doubt very much this is true. Marcia excelled at her job, and we'll all miss her." His hand swept the campus visible through a large window. "If you're looking for enemies, you won't find any out there."

"What about her husband?" I asked.

"What about him?"

"You fired a grieving man at the lowest point in his life."

"I'm afraid you're oversimplifying," Hinson said. "However highly I may think of Marcia Russell, she was found naked in a common hotel room with another man."

"I would say she paid a price way out of line with whatever she did."

"Yes. However, what she did is the issue. Our parents, staff, donors, and board members all have expectations. Teachers sign a contract to work here, and a morals clause is part of it."

"Maybe you could tell me how a man's wife getting murdered means he violated this precious clause?"

"Spouse and family behavior is part of it," Hinson said. "What our loved ones do ultimately reflects on us. In the end, Edgar Russell couldn't keep his woman in line, and I needed to fire him for it."

"I was wondering when we might get to the sexist part of the conversation," I said. "Still, wasn't expecting you to go with 'his woman.'"

Hinson waved a hand. "Forgive me. I occasionally speak colloquially. Mister Russell's wife's behavior ultimately reflected poorly on him and on The Sterner Academy. I fired him for moral turpitude."

"And now you get to hide behind a big word."

"Do you know what it means?"

"Of course I know what it means. I'll put my education against what you're teaching here any day."

"What would you have me do, Mister Ferguson?" Hinson spread his hands.

"Hire Edgar Russell back," I said, "if he still wants anything to do with you. The best thing you can do for a grieving family is show them support, not pull the rug out from under them. I'd expect someone who fancies himself as a CEO to understand basic human dynamics."

The principal showed a thin smile. "I'm afraid the school's code and his contract tie my hands. Mister Russell is free to litigate for his job if he so desires, but I don't think he would succeed." My watch vibrated for the second time, but I didn't have time to look at it. "Ferguson . . . are you Robert and June's son?"

"I am."

"I must say I expected better."

"So did I." I stood. Hinson wasn't going to indulge me much longer. "I guess sixty million a year in tuition only buys a pretty low-rent CEO."

"Good day, Mister Ferguson. I don't expect we'll need to talk to one another again."

"If we do," I said, "you're going to like it a hell of a lot less than this one." Hinson pursed his lips but offered no other reaction. I walked out, fighting the urge to dump a shelf of dusty old tomes on the floor as I left. If only he knew the restraint it took.

CHAPTER 8

"YOU DIDN'T USE much of what I sent you," T.J. said as I sat in the Mustang's passenger seat.

"Didn't really have a chance to keep looking at my watch. He's a prick, but he's not one to sit around, steeple his fingers, and ponder every word."

She started the engine and backed out of the space. With the school day over for a couple hours, teachers left the staff lot. We joined a line of cars heading down the long and winding driveway back to the main road. A man took a sprinkler apart which had been watering a stretch of grass. The grass would probably need one more cut for the year. Considering its uniform length and crisp lines whenever it bordered pavement, the groundskeeping staff must have been voluminous and well-paid.

At forty thousand a head, all things became possible.

If I talked to Hinson again, maybe I could pitch this as the school's new motto. The ones on the website weren't any better. "Did you learn anything?" T.J. wanted to know. She quickly added, "Besides his status as a dick."

"Not a lot, then," I said. "Everyone loved Marcy Russell . . . he insisted on calling her Marcia all the time, of course . . . and his hands were tied on sacking Edgar because of some moral turpitude clause from the Dark Ages." I chuckled. "You'll love this. At one point, he literally said to me, 'Edgar Russell couldn't keep his woman in line, and I needed to fire him for it.' Can you believe it?"

T.J. held the wheel in a white-knuckle grip. If her car were a manual, she might have ripped the shifter free of its linkage. "Like she was his fucking property?"

"I told you. Dark Ages."

"You think he might have had something to do with it?"

"Doubt it. The guy's an asshole, but he doesn't strike me as a killer. Probably finds the idea of having to murder someone terribly inconvenient."

"People like him just find someone else to do the dirty work," T.J. said.

"Sure," I said, "but what does he have to gain? Marcy Russell being dead and her husband getting fired don't benefit Hinson. I can't imagine he gets a bonus if the total staff count is below a certain number, and these two events got him there." I shrugged. "They both seem like good teachers. If nothing else, I think someone like Hinson realizes their value to the school and wants to keep them."

"We've talked to quite a few people today."

"Yep."

"And still no good suspects."

"Nope."

"Is the job always like this?"

"Yep."

"Is this where you mention something about us being smart and determined enough to figure it out no matter what?" T.J. said.

I nodded. "I don't need to now. You nicely took care of it for me."

She smiled. "It's what a good assistant does."

"It is," I agreed.

After confirming Gloria was at my house and didn't have anything ready to go for dinner, I picked up burgers and fries from The Abbey on my way home. There's a Fells Point location, but I try and go to the original in Federal Hill when I can. Getting carry-out meant missing out on the atmosphere and trying another beer of excellent flavor and difficult pronunciation. Enjoying dinner with my wife was a welcome trade-off.

I carried the bag of deliciousness in via the back door and set it down atop the round dining table. Gloria wandered in from the living room and kissed me. "I smell The Abbey," she said, opening the paper sack. French fry grease already turned it translucent in a few spots.

"Would you believe I cooked all this myself?"

"As much as you believed I made the lasagna."

I grinned. "Want a beer?"

"Sure." I grabbed a foreign light brew for Gloria and an oatmeal stout for myself. While Gloria tore the bag open, I brought plates and napkins to the table. As usual, she gave me a few fries from her box. A couple years ago, Gloria changed her diet and eating habits to help herself in local tennis tournaments. The modifications improved her overall fitness. While she didn't really compete anymore—tennis players are old at thirty, after all—the routine of eating like a rabbit stuck. At least she wouldn't cut the burger into tiny bites.

"Did you make any progress on the case?" she asked once we'd each sated our immediate hunger with a few bites.

"Not really. Talked to the principal of The Sterner Academy, though." I snorted. "Son of a bitch."

"I guess we won't be making a donation there?"

"Hell no," I said.

"What happened?"

I told her about Gerald Russell getting fired for ridiculous reasons after the circumstances of his wife's murder. She frowned and shook her head. "The worst part," I said, "is the principal didn't seem to care. He even said the husband couldn't keep his woman in line."

Gloria paused with a fry halfway to her mouth. "He really said that?"

"He did."

"What a prick."

"Exactly. I think T.J. is hoping he's involved somehow. She really wants him to be guilty."

"You think he is?" my wife asked.

"Of being a major asshole, yes," I said. "Anything else? I'm not convinced. He sees himself as the CEO of the school, and it's a successful, well-regarded place. I don't think he would jeopardize his image."

"He sounds like a terrible man."

"He is, but it doesn't make him a murderer. I still wanted to throw him out the window."

Gloria chuckled. "On the whole, I'm glad you didn't."

"I would grudgingly admit I am, too."

We each took a few more bites. I added in some fries. I was down to less than half my burger. About three-quarters of Gloria's remained. She would probably put half away for leftovers—then forget about it for a couple days and get mad at me for eating it when I felt it obvious she wasn't going to. "I heard from the reporter again," she said after a swig of beer.

"Setting up the interview?"

"Nothing definitive yet. She wants to expand it more into my personal life, too. More of an article about me overall versus just the business."

This is exactly what I figured would happen. Puff pieces needed to be about people to be resonant. Now, I needed to walk a fine line between not wanting some journalist trampling all over our privacy and being happy for my wife. "They couldn't pick a better person to do a feature on."

She blushed. "I'm sure they could have . . . but thanks." After another minuscule bite, she added, "You know this means you might get included?"

"I know," I said.

"You're all right with it?"

"With a mention, sure. I'd rather not have my picture in the paper."

"You want to keep your ability to go undercover?"

"Part of it, I guess," I said. "In general, me getting recognized doesn't make my job easier. I also don't want someone to read this article and decide to come after you to get to me."

"Maybe I'll have her mention you're a superhero," Gloria said.

"With the right mask and cape, we could even run my photo."

"I get your concerns," my wife said in a tone suggesting she didn't really understand but was making the effort. "I'll let you know when the interview happens in case you're able to make it."

"Can I show up in a mask and cape?"

"No."

"I'll try to be there anyway," I said.

————

The next morning, I woke up before Gloria. Part of her fitness routine involved getting up earlier than before, but my feet still hit the floor well ahead of hers most mornings. I changed into my Under Armour running attire—including a light jacket for the autumn chill in the air—and hit the mean streets of Federal Hill. I used the four or so blocks it took me to get to the eponymous park as a warm-up. When I got there, I was ready to go.

As usual, I wasn't alone. The combination of a convenient location for residents and spectacular views across the harbor made Federal Hill Park a popular spot for walkers and runners. I soon settled into a nice rhythm behind a blonde woman with a bobbing ponytail and tight yoga pants. Unlike most people out exercising at the beastly hour of eight-fifteen, I didn't wear headphones. Being music-free allowed me time to ponder my current case and also be alert for people trying to waylay me—which has happened several times.

After about fifteen minutes, the woman ahead of me broke off the path and headed back into the neighborhood. Once I hit thirty minutes, I did the same. Running was a little easier before I got shot on the other side of the harbor nearly two years ago. It cost me a lung lobe, and my fitness never quite reached its prior levels. Still, I figured ninety-five percent of where I'd been before was better than most. It took me a few months of hitting the pavement, but my times and distances now were pretty close to my earlier marks.

As I walked back up Riverside Avenue, I scanned for goons and criminals. Over the years, I've been assaulted a few times, nearly run over twice, and fired at once. There were few people and cars moving along, and none of them looked like they wanted to punch me or turn me into street pizza. I unlocked my front door and headed to the basement to conclude my workout. The ceiling height made it difficult for me to stand up straight, but it was the best place in the house to set up a weight bench.

After another fifteen minutes of pumping iron, I headed upstairs for a much-needed shower. When I came back down in clean clothes, Gloria sat in the kitchen drinking coffee. "Morning," she said with a smile. Even with no makeup and her chestnut hair looking very much like she'd just slept eight hours, my wife was still the most beautiful woman I'd ever seen.

"Morning." I leaned down and kissed her as I walked by to get coffee.

"I've been thinking more about the interview and article."

I'd hoped our discussion about it last night represented the end, but apparently not. "What about it?"

"Well . . . I didn't exactly live the most productive life until a couple years ago. This is supposed to be a good piece for the company, and I don't want people to find me unrelatable."

"Our parents have money," I said. "Most people already can't relate to us. It's about bridging the gaps."

"You've always seemed to do it pretty well."

I shrugged as I joined her at the round kitchen table. "I've always had the ability to talk to people."

"I haven't," Gloria said. "I could use some pointers."

"You're the ripe old age of thirty now."

She grinned. "Don't remind me."

"How many people reading this article knew for certain what they wanted to do by thirty?" I said. "Hell, some people never figure it out. Others just take over the family business because it's been expected of them their whole lives. You started working on this at least three years ago and seriously about two. There's your focus. It took a few years after college to figure out what you wanted to do, you found fundraising, and you liked helping people so much you started your own company."

She nodded slowly. "That's really good. If this whole PI thing doesn't work out for you, you could always go into PR."

"There's no need to be mean," I said.

Gloria chuckled. "You making breakfast? I think I'm going to work at my house today, so if you're not, I can always pick something up en route."

I glanced at my watch. No way to make it in by nine unless I left right now and set the land speed record on the drive. I would endure a glare from my assistant when I arrived. "I think I'll pick something up, too."

"All right." She stood, took a few steps to stand in front of me, and kissed me like she meant it. "Try not to get in too much trouble on this case."

"Who, me?" I said.

CHAPTER 9

I ARRIVED with breakfast sandwiches and hash browns to find I'd beaten T.J. to the office.

This rarely happened. She was almost always here by nine. I sometimes rolled in later, so I didn't care if she did, too. The air remained crisp as I crossed the lot. It would get warmer later but still be pleasant and temperate for fall. I walked into the shop, headed to the right, and climbed the metal stairs. Inside, I reached into the bag of food, took out a breakfast sandwich and hash brown for myself, and set the paper sack on T.J.'s desk.

A car pulled in below. This was probably her. I set the coffee maker to brew. Priorities. Footsteps came up the stairs. They thunked too hard on the metal to be T.J.'s, and I thought I heard two distinct sets. I was still shrugging out of my coat when the door burst open. Two suits hustled in, both built like linebackers stuffed into ill-fitting jackets. Heavy brows hooded their dark, deep-set eyes. The brass glinting on the knuckles of the goon on the right answered the question of why they were here. They both wore their hair short, and the similar colors made me wonder if they were related.

"You two brothers?" I asked. They frowned and looked at each other. "Cousins?" They turned back to me, expressions mostly blank but trying to convey menace. "Does the family tree actually fork at some point?"

The one with the brass knuckles took the bait. "Listen here, asshole, we—"

"So your parents *were* related?" I said, cutting him off.

While the first man fumed, the other one put a hand on his chest. "You know the deal," he said. "Back off, and we'll leave."

"Back off what?"

"You know what."

"I think anyone who's serious about getting me to abandon a case would send more than you two clowns," I said.

The crack compelled the brass man to take a swing at me. It wasn't his best work—at least I hoped not. The punch was all arm. Maybe he was hoping the metal on his fist would find the mark and end this quickly. I rocked back, however, and he hit only air. I kicked him in the side, making him stagger forward while his friend moved to fill in the gap. I blocked a couple of his punches before his eyes flicked toward his buddy. They were going for some kind of setup.

And I was going to let them.

When my foe grabbed me, I didn't resist too much. Enough to keep him from setting his feet, which would be important in a couple seconds. The first guy made sure I could see the brass knuckles as I squirmed. The goon holding me tightened his grip, but rather than plant his feet, he moved when I did. Light glinted off the metal as the first man drew his fist back. When it was time for him to bring it forward, I shifted my stance, threw my weight to the side, and spun.

Because the guy holding me never set his feet, he couldn't offer a lot of resistance. He came along for the ride and made some tortured sound like a cross between a moan and a grunt when the weaponized fist slammed into his back. I felt the impact through his body. His grip slackened, and he crumpled to the floor. The guy who threw the punch stared with wide eyes. I punted him hard in the balls, and he doubled over.

"Don't you puke in my office," I said to the one who took the punch as I dragged him toward the door. His face was a mask of pain tinged with green. "The school send you?" His expression didn't change. "Some councilman?" Nothing. "Piss off." I hoisted him upright and tossed him down the stairs. He bounced off a few on the way down before landing in a heap at the bottom. His head lifted weakly, then hit the floor again.

Before I could go back inside, the remaining goon barreled out the door, murder in his eyes. He threw a hard punch at my face, forcing me to step to the side to avoid maxing out my dental coverage. When he fired off another right cross, I deflected his forearm and seized his wrist. We strained against each other. His sour breath washed hot over my face as he bared his teeth. He was stronger than me, and he would win this part of the battle if he were patient enough, but he wasn't.

I knew a headbutt was coming, and I moved my right arm into the way. His forehead slammed into my elbow, which hurt us both. He blinked rapidly to clear the cobwebs, and the lower half of my arm went numb. I put my foot behind his knee, leaned forward, and pushed his right arm. It was enough to send him toppling to the hard metal landing. Before he could get up, I stomped on his hand and ground my heel into it. A bone cracked, and he howled in pain.

"I think you two have overstayed your welcome," I said. "Unless you want to tell me who sent you here this morning."

"Eat shit," he growled through clenched teeth.

"Wrong answer." I moved my foot from his hand and kicked him in the face. It wouldn't put him out, but I didn't need it to. The goon at the bottom of the stairs rose to unsteady feet. Using mostly my left arm, I hefted this one up by his jacket and sent him down the steps via the express route. The guy below stared with wide eyes as his friend tumbled down and barreled into him. They both ended up on the landing in a tangle of arms and legs. "Tell whoever sent you to fuck off."

It took them a couple minutes and a fair bit of struggle, but they both made it back to vertical and hobbled toward the lot. I walked back into the office. The coffee had finished brewing. "Perfect timing," I said.

———

Shortly after my two uninvited guests left, more footsteps ascended the stairs. They sounded like T.J.'s, and sure enough, she came through the door a moment later. "Who the hell were those two guys?"

"Salesmen," I said. "Told them we didn't need a vacuum cleaner."

"The way they were walking makes me think they got tossed down the stairs." I remained silent. T.J. grinned. "They must have been very persistent salesmen." She hung her coat on the rack inside the door.

"Some people just can't take 'no' for an answer."

T.J. headed to her desk and spotted the bag. "You got me breakfast? Thanks."

"I made coffee, too." I moved to the machine and poured myself a fresh cup. "Those two idiots left right as it finished brewing."

"Let me guess," my assistant said, "the principal sent them to convince us to back off."

After adding some milk to my java, I sat at my desk again. "Two problems there," I said. "One, we can't presume the principal sent these two assholes. Two, if he did, he only knows about me."

"It had to be him."

"He's not the only person we talked to yesterday. Edgar Russell."

"His wife got killed," T.J. pointed out. "I doubt he paid a couple goons to keep us from figuring out what happened."

"It's unlikely, but people kill their spouses . . . or have them murdered . . . every day in this country." When she grimaced, I added, "Let's back burner him for now. I don't think he had anything to do with it. We also spoke to four members of the county council. My guess is they told other people in the building we were there and why."

"You suspect someone on the council?"

"Honestly, I don't suspect anyone right now," I said. "We don't know enough yet, and we haven't exactly found a smoking gun. I'm simply saying we can't presume the principal is behind the surprise visit this morning."

"He's an asshole," T.J. said.

"Agreed."

"He's the last person we talked to."

I shrugged. "True."

"And I'm sure that fancy school pays him well enough to afford a pair of goons."

"No doubt, but none of those things mean he did it." T.J. frowned as she unwrapped her breakfast sandwich. "We can put him on the list. He's a possibility, but there's no way we can say he's a certainty at this point."

"I guess your two guests didn't tell you anything useful?"

"Nothing. One of them wore brass knuckles. I'm glad they found me and not you."

"Yeah." She nodded. "Me, too."

"I guess you're going to dig into the principal?"

"And the school," T.J. said. "You told me he feels he's the CEO. I've watched enough movies to know CEOs usually have to deal with a board of directors. Maybe he didn't send anyone, but they did."

"Worth looking into, I guess," I said. "Knock yourself out."

"What are you going to do?"

"This coffee isn't going to drink itself."

"That's it?"

"I'm delegating. All good bosses know how."

"Uh-huh," T.J. said. She wiped her fingers on a napkin and then did some typing. "I talked to Melinda recently. Basically told her how this fancy school wasn't my world. I guess it got in my head a little."

"It's not my world, either," I said. "I went to private schools but never to a place like Sterner." I chuckled. "We did enjoy beating them in lacrosse, though. They had a couple good players but never much of a team."

"So your fancy school was better at the rich white kids' sport than an even fancier school?"

"I wouldn't know. I didn't play golf."

She chuckled and got back to work. Once her breakfast sandwich and hash browns were gone, the typing became faster. Suddenly, it stopped. I glanced up, and T.J. stared at the her screen with wide eyes. "What is it?"

"You need to come and see this," she said. I walked across the office to her desk. Her laptop displayed a Sterner Academy page. True to what she told me, my assistant looked into the board of directors. "Scroll down."

I did. The page was a list of names. Some bore photo accompaniment, and others did not. Toward the bottom, I stopped and recoiled. The left-hand column held a picture of my father. Beside the photo, the page said *Robert and June Ferguson, The Robert and June Ferguson Foundation.*

"Shit," I said.

CHAPTER 10

I ARRANGED to meet my parents for lunch. They did a lot of good work for charity, but supporting The Sterner Academy seemed like a serious misstep, and not solely because few students who attended needed any form of assistance. The odious principal represented a big black mark against the place— now, I understood why he mentioned my parents when learning of my last name. I hoped I could convince them to resign, but if they felt this was one of their pet causes, I knew the conversation would be long and frustrating.

If only the bistro served alcohol.

I stepped inside, scanning the room for my parents. My mother chose one of her usual spots—a small table tucked into the back corner. The place was near their house in Roland Park and only held about a dozen tables. So far, the lunch rush hadn't materialized. As I approached, my father spotted me and lifted his hand in greeting.

"Coningsby, dear!" my mother said. She stood to give me a hug. "So glad you could make it. We were just looking at the menu."

My father smiled as I slid onto a chair opposite them. This table would accommodate two people easily, three with relative ease, and four if they were thin and ordered small plates. "Hi, son," he said. "How's the business going?"

"Oh, you know. Always have to sift through a roomful of crap to get to a nugget of truth." I picked up the menu, avoiding their eyes. We made small talk until the waiter came to take our order. My mother chose a Cobb salad, my father nodded and picked the same thing. I went for a burger and fries. This was my first time eating here. Any place which can't make a good burger and fries doesn't deserve a second visit.

As soon as the waiter dropped off our drinks and disappeared again, I cleared my throat. "I'm glad you were able to meet me today," I said, "but I have to confess this isn't entirely a social call."

"I got the feeling," my father said. "What's going on?"

"I guess you heard what happened to Marcy Russell?"

"Terrible," my mother said, shaking her head and offering a delicate sniff. She never liked me working murder cases. I figured the very idea of a dead body offended her sensibilities.

"Do you know where she worked?" I asked.

My father bobbed his head. "The Sterner Academy."

"Where you're on the board."

"We're on more than one, son. What's the problem here?"

I answered his question with one of my own. "What do you think of the principal?"

He shrugged. "Hinson seems like an okay guy. Not the warmest and fuzziest, I admit, but he makes a good administrator." He paused. "Are you working on Marcy Russell's murder case?"

"More or less," I said. "The Ellicott family hired us. He's the councilman who was found dead with her."

"What does this have to do with the Academy, Coningsby?" my mother asked.

"I didn't even know you were involved with the place until this morning."

"You have some issue with it, son?" my father said.

"I'm a little curious how you came to be on the board of a school I didn't even consider let alone attend."

My father pushed his glasses up his nose. They were his only concession to age. He'd let gray creep into his dark hair, and the ratio now sat at about fifty-fifty. By contrast, my mother's hair color came from a bottle for years. It was a perfect match for how it looked in the memories of my youth, at least. "Our foundation has placed a few students there, son. A couple a year for a while now. It's not the only school in the area we work with."

"You'd know this if you stayed involved with the foundation, Coningsby," my mother added.

I didn't take the bait. They'd severed the relationship over concerns about my safety after I got shot. On the whole, I couldn't blame them, and my business had turned out well since I struck out on my own. Rather than let this devolve into an argument, I said, "Let me tell you something about your man Hinson. He fired Edgar Russell over what happened to his wife 'Conduct unbecoming a teacher.' Then, he had the nerve to tell me a widower should have kept his woman in line. When I pressed him, he didn't exactly walk it back."

The waiter dropped off our food, refreshed the drinks, and wandered away again. Two people took the table beside us. While I ate my burger—it was good enough for me to want to come back—my father lowered his voice before answering. "Like I told you, he's not exactly warm and fuzzy."

"Dad, he's an asshole."

"Coningsby!" My mother frowned. "You may not like the man, but it doesn't mean he did something wrong."

"So you're okay with what he did and his justification for it?"

"Well, I—"

"Because if you are, by all means, keep your precious board seats. Wouldn't want your rich friends to think you weren't funneling kids into an elite school, after all."

"We didn't know he fired Mister Russell," my father said. "I think it's an overreaction. You're coming at this like you think Hinson was involved somehow."

"T.J. does," I said. "I'm not convinced. We can't rule him out at any rate. I believe you should reconsider where you devote your money and attention. If this goes south fast—and it might—I don't want to see your foundation caught in the blowback."

"We'll think about it, dear," my mother said. "I'll certainly have a question or two for Mister Hinson. He'd better make time for members of the board."

"He told me he fancies himself as a CEO." I shrugged. "I'm not sure how eager he'll be to listen."

"You're going to keep digging?" my father said after a bite of salad. It looked good, and the hard-boiled egg was perfect. I'm not much for entree salads, but I'd consider it.

"I am."

"Let us know how it's going."

"I will," I said.

I was in the car and headed back to the office when my phone rang. T.J.'s name and number displayed on the infotainment screen. I pushed the button on the wheel to accept the call. "I didn't bring you anything. There's two sets of leftovers in the fridge."

"First of all, rude," she said. "Just because there's already food in the fridge doesn't mean you shouldn't bring me lunch."

"I picked up breakfast. One meal a day is all I cover. It's in your contract. What's the second thing?"

"I think we want to head over to the Russell house again."

"Why?"

"The son is there this time. Edgar called a couple minutes ago."

"The life of an entrepreneur is unpredictable," I said. "All right. I'll swing by and get you, and then we can go see them. You sure the son is still going to be there when we pull up?"

"Edgar thinks he will," T.J. said.

"Let's hope he's right."

"What are we going to ask Gerald?"

"Probably a lot of the same questions we put to his dad. People don't tell everyone in their lives the same things. They'll share different stuff with a friend versus a spouse versus their child."

"That reminds me . . . we should talk to some of Marcy's colleagues."

"We should," I agreed as I stopped at a red light. "The challenge will be getting into the school again. The principal has probably ordered all the lettermen to rush me on sight."

"Gotta look out for the golf team," my assistant said. "They probably have their five-irons ready to go in case you get spotted anywhere on campus."

I chuckled. I'd bet good money Hinson told someone about me. It was impossible to say if he sent two goons to my door this morning—doing so seemed a bit unsavory for the image he wanted to project. Still, talking to Marcy Russell's colleagues could prove useful. We would simply need to find a way to do it away from the prying eyes and ears patrolling the venerated hallways of The Sterner Academy. "Let's try to get her coworkers soon. We'll figure something out. I'll see you in about ten minutes."

"You got it, boss," she said and ended the call.

Eleven minutes later, I pulled into the lot. T.J. climbed in, and we were off for another trip to Middle River.

———

We pulled up in front of the Russell house. This time, a dark red Tesla Model 3 sedan which had not been present before sat at the curb. If you were going to claim entrepreneur status, might as well drive something which looked the part. I stopped the S4 just behind it. T.J. and I climbed out and walked to the front door. I knocked, and Edgar Russell answered a moment later. "Good, you're here. Thanks for coming."

"I'm glad you called us when Gerald was around," I said as we headed inside.

"He's in the kitchen."

We walked down the hall. A young man stood at the kitchen counter. He was short, overweight, and dressed in faded jeans and a plain black T-shirt. He looked more like a junior software developer than someone in business for himself. "You must be Gerald," I said.

He eyed us both suspiciously, and his expression didn't improve when his gaze landed on his father. "Who are you?"

I showed him my ID. He spent maybe a second reading it. "You hired a PI?" he asked his dad.

"Other family did."

This made Gerald smirk. "So now you're here on behalf of some rich guy to smear my mother's name."

"We're here because it's foolish to presume the councilman was the sole target," I said. "The odds of your mother being in the wrong place at the wrong time when she didn't live or work near the crime scene are infinitesimal. I think whoever killed her and Raymond Ellicott wanted them both there." I shrugged. "You can help us or not."

He nodded. "All right." Gerald pushed a glass of wine toward his father. "Dad, you need to take a load off. Have a drink."

The older man frowned at the offer. "Little early in the day for me, son."

"Fair, I guess." Gerald shrugged and took a swig himself. "What can I do for you?"

"Start by telling us a little about yourself," T.J. said.

He waited a few seconds before answering. "All right. I'm twenty-four and just finished a master's in education. I don't want to go into teaching, though. My parents have done it for years. Seems like there's no money and tons of heartache in it. Don't give me a look, Dad. I heard you and Mom complain about things enough."

"Not our students," Edgar said. "There are other parts of the job I could do without, sure. It's really about the kids for me . . . just like it was for Marcy." He closed his eyes, and a few tears leaked out.

"Here you go, Dad." This time, Gerald grabbed a longneck from the fridge and set it in front of his father. "Your favorite."

Edgar looked at the bottle and sighed. "It's still too early in the day for me." He glanced at T.J. and me. "This has been a trying few days . . . made even worse by Hinson. If I start drinking, I'm not sure I'd be able to stop."

The son frowned and changed the subject. "Funeral is set, though, right?"

"Yes," Edgar said. "Next Monday."

"Good."

"You ever have any dealings with The Sterner Academy?" I asked Gerald, who still moved around in the kitchen.

"Me? No. Like I told you, I've never really wanted to get into teaching."

"Yet you got a master's in education."

"If I got one in history, I wouldn't be forced to work in a

museum." He shrugged. "You can do a bunch of things with the theory. It doesn't mean I need to teach kids."

"You might be good at it if you cared enough," Edgar said. He teared up again. "Marcy won an award, and it's like none of it even matters. Goddamn place. I can't believe I gave them so many years."

Gerald fetched a glass from a cupboard, filled it with cold water from the refrigerator, and set it before his dad. "Can't be too early for water. Come on, Dad. You need to stay hydrated. I'm sure you really haven't been."

"Probably not." Edgar grabbed the glass and took a long pull. "Thanks. Hell, I probably haven't been eating enough, but I don't suppose you want to cook anything?"

"Not really my jam," he said.

"I'll cook," I said. "I enjoy it."

"I couldn't ask you to," Edgar said.

I put up a hand. "It's fine. Mind if I check the fridge?"

"Help yourself."

I opened it and found reserves were pretty low. The fresh vegetable situation was dire. No meat—fresh or sliced from a deli counter—in sight. The carton of eggs remained good for another two weeks, and there were six. A package of Muenster cheese hadn't molded yet, setting it apart from the mozzarella. At the bottom, a new-looking loaf of bread sat alone on a shelf. "How about omelets and toast?"

"For lunch?" Gerald said.

"You want something else, come in here and make it." He scoffed, so I got busy. Once I set a pan to heat and cracked the eggs, I beckoned T.J. into the kitchen. "Can you start toasting the bread?" She said she would. I found an onion and diced it. A couple pats of butter in the pan melted and sizzled, and I dumped the onions in. A couple minutes later, the eggs followed.

T.J. worked the toaster and the butter, and we soon presented a simple lunch to the Russell men.

"Thanks," Edgar said. He cut into the omelet right away and started eating.

I held Gerald's plate above the counter. "Your mom talk to you about Sterner?"

"Why would she talk to me when my dad worked there, too?"

"Because people don't tell everyone in their lives the same things. She might share different details with you." I set the plate down, and despite his earlier gripes about the menu, he also dove right in.

"She never really did," he said around a mouthful of hot egg. "Maybe she knew I wasn't really interested in the classroom side of things." The young man added a shrug. "I wish I could tell you something more helpful."

"Me, too," I said. We left a few minutes later.

"The son is kind of a prick," T.J. opined once we were back in the car.

"I guess."

"You don't think he was? He didn't even seem to be broken up about his mother's murder."

"Everyone grieves differently."

"It was nice of you to make them some food, at least."

"Someone needed to," I said. I fired up the engine and pulled away from the curb. We hadn't learned much of anything from this visit. Marcy Russell's funeral the following Monday created a deadline in my head. I didn't want Edgar to bury his wife without knowing who killed her.

We had five days to figure it out.

CHAPTER 11

T.J. COLLAPSED onto her secondhand couch, kicking off her shoes with a sigh of relief. It had been a long day at the office and out in the field, capped by that strange meeting with Edgar and Gerald Russell. She couldn't stop thinking about the odd dynamic between the two. Edgar was clearly devastated by his wife's murder. His eyes were bloodshot, his face looked thinner than in the Sterner staff photo online, his clothes disheveled. He could barely speak about her murder without choking up. T.J.'s heart ached for the poor man.

But then there was Gerald.

He never really did anything to comfort his father except offer him a few drinks. No displays of empathy or even basic camaraderie. When Edgar began crying, Gerald didn't even bother to hand his father a tissue. He answered any questions without an ounce of feeling. C.T. was right—everyone grieved differently, but Gerald's complete lack of sorrow or emotion unsettled her.

Shouldn't he be more upset that his mother was dead? Murdered in fact? Even if they hadn't gotten along, he should want her killer caught. Maybe Gerald simply wasn't as emotional as his father. Still, T.J. expected to see some hint of loss in his eyes —or at least a bit of fatigue or stress in his face. But no. Gerald stopped playing entrepreneur long enough to turn up, look bored, and manage to be useless.

Even the news of his father's firing didn't make a dent. He must have already known. "Still," T.J. muttered to her empty apartment. "I'd be pissed." Edgar losing his wife under such circumstances was already a devastating blow, but Principal Hinson piled on when he fired the man on dubious grounds. Gerald still lived at home and didn't show any acumen in their brief encounter. He probably depended on his dad to some degree.

Why wasn't he angry?

Maybe he was in shock and still processed the whole mess. Even if the young man had never experienced the loss of someone close to him before, that explanation didn't sit right with her. The silence offered no answer. In moments like these, she missed the noise and energy of the office. So far, Gerald was a conundrum that T.J. couldn't quite solve. In her past job, she'd spent time with too many men and developed an ability to read them to some degree. The indifference in Gerald's gaze in the wake of such a tragedy gnawed at her.

T.J. got up and padded to her living room window. Street lights were already on, and even though dusk hadn't descended yet, each one lifted a little bit of gloom. Finding bright spots in the darkness was important. She'd learned to over the years. Edgar was figuring it out now. Gerald remained an enigma.

T.J. wasn't one to jump to conclusions, but she couldn't shake the feeling that there was more to Gerald than met the eye. She wasn't suspicious . . . not yet. She didn't know what was off about Gerald, but she was going to find out.

———

T.J. used her own laptop to do a little sleuthing.

She paid attention when C.T. shared tools and tips as he did so often. In the last few months, she'd completely reconfigured her computer to allow for some of the more interesting searches and activities the job required. Her work inbox showed a couple new emails. One was junk, but the other was from Gonzalez. The message only said, *These got logged into evidence at the scene but only reported on after you collected all the printouts.* The email contained a link to a secure Baltimore County site.

T.J. discovered the report covered a pair of prepaid cell phones recovered in the hotel room. She remembered reading allusions to phones in other documents but presumed they referred to the dead peoples' normal devices. Why would a man and a woman who didn't know each other both have prepaid mobiles at a seedy hotel? Were the two actually familiar with each other and managed to hide the connection from their families and friends . . . as well as the police and a PI's office?

The details on the phones were few. They were well-known and reliable Android models available at stores across Maryland and other states. Interestingly, each only held a single contact entry—the other number. T.J. frowned. This definitely pointed to the councilman and the teacher knowing each other. If they did, it would upend the entire case.

Had Raymond Ellicott been yet another man willing to step out on his wife? T.J. had seen—and, unfortunately, been paid to spend time with—plenty of that type over the years. They didn't come from any particular walk of life. Some people remarked about it always being the quiet ones or the folks no one would expect. In T.J.'s experience, no group or class held a monopoly on cheaters.

She kept going in the report. The second page held an undated text exchange beginning with the phone attributed to Raymond Ellicott.

I'm at the hotel. Come to room 115 and look sexy for me.

I'm on my way, baby. Gotta wear a jacket for the cold, but make sure you open it when I walk in.

You're so fucking hot. I swear I wish I wasn't married sometimes.

Me too, but let's not talk about it. We should enjoy our time together. We don't get enough of it.

Maybe we should make sure to schedule more.

Ravage me tonight first. Then we'll see.

"Wow," T.J. said to her apartment. "Pretty tame." And it was. She'd been paid to send much racier messages—with lewd photos attached—as part of a "girlfriend experience" package Weasel Boy offered certain clients. This exchange held no pictures, one curse word, and very little in the way of heated talk.

She closed the file not knowing what to think about where their case stood. Her thoughts returned to Gerald Russell and how weird he acted at home with his father. She stood and grabbed her keys. Keeping an eye on their house for a while couldn't hurt.

———

T.J. parked the Mustang down the street from the Russell residence, killing the lights as she pulled to the curb. She settled in to keep watch, curiosity nagging at her. Something about this case—and Gerald in particular—didn't sit right with her. Even allowing for people to grieve in their own ways, his behavior was odd at best. The curtains of the house were drawn, making it difficult to see within.

T.J. drummed her fingers on the steering wheel, eyes fixed on the darkened house. She wondered about Gerald's relationship with his parents. Did they get along? Had things always been strained or just more recently? Maybe she and C.T. should have put these questions to him. They'd run the risk of being perceived as insensitive, but it didn't really matter. They didn't work for the Russells, after all.

Then, there was the matter of Edgar's firing. Both he and Marcy served as faculty for The Sterner Academy for years. Model teachers. She gets murdered under admittedly unsavory circumstances, and out comes the morals clause like a hammer. The timing of it all seemed suspicious—not to mention Principal Hinson telling him he couldn't keep his woman in line. "Chauvinistic prick," she muttered in the car.

The pieces weren't adding up, and it was T.J.'s job to make them fit.

After over an hour of observing no action, T.J. was beginning to get antsy. Just then, movement caught her eye. A car drifted along the street toward her, and its headlights soon hit her mirror. T.J. slid down in her seat, watching as the black sedan came to a stop in front of the house. The front door swung open, and Gerald emerged. He locked up behind himself before pulling out his phone and hustling to the driveway. The vehicle sported an Uber sticker in the window. Gerald leaned forward and said something brief to the driver—probably confirming his name—before opening the rear door.

As Gerald left his Tesla at the curb and hopped in, T.J. tapped out a note on her phone with the make and model of the other car. It pulled away before she could get the plate. T.J. fired the Mustang to life and pulled out after it. She trailed the Uber at a reasonable distance as it wound its way through the residential streets of Middle River. Where could Gerald be off to on a random weeknight? And why would it be more important than spending time with his grieving father?

The more T.J. dealt with Gerald, the less she liked him.

As they approached the traffic light at Eastern Avenue, she edged closer to try and catch a glimpse of the Uber's navigation screen through the rear window. The light turned red. T.J. stopped and expected the sedan to, as well. Instead, it accelerated through the intersection. The driver of an approaching minivan expressed her displeasure with a loud and long horn honk.

T.J. wondered anew where Gerald could be headed at this hour. Why the need for secrecy? Her pulse quickened. It could be nothing. She tried to remember people dealt with grief in their own way. Maybe Gerald headed out for a night on the town with his friends. He probably needed it. She flashed back to her own unexciting twenty-first birthday as the light turned green. She was a good two minutes behind the sedan, and it could have made any of a series of turns. T.J. kept going down the main drag but didn't see the black car again.

"Dammit," she muttered. T.J. turned around at the next light and drove slowly back the way she came. She looked into each connecting street. No luck. Whoever drove the Uber knew what was going on and spotted the tail to make sure to lose it before going wherever they were actually headed. T.J. smacked the steering wheel in frustration. She should've stayed farther back. Getting the plate number instead of trying to see the screen would have been a good move, too. These were rookie mistakes, and she didn't think of herself as a rookie.

Cursing under her breath, T.J. contemplated her next course of action. Should she drive around hoping to randomly spot the Uber again? That seemed like a long shot. She decided her best bet was to go home. She and C.T. could review the new evidence Gonzalez provided and talk about what Gerald's actions might mean in the morning.

CHAPTER 12

MY LUNGS WERE BURNING by the time I turned onto Riverside Avenue. I slowed to a walk to catch my breath. Baltimore's autumn mornings had a way of waking me up, a cold slap of reality which only grew more chilly at the approach of winter. As I neared my house, a dark sedan pulled away from the curb. The windows were tinted too dark to see inside. I paused and checked for other vehicles or people on foot, but nothing else seemed out of place. Could have been an overnight guest from one of the rowhouses nearby. Still, I made a mental note of the make and model—some new Kia sedan—as I walked up the front steps.

Inside, the smell of coffee greeted me before my wife could. She was awake, yawning at the counter with a robe covering her pajamas. "Morning," she said with a sleepy smile.

"I didn't think you'd wake up until the bacon hit the pan," I said. Gloria poured me a mug of java, and I happily accepted it.

"I heard a car drive by." She shrugged. "They don't normally wake me up. Maybe I was already coming to." I thought about the Kia I saw pulling away. The company wasn't known for big noisy engines, and the car I saw sounded no louder than many others on the road.

Gloria grabbed a seat at the kitchen table. I needed a shower, but with her already awake, I might as well make breakfast first. "Did you talk to your parents?" she asked while I rummaged in the fridge.

"Yep."

"Are they resigning?"

"Nope."

"Are you feeling monosyllabic about the whole thing?"

"Yep," I said.

She chuckled. "You surprised?"

"Not really." I found some fresh sausage and a pack of eggs which still had a week to go. "I didn't expect them to leave in a fit of outrage, storm The Sterner Academy, and resign after smearing Hinson up and down the halls. It would have been great, but I didn't think it would happen. They don't do things at speed." I set a pan to heat on the stove.

"They're thinking about it, though?" Gloria asked.

"Yes. Probably trying to look into it themselves even though their son is the smartest PI working in the city."

"Maybe they're worried they can't afford his rates. Someone so brilliant must be expensive."

"I'm sure he would give them a family discount," I said. Once a pat of butter melted in the pan, I cracked two eggs to fry and stuffed four sausage patties into the rest of the space. Half a loaf of sourdough remained in the bread box, so I put two slices in the toaster. Another swig of coffee gave me the energy to keep going.

"I'm sure this isn't easy for them," she said. "Heck, my parents would probably do the same thing. They'd probably want to let things play out."

"I guess." I flipped the eggs and pork patties. "In the end, maybe Hinson will just be an asshole who used some arcane morals clause to kick a grieving man to the curb. If the school stays out of the bad part of the news cycle and keeps making money, he'll probably get a new contract out of it."

"You think he's involved?"

"I don't know who is at this point," I admitted. When the toast popped up, I buttered the pieces and then made two plates. I carried them both to the table, topped off my coffee, and joined Gloria. "He might be dirty. I kind of hope he is. I enjoy sticking it to guys like him."

"I'm sure you'll figure it out." She squeezed my hand. "If you do it quickly, you can tell the reporter about your latest triumph."

The damned interview. It was tomorrow, and I'd forgotten about it. It would be good for Gloria and her company, so I would grin my way through the whole thing. "Let's hope I have something good to say, then."

———

When I pulled into the lot, T.J.'s Mustang was already there. Things were operating more correctly in the world today. As I stepped out into the sunny morning, I hoped this positive trend would continue. Principal Hinson would confess to whatever he did, or maybe he'd climb up to the top of a tower at The Sterner Academy and hurl himself off. I figured neither was likely no matter what he did, but good weather and the promise of more fresh coffee filled me with a little irrational hope.

It dimmed quickly when I remembered the welcoming committee I'd gotten recently. Those two had clearly been staking out the office and waiting for me to arrive. If a couple of different goons showed up today, they would have found T.J. and not me. I bounded up the metal steps two at a time and threw the door open. No musclemen waited. T.J. sat behind her desk. She leaned out from behind her screen. "Why'd you run up the stairs?"

"In case whoever sent the first two assholes tried again," I said.

"Quiet morning so far, boss." She grinned. "But not a quiet night. Did you see Gonzalez sent us something?"

"No."

"You don't check your email at night?" she asked.

"Sometimes. Other days, I like to have an actual boundary between my job and the rest of my life." Gloria already worked from home—one of our houses—every day. As much as she loved her job, I also knew there were times she struggled to leave work behind her and enjoy an evening with her handsome husband.

I figured I would leave my wife's sometimes poor work-life balance out of the upcoming interview.

"It's a doozy. You should take a look."

"Sure," I said as I headed to the coffee pot. "Right after another cup of morning magic." Hot java in hand, I sat at my desk, woke up the laptop, and logged in. Sure enough, Gonzalez sent an email last night. His extremely chatty message read, *These got logged into evidence at the scene but only reported on after you collected all the printouts.* "I'd been wondering about phones. Unless there's been a robbery, it's hard to believe anyone is found without one today."

"Check the report," T.J. said.

"Must be juicy."

"I saw it last night."

"You know you don't need to work when you're off the clock, right?"

She shrugged. "Something was nagging at me. I don't trust the son . . . Gerald."

"And this compelled you to check your email?" I asked.

"I wanted to look a few things up," my assistant said. "Happened to see a new message."

I got the feeling there was more to the Gerald situation, but I let it go for now and followed the link Gonzalez provided. Like a modern police department, the BCPD did a lot of things online. The page I landed on looked like SharePoint. Easy to lock things down to certain internal users based on group membership or rights, and it was simple to grant read-only access to outsiders like me. The devices in question were common Android burners available in a couple hundred stores across the state and probably ten within a reasonable distance of the hotel.

The notes marked the investigation into the phones as ongoing. I saw no report of fingerprints or other DNA yet. Each held only one number in storage, and of course, it belonged to the other in both cases. I didn't like this turn of events. All our work had been predicated on the fact Raymond Ellicott and Marcy Russell didn't know one another. If they did—especially to the degree they bought exclusive burners and went to a no-tell hotel —then we would need to start over.

Call logs were empty. Curious. There were only a few texts. Maybe they'd recently acquired the devices. I read the conversation beginning with the phone the BCPD assigned to Ellicott.

> I'm at the hotel. Come to room 115 and look sexy for me.

> I'm on my way, baby. Gotta wear a jacket for the cold, but make sure you open it when I walk in.

> You're so fucking hot. I swear I wish I wasn't married sometimes.

> Me too, but let's not talk about it. We should enjoy our time together. We don't get enough of it.

> Maybe we should make sure to schedule more.

> Ravage me tonight first. Then we'll see.

"Ravage me?" I wondered aloud.

"No one's ever said it to you?" T.J. asked with a chuckle.

"I don't think anyone's said it in a hundred years." I read the exchange again. "This is the tamest version of sexting I think I've ever seen. Where are the racy messages? The pictures?"

"I wondered the same things." T.J. wheeled her chair to my desk.

"It's like a couple of prudes wrote these messages because they heard the young people were sending spicy things to one another."

"Well, these people are both in their forties. Much closer to your age than mine."

I chuckled. "The whole thing just sounds . . . off somehow."

"You think they didn't write these texts?"

"Impossible to say. It's interesting, however . . . the report doesn't show date or timestamps. Someone could have killed both victims and created the conversation after they were dead to send police down the wrong road."

"Maybe," T.J. said. "Want to know what's going on with Gerald?"

I frowned, wondering where she'd gotten this information. "Sure."

"I went to the house last night. Don't worry. I parked up the street. They didn't see me . . . especially not with the curtains drawn."

"What happened?"

"Gerald left in an Uber . . . not his own ride. I let them get a little ahead and followed. The car lost me at a light, though, and I couldn't find it again. It's like the driver knew I was behind him."

"You think he's being secretive?" I said.

"Sure looks like it."

"Maybe he's sneaking out to meet his girlfriend." She rolled her eyes. "Yes, it's possible he's up to something shady. I didn't like the way he acted when we were there, either."

"I think we should keep an eye on him."

"Maybe." I tapped my screen where the world's tamest text exchange between two supposed lovers occupied much of the real estate. "I'm really curious about this. It reeks of a setup, but we need to be sure."

"This is going to involve a couple of uncomfortable conversations."

"It is."

"Good thing your name is on the door, then," she pointed out, wheeling back to her own desk.

"Yes," I said. "Lucky me."

———

I didn't look forward to the conversation, but we needed to do it. I called Susan Ellicott. "Mister Ferguson, it's good to hear from you."

"Please, call me C.T. I have some—"

"Let me get Paula. Hang on." I was about to tell her we didn't need Paula. Having one woman mad at me at a time was enough. I learned this when I tried to date multiple girls at the same time in college. It took a few iterations to drive the point home then. I'd smartened up in the intervening years. A moment later, background noise filled the line. I guessed we were now on speaker, and Susan confirmed this. "Okay, Paula's here with me, and you're on speaker."

"Hi," Paula said.

Before I could raise a sensible objection to the arrangement, Susan spoke again. "Are you calling to give us an update, C.T.?"

In a manner of speaking, I supposed I was, but I didn't want to get their hopes up with a confirmation. "More of a question, really," I said. "We've talked to a lot of people, including the family of Marcy Russell."

"Those poor folks," Susan said. "I know exactly what they're going through."

She didn't, but I wouldn't belabor the point. "They've told us pretty much the same things you did. No connections between the two victims."

"I'm not sure I like where this is heading," Paula said in an ominous tone.

"County police shared some new evidence with us," I said. "It took us a while to sift through everything they gave us at first, but I never saw any mention of cell phones recovered at the scene."

"I presumed they were taken," Susan said. "A robbery."

"Both your husband and Marcy Russell had cash and jewelry on them. It's not like a robber to leave something like a ring behind."

"What are you saying, C.T.?"

"The new evidence was two burners. Not in the initial report because the BCPD sent them out for analysis. Apparently, they came back last night. Cops ran the records for their real phones. No sign they ever talked. " I took a deep breath. "There's no delicate way to ask this, so I'm just going to go ahead. Are you sure Raymond didn't know Marcy Russell?"

"As sure as I can be," Susan said.

"He never talked about her," Paula added.

If Raymond and Marcy were carrying on an affair, this wouldn't be surprising. Only the most colossally stupid married man would mention his mistress to his adult daughter. "Each phone had only the other as a contact," I said. "There was a text exchange in the police report. It's . . . tame, but it suggests they knew each other."

No one said anything for a few seconds. When Paula answered, I could hear the tears. "How well?"

"Well enough to arrange the rendezvous and talk about looking forward to it."

The line went silent. One of the Ellicotts probably muted their end of the connection. I did the same with ours. "Let's see if they give us a pink slip," I whispered to T.J.

"You think they would?"

"We've raised a suspicion which would upend everything they knew about their husband or father. It's a possibility."

Before T.J. could answer, the Ellicott ladies came back on the call. "I don't buy it," Susan said, and her tone suggested she would not entertain further suggestions to the contrary. "There's no reason Raymond and this woman would have crossed paths, and he wouldn't cheat on me. Do you have anything else to go over?"

"We're pulling on a few strings," I said. "Nothing definitive yet. Someone sent two alleged tough guys here the other morning, so we rattled the right cage somewhere along the way."

"All right. Please let us know if there are any *facts* we should be aware of."

"We will."

Susan ended the call. "At least she didn't fire us," T.J. said.

"And the Russells can't. It's the worst win-win in history."

"It still counts," my assistant said.

I wished I could share her optimism.

CHAPTER 13

BECAUSE WE HADN'T INFLICTED enough harm on ourselves, T.J. and I called Edgar Russell next. Before I tapped the green button on my phone screen, I said, "We're not going to mention Gerald leaving last night. He doesn't need to know you followed him."

"His driver seemed to know someone was back there," she said.

"Let the identity remain a mystery, then." I tapped the button, and Edgar answered after a couple rings.

"Do you have a break in the case already?" he wanted to know.

"Not exactly," I said. "Is your son there?"

"He is. I think he might even be awake." He moved away from the phone, but we still heard him shout for Gerald loud and clear. A minute later, they both came back. "We're here now."

"As you know, the Ellicotts hired us," I said. "We've always proceeded as if there were two victims who were equally likely to have been in someone's sights."

"You can get to the point, C.T.," Edgar said. "Between Marcy's murder and Hinson kicking me to the curb, I've gotten used to hearing bad news recently."

"The county police logged two burner phones into evidence recently," T.J. said. "They weren't in the report we read because they'd been sent out for analysis."

"Are the results back?" Gerald asked.

"Yes," I said. "It's . . . not a positive development. Each had one number in the contact list, and it belonged to the other phone. There's no call history between them, but there's a text exchange. It suggests they knew each other well enough to plan their meeting at the hotel." I paused. Silence prevailed. "There's nothing racy or indecent. It's the most PG-rated thing I've read in quite some time, actually."

"Is there any evidence Marcy knew the councilman?" Edgar said.

"Dad, the phone records are telling us she did," Gerald put it.

"No. No, I don't believe it. Is it possible someone could have added those messages after . . . after they . . . "

"Yes," I said. "These are the kinds of devices you can get anywhere. It would have been easy for someone to buy them, create the text chain, and make it look like Marcy and Raymond carried them."

"Were they robbed?"

"Their personal phones weren't recovered," T.J. said. "Cash, credit cards, and jewelry were intact. It makes robbery unlikely."

"Sounds like it lends credence to my idea," Edgar said.

"I don't know, Dad," Gerald added. "We can't possibly know every person Mom encountered."

"I'm not buying it." Edgar's voice was firm.

"I don't know if I am, either, but it's interesting evidence."

"If your mother could hear you now, she'd be disappointed."

"Well, she can't, can she? She's dead!"

"You think I don't know—" I hit the red button to end the call. We didn't need to intrude on the Russells more than we already did.

"Don't try to put a positive spin on this one," I told T.J.

She shook her head. "Don't think I could. Gerald sure seems like a scumbag. He's ready to believe the worst about his mother."

"We need to know more about her. Maybe some of her coworkers would want to talk to us."

"You think they'll know anything?"

"Considering how shallow our knowledge pool is right now, it can't hurt."

"All right," T.J. said. "I'll see if I can set something up without raising the alarm at The Sterner Academy."

Normally, I might not care what attention we attracted. Considering the waters of this case were rife with sharks—and we didn't know which were the great whites—I agreed with my assistant's need for discretion. Even if Principal Hinson were just a massive jerk, he didn't need to know anything about what we did.

———

A little while later, T.J. clapped her hands, jarring me out of another unproductive look at the BCPD's work. "Yes! I got three of Marcy's colleagues to talk to us."

"How?"

"You told me most email addresses are easy to guess," she said. "Sterner only publishes a few they want the public to know. It's firstname dot lastname . . . maybe there's a number added for really common ones. Anyway, the directory of teachers and their credentials is available online, so I figured the same format would apply. I emailed a bunch of the ones who worked with Marcy."

"Is her bio still up?" I wondered.

"No."

"Interesting."

"It is," she agreed. "I sent a Zoom link. They're going to join us shortly."

"In the middle of the day?"

T.J. shrugged. "Two of them are free this period, and one's cutting out on a planning session."

In a role reversal, I wheeled my chair to T.J.'s desk. "Good work on the emails," I said.

"You could've done it."

"I figured my time was more valuable brooding over the evidence." She'd mentioned doing something at Sterner, so I wanted to give her the chance. If nothing happened by the afternoon, I would have taken the same steps my assistant did. It was good to see her learning on the job. She made a better student than I did a teacher.

"Uh-huh," T.J. said.

Her Zoom window indicated another party joined the room. T.J. clicked to admit the new arrival. Three women sat in a vehicle whose roof height suggested a nice SUV. A car like my Audi was probably the baseline to get into the staff and faculty lot at The Sterner Academy. American cars probably got towed within an hour. Can't have parents and boosters thinking the teachers drive anything less than the best. The plush headliner around them was a light tan, matching the leather seats.

No one held the phone, so I presumed it was in some holder or mount on the dashboard. Height was difficult to gauge with everyone seated, but the woman behind the wheel's hair came closest to the roof. She spoke first. "Hello?"

"Hi, we're here," T.J. said. "I'm the one who contacted you. This is my boss C.T. Ferguson."

"I'm a private investigator looking into the whole mess," I added.

The driver was a pretty brunette who appeared to be around my age. "Looking into it for whom?"

"The councilman's family hired us, but we're not presuming who the more likely target was. This crime had two victims."

"More if you count their families," the passenger said. She was a blonde with a round face.

"Sorry," the one behind the wheel said. "I should probably introduce everyone. I'm Clarissa Van Buren. I taught with Marcy most days. We were on the same team. Next to me is Penelope Whitestone." The woman in the passenger's seat offered a curt wave. "Behind us is Rosalind Fairweather." A young teacher with hair the same shade of chestnut as Gloria's leaned in from behind and smiled. All of them dressed in a manner managing to be both professional and conservative at the same time. It wouldn't have surprised me to see those two terms in the Sterner rulebook—and probably more than once.

"We all want to see whoever did this caught," Penelope said.

"Same here," I said. "We've been operating under the presumption Marcy and the councilman didn't know each other, but the police just got some evidence to suggest otherwise. Did she mention anything about him or anyone else in his position?"

"Not to me," Clarissa said. The other two shook their heads in agreement.

"I don't think she was interested in politics," Penelope added. "Or politicians." In the back, Rosalind lowered her head for a second.

We would come back to her.

"Can you think of any reason she would have been at a hotel?" T.J. asked.

"No," Clarissa said. "It's not near the school or her house. I can't see her going out of her way to that part of town."

"Neither Marcy nor the councilman had their phones on them when their bodies were found," I said. "They still had other valuables, so it makes robbery unlikely. The police think the bodies might have been moved and posed there." Even if they didn't, it was my current working theory. Might as well try it out. "I know it would seem unlikely for a teacher to have enemies, but can you think of anyone?"

Penelope leaned in and shrugged. "We have parents who get on our cases every now and then. It's usually over a grade or an assignment. Something they think their genius child should have done better on." She snorted, and her two colleagues rolled their eyes as if on cue. I wondered if they took this show on the road. "Nothing ever comes of it, though. The worst threaten to rat us out to the principal. Even if they do, we don't get in trouble as long as we're doing our jobs. At some point, it's on the kids to learn."

"It's worse when you're new," Rosalind said. "There are parents who think the money they pay allows them to push you around. I've been doing this for five years now. I know that's not a long time compared to some of my colleagues here, but I'm not fresh out of college, either."

"Did Marcy attract any particularly nasty attention?" T.J. asked. "Or someone who just wouldn't let it go?"

All three women shook their heads. "If she did," Penelope answered for the group, "we never heard about it."

"She would've told us," Clarissa added.

"Anything else you can think of?" I said. I remembered Rosalind's head drop earlier and thought it might be significant. I needed her to think the same. "Doesn't matter what it is. Details people think are unimportant can break a case wide open."

In the front seats, Clarissa and Penelope looked at each other and both shrugged. "Maybe," Rosalind said a second later.

"You can tell us," T.J. said.

"It's probably nothing. A few months ago, she was pissed about something. I'm not sure what. I don't think I'd ever seen her angry like that before. I asked her what happened, and she wouldn't get into it." She paused for a small chuckle. "Then, she said the weirdest thing. 'Maybe I'll surprise them all and run for the school board.' We laughed about it. I never heard her mention it again."

"Sterner is a private school," I said. "I wouldn't think you're subject to the whims of the county school board."

"We're not," Clarissa said. "There are standards every school needs to meet, but I think parents choose to send their kids here because we're not merely any old county school."

"Who would want to be on the board, anyway?" Rosalind wondered. "It's all gotten so political. You endure long hours of loud jerks yelling at each other."

"We're going to need to get back." Clarissa looked at her watch. "Fourth period is almost over."

"I think we have what we need," I said. "Thank you all for talking to us today."

The teachers bid us adieu and ended the video call. "The school board," T.J. said. "That's new."

"And surprising. Why would someone who teaches at a place like Sterner care about what goes on in the county? The whole point of private schools is they don't have all the oversight."

"We keep learning things that are making this harder."

"Yes," I said. "Let's hope the rest of the day is easier."

When T.J. went out to pick up something for lunch, I called Edgar Russell back. "I'm sorry about earlier," he said. "It's a tough situation, and I don't think Gerald is handling it well."

"There's no easy way to get through things like these," I told him.

"Do you need Gerald for something? I'm . . . not sure he's still home."

"No. I wanted to get your take on Anthony Hinson." Edgar

didn't say anything, so I continued. "I'm sure you hate him right now, and I get it. He rubs me the wrong way. I don't know if he's involved at all, but he's a prick, and I want to know what you think about him."

Edgar sighed before answering. "You're right. He's a prick. He can turn on the charm when he thinks it will benefit The Sterner Academy . . . or himself . . . but if he thinks he doesn't need something from you, he's basically an ass. He wasn't bad to deal with as a principal."

"All in on the school?"

"Sort of. I got the feeling he always had something else going."

"Like what?" I asked.

"I don't know. Hinson was always great at promoting Sterner, but he talked himself up at the same time. I never got the impression he was angling for another job, so he must have been trying to get his name out there. I just don't know for what."

I thought about broaching the topic of Marcy's potential run at the school board but decided against it. Among the dreary menu of burying his wife, dealing with his son, and losing his job, Edgar Russell didn't need someone sliding anything else onto his plate. "Maybe I'll shake the tree and see what falls out," I said. "Thanks for your time." I ended the call and got to work.

In addition to hacking into things and pissing people off, investigating potentially wild tangents might have been my best skill as a detective. I pulled up the puffed-up biography of Anthony Hinson on The Sterner Academy's website. Teachers got a paragraph or so for a writeup before the list of their bona fides. Staff enjoyed quite a bit more, and Hinson made sure to capitalize on the extra real estate.

In the constellation of educational luminaries, Anthony Hinson shines as a bright and constant star, steering the venerable ship of The Sterner Academy with unparalleled grace and wisdom. Serving with unrivaled distinction as Principal, Dr. Hinson has forged a beacon of excellence, lighting the path of knowledge for the promising young minds that grace the Academy's halls.

A paragon of intellectual prowess and visionary leadership, Anthony Hinson embarked on his luminous journey with a summa cum laude distinction from Yale, where he majored in Educational Leadership, subsequently achieving a Ph.D. that echoes his indomitable thirst for knowledge. His prodigious academic journey is rivaled only by his voracious appetite for fostering excellence in others, a trait finely honed through years of meticulous training and experience.

During his tenure, The Sterner Academy has blossomed into a veritable Eden of learning, where students are nurtured to become not just leaders, but pioneers of the future, equipped with the acumen to navigate the complex labyrinth of the modern world. Under his stewardship, the Academy has secured numerous accolades, transforming into a haven where innovation meets tradition, a place where young minds are cultivated to their fullest potential.

But Dr. Hinson's accomplishments transcend the walls of the academy. A revered thought leader in the educational sphere, he is often sought after as a keynote speaker at conferences, where he dazzles audiences with his profound insights and avant-garde approaches to education. A prolific writer, his scholarly articles grace the pages of prestigious journals, setting the gold standard in educational discourse.

"What a reeking crock of shit," I commented. I stopped reading when the nausea became too great. T.J. would be back with lunch soon, and I wanted it to stay down. The Sterner Academy clearly let Hinson write his own bio and didn't appear to provide so much as a cursory edit. The flowery paragraphs probably impressed people who valued the things in them. As far as I could tell, it was all hot air. In reality, Hinson ran a fancy private school which catered to Baltimore's elite and charged tuition rivaling many excellent colleges. If he simply stayed out of the way, the place would probably do fine coasting on reputation and whatever work the assistant principals did.

I scrolled to the bottom and saw one thing which jumped off the screen at me: Hinson was a member at the Roland Park Country Club. An odd place for someone so devoted to education, but it would be exactly the right venue to hobnob with people promoting money and opportunity without the pesky demands of oversight. I called the club and got connected to someone in the main office. "I'm sorry to bother you," I led off, "but Anthony Hinson invited me to an event, and for the life of me I can't remember when. I'd try to call him myself, but he's a principal."

"No problem, sir," the cheery woman said. Customer service operators tended to be helpful. It was in their job description. At a ritzy country club, they would trip over themselves to do it. "Mister Hinson has a dinner on the books for four-thirty today."

"Well, I guess I'd better find my tux." She giggled politely. "Thank you," I said, and I broke the connection before she could ask any follow-up questions. I needed to be in attendance at Hinson's *soirée*. A significant roadblock presented itself: to get in, I needed an invitation from an existing member. Good thing I knew one.

"Absolutely not," my father said when I posed the question to him.

"I wouldn't ask if it weren't important, Dad."

"I know you think Hinson is shady. I agree it seems he acted in bad faith, but it's no reason to crash some event."

"I won't be crashing. You and I will be there having a drink and rubbing elbows with your rich friends. It just so happens Hinson will be talking to a bunch of assholes nearby."

"You'll make a scene," he said.

"*Moi?*"

"Yes, you."

"I'll be the picture of decorum." My father said nothing. We both knew I was lying. I had every intention to make a scene and embarrass Hinson. My father's silence conveyed his understanding of the situation. "It's vital to the case, Dad. Two people are dead. Maybe Hinson's not involved, but there's something shady around him. I need to see what it is."

"All right," he said after a moment. "Meet me there at four-fifteen."

"Thanks, Dad."

"Don't thank me, yet. If the club fines me, you're paying it."

"It'll be worth it," I said.

CHAPTER 14

AFTER LUNCH, I filled T.J. in on the plan. "I wish I could come with you," she said. "The smug prick."

"You mean Hinson, right?"

She chuckled. "I think I'll leave it vague. Kinda surprised your dad agreed."

"Me, too," I said. "I'm sure someone will shake a finger at him or maybe *tsk* a few times. I'm actually going to try and be on some decent behavior at least. How long it remains is up to Hinson and whoever is there with him."

"You didn't get any other details about the dinner?" she asked.

"No. Places like the country club have to factor member privacy in. Their folks will be helpful, but they're not going past the basics unless you give them a compelling reason, and me cold-calling doesn't come close."

"You wearing a tux?"

"Suit," I said. "Might even style my hair a little and go for the Harvey Specter impression."

"Who?"

I sighed, leaving my assistant with the homework of watching *Suits* while I headed home early to change. Gloria wasn't there—

probably working at her own house or scouting a location some-where. Some aspects of her job sounded very exciting. Others . . . not so much, though I supposed the same was true of mine. Tossing a couple of goons down the stairs got the blood moving a lot more than hours in a car staking out someone's house.

I opted for a dark gray Tommy Hilfiger model, pairing it with a plain white button-down and sharp red tie. I reached the country club early and let the valet take my S4. Belonging to the model's previous generation, it was one of the few in the States with a manual transmission. This required a second person—who could actually operate the third pedal—to take the car. Scanning the lot where they left vehicles, I didn't see my father's silver Lexus. I hoped he wouldn't faint when he realized I was early.

A few minutes later, he handed the keys to his LS to the same valet who took my car. We walked up the paved path together. The building was two stories and brick with a slate gray roof and windows trimmed in white. A large brick archway led to the main doors. "How luxurious," I said as we passed under the arch.

My father ignored me. He'd probably be doing plenty of it today. "Robert Ferguson and guest," he told the gentleman inside the entryway.

"Very good, sir," he said, suggesting he'd brushed up on his Wodehouse before taking the job.

"You know Jeeves back there?" I asked when we were out of earshot.

"No," my father said. "I take it we're headed to the restaurant?"

"I didn't come here for the duckpin bowling."

He smirked. "I'd probably still beat you. Your mother and I did well in a fifty-five-and-over league last year."

"When you're ready to try with the bumpers up," I said, "you know where to find me."

My father smiled, and I followed him to the restaurant. He told another guy who we were. Jeeves number two offered the same response. I'd been to the club a few times with my folks, but it had been years since I'd taken a meal here. The restaurant floors were tan tile with gold inlays. Mahogany beams ran along the ceiling in stark contrast to the off-white paint. A similar color scheme prevailed on the tables and their cloths. Real napkins enveloped silverware. The whole scene almost made me want to get a fancy sales job so I could afford the membership.

Almost.

From the bar, I spotted a reserved area which looked like two or three tables shoved together. My father ordered a rum and soda, and I opted for a beer. He put the usurious fee for our drinks on his tab, and we headed to a vacant table near where Hinson would hold court. We were close enough to see every-thing—and maybe hear what went on, as the place wasn't crowded at four-twenty-five—but I made sure to stick my dad between me and the VIP area.

Shortly after the appointed time, Hinson and seven other men all dressed to the nines walked in and strode to the reserved space like they owned it. One man wore glasses with red frames, but everyone else opted for a sedate and professional look. I sat lower in my seat and shifted to the right a little so my father's head would screen Hinson's view of me. He didn't raise the alarm, so I figured we were good. The party ordered a round of drinks and engaged in the kind of small talk rich and powerful men make. Someone bought a company, another paid cash for a vintage Porsche, and a third man was fucking both his secretary and the college intern behind his wife's back. The last story earned the most guffaws and attaboys. I wasn't surprised.

As five o'clock neared, more people filtered in, including a pair who sat between us and Hinson's VIP spot. The added noise made eavesdropping harder. An additional tuxedo-clad server patrolled the dining room. I leaned forward—which came with the added benefit of keeping me low enough to avoid being seen —and listened as best I could.

"We'll be at the funding stage soon," Hinson said. "I expect a successful trial, and then we'll open things up for a few select investors." He talked a little longer and even fielded a couple of questions but never mentioned the product. I supposed the men he invited already knew.

"This is my cue, Dad." I stood.

"Remember," he said, "you're on the hook if the club fines me."

"Yup." I approached while Hinson talked more about investments, percentages, and potential terms. I came from his right side as he faced the small audience, so he wouldn't see me at his four o'clock. "Wow, I think I'd like to get in on this." The seven other men frowned at my interruption. Hinson turned. Recognition pulled his brows into a furrow, and he glowered at me. "How much does it take to get in on the ground floor? I probably have a hundred in cash on me today, but I have a platinum AmEx, too."

"Mister Ferguson," he said through clenched teeth. "How did you get in here?"

"Apparently, they'll let anyone join this place."

"I'm in the middle of a meeting."

"I'm looking to expand my portfolio, Tony." The nickname earned me a fresh scowl. "What's the product? I want to make sure I'm properly diversified."

"We're not open to investors yet," he said, summoning some professionalism as his face reddened.

"Take a hike, pal," one of the men at the table said as he stood. He was about my height though heavier and at least fifteen years older. This aggressive gentleman did not wear the red glasses. "Private event."

"And a private club," I pointed out. "Yet here I am."

"You want to do this the hard way?" I shrugged, and he came toward me. I figured my father was covering his eyes somewhere behind me, hoping no one pegged him as the member who brought a disruptive guest. My antagonist fired off a quick jab and then a cross. Someone in their first week of karate class could have blocked both. I did so easily.

"Let's not make a scene, Zeb," Hinson said in the same tone he might use to tell students to stop running in the hallways.

"Yeah, Zeb," I said. "Besides, I'm going to go on offense if you try to hit me again, and I don't think it would end well for you."

"We'll pick this up another time." Hinson recovered his phone and thrust it into his pocket. "Forgive the intrusion, gentlemen." He walked the long way around the table. I let him go. Zeb glared at me. All the other men did.

"He's a snake oil salesman, guys," I said. "I just saved you a lot of money." Their expressions remained uncharitable. Zeb harrumphed and sat again. I wondered if he was Hinson's connection to the two goons who visited me a couple days ago.

———

I walked away from Hinson's group and rejoined my father. He sat alone at our table. Sure enough, he made sure to face away from what transpired behind him. His glass was now empty. I was surprised he didn't order another. "Well, the room was treated to quite a spectacle," he said as I took my seat.

I snorted. "Blame Hinson's asshole friend. I'm not the one who started throwing punches. I didn't even attack back, Dad. You should be admiring my restraint."

My father sighed. "From what I heard, son, you seemed to enjoy antagonizing Hinson."

"I didn't antagonize anyone. I wanted to know what the product was. Still do, really. It might matter to the case. Zeb took a swing at me for asking a couple basic questions about their little investment club."

"I just don't think you'll win anyone over with confrontation." He picked up his glass and frowned at the ice remaining in the bottom. "Besides, no matter your low opinion of Hinson, there's nothing untoward about him soliciting funds. You took enough business classes to know how many products get their initial kick from family and friends investing."

I leaned forward, torn between needing to be heard over the growing crowd and the desire to keep my voice down. "Sure, but what's he actually collecting investments for? I'd like to know the nature of the product. What if it creates some kind of conflict with his job? There's zero chance he's ethical enough to give a shit about a conflict of interest."

My father waved a hand. "You're making assumptions. We don't know what it is. It could be completely unrelated."

I took a swig of my beer. It had grown to room temperature, and this diminished my enthusiasm for finishing it. "Maybe. You're going to some decent lengths to defend this guy, Dad. I still think you and Mom should resign from the board." He didn't reply. We sat in tense silence for a minute. I knew my father disapproved of my tactics, but he also knew I couldn't come to a place like this and not challenge Hinson. Even if I wouldn't credit myself with making a scene, one ensued.

Finally, my father sighed again and stood, fastening the top button of his jacket. "All right. I think I've had my fill of excitement. The club probably has, too." I rose as well, and we headed for the exit. The dining room buzzed with an ever-expanding crowd, and part of me wondered how many people discussed the brief scuffle between me and Zeb. I glanced behind me and didn't see Hinson at his reserved table. Maybe he beat a hasty retreat. His carefully cultivated image might have taken it on the chin a little today.

We stepped out into the increasing chill and approaching dusk. Valets rushed to retrieve our vehicles once we handed them the tickets. I turned to my father. "You know I'm right about Hinson. Resigning from the board is the only logical and ethical move."

He regarded me with tired eyes. "I understand your concerns, son. We don't know what tonight was about, but it's not black and white. You may not like him, but he's done considerable good for The Sterner Academy."

"A place like Sterner can pretty much run on its own," I said. "As long as you don't have an idiot steering it into an iceberg, it'll keep going."

"I think you're understating the job," my father said. "Look, your mother and I will consider everything you've said. We've been on the Sterner board for a few years, but we're not married to the place. If we find out something bad is going on—"

"How are you going to find out, Dad? Hire an investigator?" He rolled his eyes. "Maybe you should try trusting the one in your family."

"You might be too close to this."

"Forget it," I said, holding up a hand. "I'm trying to keep a bad situation from blowing up in your face. You and Mom do a lot of good work. There's no need to get caught in the blowback here." Before my father could respond, the valet arrived with my car. I tipped him a five and climbed inside the black S4. My father still frowned, probably considering what he wanted to say. "Goodnight, Dad. Let me know when you come to your senses." I pulled away, watching my father recede in the rearview mirror.

I'd hoped seeing Hinson in action would spur him to resign but no dice. He seemed to want actual proof of wrongdoing, and I had no idea how he expected to uncover this himself. If Hinson were involved in the murders of Raymond Ellicott and Marcy Russell, we would make him pay for it. Maybe my parents would even end their involvement with Sterner before it became problematic.

It was a challenge for another day. Tonight, I headed home feeling I'd at least rattled Hinson's cage. The jackass scurried off after I crashed his little investors party. Maybe someone there would reconsider parting with his money. It was a small victory, but I would take it.

For now.

———

Gravel crunched under my tires as I passed through the country club gates. Once I was back on asphalt, I grabbed my phone off the passenger seat and called T.J.

"Hey, boss, how'd it go?" she answered.

"About as well as expected. Which is to say . . . not very well at all."

T.J. chuckled. "Did you at least get some good intel on Hinson?"

I wished I did. Other than the aggression shown by one of the man's friends, I came away with more questions and few answers. "I learned he's just as much of a pompous windbag when speaking to a group as one-on-one," I said as I checked for tails. No one followed me. "You should read his bio when you're not hungry. On the whole, I'm not sure this was a useful outing. He made a sales pitch I couldn't hear much of, and one of the potential investors threatened me."

"At the country club? Wow, membership standards are slipping."

"Don't tell my father. I think he's expecting to get a fine in the mail for the scene he thinks I caused."

"Sounds like you don't know much more than you did before you put your fancy threads on," T.J. said.

"Unfortunately, you're right," I said. "It was fun to wind up Hinson, at least, though it does make learning more about him a little more challenging. He'll never let me within a mile of The Sterner Academy now. We need to know what he's up to. After our latest encounter, there's no easy way I could get back inside and look around."

T.J. was quiet for a moment. "What about me?" she finally said. "Hinson doesn't know me. We've never met. Maybe I could pose as a prospective parent or something. They might even give me a tour of the place."

"I like your attempt at problem solving, but it doesn't work. You're way too young to have a kid old enough for Sterner."

"I'm twenty-one. I could pass for a couple years older."

"Maybe," I admitted. "This is going to sound judgy . . . but women who have kindergarten-aged children while in their early twenties almost certainly can't afford to send their tykes to Sterner."

She sighed. "You're right. That does sound judgy."

"It was a good idea. We'll figure something out. There's got to be an opening somewhere. If we can't go in person, there are ways to get into his computer."

"If he's keeping whatever we care about on his work PC," she said.

"Fair enough. He might not."

I made a turn and headed toward I-83 and Gloria's house. "We'll keep digging. If there's a startup, we should be able to find the records. The guy who took a swing at me was Zeb. Probably a nickname, but if we can uncover something, it might get us to more of the men involved. Maybe we can leverage one of them if we can't get to Hinson directly."

"Good plan, boss," T.J. said. "I'll start first thing tomorrow."

I knew she would, and I hoped she wouldn't lay the ground-work tonight. While smart and eager to learn, T.J. lacked experience, and this sometimes led to preventable mistakes. We couldn't have a bunch of unforced errors if we wanted to take down Hinson . . . or whoever was responsible for the double murder at the heart of our investigation. "All right. See you then." I ended the call and tossed my phone onto the seat beside me. Checking the rearview mirror, I saw only unfamiliar vehicles behind me. No one had decided to follow me from the club.

As I headed north and the sun dropped close to the horizon on my left, I turned my thoughts back to the problem at hand. T.J. was right, we'd figure something out. I couldn't get into the school. She might be able to, but not in the guise of a prospective parent. I thought about asking Gloria to do it but dismissed it just as quickly. My wife had enough on her mind and her plate, and I didn't want to put her in danger in case Hinson smelled a rat.

Worrying about it more tonight wouldn't get me anywhere. T.J. and I would dive back in tomorrow fresh and ready. If we didn't have an easy way to get back onto campus and inside the main building, I could always craft a special email to send my favorite principal. Spear phishing when the target was a massively self-important prick never presented a challenge. A little puffery, and Hinson would open the message.

I got off at Falls Road and headed toward Brooklandville. Gloria would be hungry. I was, too. I'd never eaten anything at the club. As I drove past her street in search of delicious take-out, I checked the mirrors again. No suspicious cars followed me.

I wondered how long this would remain true.

CHAPTER 15

EARLY THE NEXT MORNING, I drove through the stately iron gates of The Sterner Academy and up the unblemished driveway. It made me wonder if some company came in and paved it every summer just so parents' Bentleys didn't have to drive over pock-marked asphalt. I followed the signs to visitor parking. The campus still looked like something out of a brochure. The faculty and staff lot was packed with expensive cars. Local Mercedes and Land Rover dealerships could have filmed commercials here.

I'd arrived about an hour before first period began. Still, students dressed in the school's signature navy blazers and khaki pants strolled along the pristine pathways, backpacks slung over their shoulders. I wondered how many had known Marcy Russell. I needed a plan to get around campus. Hinson would have me removed on sight. I wondered if he circulated photos of me to the security staff. Venturing into the buildings would be risky.

Skirting the perimeter might lead me to fewer people who knew Marcy Russell or could tell me something useful, but I would stick to it at first. I hopped out of the S4 and headed toward the athletic fields. A few enterprising students ran on the track. A man with a stopwatch in hand observed some of them.

He was about my height, a few years older, and a little brawnier, with brown hair and round glasses. His dark eyes narrowed as I approached, and it made me wonder if he recognized me. "You need something?" he said in an unfriendly tone.

"I'm investigating the murder of Marcy Russell."

"Terrible thing. She was a good lady."

"You the track coach?" I asked.

He shook his head. "Ronald Lobdell. Lacrosse." He did not offer his hand.

I considered telling him about my own lacrosse success, but I also didn't want this to turn into a pissing match. Unless he'd also been a collegiate champion, he could interpret something I said as one-upmanship. He'd probably be right on some level, and at the moment, I needed him not to hate me and report me to security.

"Did you know her well?"

He shrugged. "Not really. I only teach a couple gym classes, so we didn't cross paths in the buildings often. She was always nice to me when we did. Students really seemed to like her."

I studied him, searching for any tells or signs he was holding something back. Coach Lobdell managed to hold my gaze while continuing to look unhappy. "Any thoughts on who could've wanted to hurt her?"

"Wish I did." He glanced down at his watch. "Listen, I gotta get these kids moving. Some of them won't be ready for lacrosse in the spring."

"Sure," I said. "Good luck." He grunted, and I headed farther down the path. Behind me, Lobdell barked at a couple students, telling them their times wouldn't cut it when the games counted. I never broke a sweat when we played against Sterner in high school, and the degree to which I still followed the local lacrosse scene told me things remained largely the same.

After about a hundred more yards, I spotted what looked like a shed behind the main building and near one of the three base-ball fields. Compared to the rest of campus, it was ugly and drab. In reality, it was a typical shed, but I couldn't believe the boosters at Sterner wouldn't have demanded a posh brick building go up in its place. The door opened, a groundskeeper walked out with an edger in hand, and he locked up behind himself. He looked to be in his sixties, leathery skin still tanned from hours spent tending the grounds.

"Morning," I called out as I approached. He fired up the tool before I shouted, but it hadn't gotten loud yet.

The man killed the edger and lifted his safety goggles. "You lost?"

"Not all who wander are lost," I said. He stared at me. Not a Tolkien fan. "I'm looking into the murder of Marcy Russell. Did you know her?"

He nodded. "Sure did. I've been here a long time, but my job is pretty invisible unless something goes wrong, but Marcy was always nice to the staff. Good lady. Terrible what happened to her."

"Sure is. You mentioned you'd been here a while. Did you know Marcy well?"

He waffled his hand. "We'd chat whenever I was working near her classroom or if she saw me outside. She was one of the good ones. I wouldn't say we were close, though. We didn't hang out away from here."

"No one seems to have a bad thing to say about her," I said. The groundskeeper nodded. "You have any idea who'd want to hurt such a beloved person?"

"No idea. I wish I did." He hefted the edger. "I got a shed full of power tools for the bastard who did it."

I admired his candor . . . and his means of getting justice. The man told me he'd worked here for quite some time, so I shifted gears a little. "What do you think about Principal Hinson?" He spat on the ground, and I had my answer. "I'm not saying he's involved, but I also haven't ruled him out."

"What do you need?"

"You know anyone else I could talk to?"

"Maybe Rachel Heaton," he said. "She's the PTA president."

"And she has an office here?" I asked.

"Of course."

I went to a nice private school, and our PTA president barely put in an appearance. The Sterner Academy collected money from some wealthy and indiscriminate people. "Is she in the administration building?"

"Yes."

I winced. "I'm trying to avoid it. If Hinson sees me asking around, he's going to sic the dogs on me."

He nodded and gestured for me to follow him, so I did. We took the long way to avoid passing too many windows in the admin wing. At a plain exterior door, he stopped and pulled out a ring full of keys. "Her office is the next on the right. The principal and his people can't see you at this part of the building. I'll leave this unlocked for a while. Just come out the same way."

"I will. Thanks."

"I hope you find whoever killed Miss Russell." He walked away. I pushed the door open, stuck my head in, and looked both directions. The hallway was wide, polished, and empty. I slipped in and let the door close quietly behind me. Sure enough, the next office belonged to Rachel Heaton. The door was open at about a forty-five-degree angle. I knocked.

"Come in," called a brisk female voice.

I entered a spacious office. It only had one window, but it was massive, and it offered a nice view of the campus. Despite being much nicer, it reminded me of my setup. Two desks stood in the space. One was plain and empty. The other was an impressive oak number I would have been glad to steal while no one watched. A tall, slender woman sat behind it. She kept her blonde hair cut at the chin, and she appraised me over the rims of her glasses. Despite the professional pantsuit she wore, I guessed the older male students compared her to a hot librarian. "You don't look like a parent."

"I drive an Audi," I said. "Seems like a good first step." She grinned. "Rachel Heaton?"

"That's me."

I thumbed over my shoulder. "You mind if I shut the door more?" She shook her head, so I pushed it enough to leave it open a crack. "I'm a private investigator." I sat and showed her my ID. "I'm looking into the murders of Raymond Ellicott and Marcy Russell."

"I wish you good luck, then." A warm smile came to her face and then left just as quickly. "Marcy was wonderful. An excellent teacher. She expected a great deal of her students, held them to account, and got on well with their parents. It's a delicate balance."

"I'm sure."

"If you came to me for insight, I'm afraid I don't have much. I liked Marcy, but we didn't talk every day."

"You don't know of anything going on with her?" I said.

"No."

I remembered an earlier conversation T.J. and I had with a few of Marcy's fellow teachers. "Did she ever mention anything to you about running for the school board?"

Rachel Heaton recoiled as if I'd shown her a snake. "How do you know about that?"

"I'd love to tell you it was my own brilliance, but a few of her colleagues mentioned it."

"Not many people knew that," she said.

"Did Marcy say what spurred her to run?"

"The curriculum."

"What about it?"

"She thought it was going to change here, and that the county would eventually follow suit. She liked the current one and wanted to keep it."

"You think it's possible someone killed her over this?"

Rachel Heaton shrugged. "Curriculum development is a multi-billion dollar business if you do it right. Even if you only do it pretty well, it can be worth millions, and one of the large companies might come and gobble you up. Wasn't the councilman big on education, too?"

"He was," I said.

She spread her hands. "I feel like I'm stepping on your toes a bit, but that might be the connection."

"Maybe. I'd love to get into the school and poke around, but Hinson would have me tossed out before I got very far."

She wrinkled her nose at the mention of the principal's name. "Do you think he had something to do with it?"

"I don't know." I didn't divulge anything about the country club. Rachel didn't seem like a fan of Hinson, but they worked in the same building, and professional loyalties can be hard to predict. "I get the feeling something is going on with him, though."

"You have a card?"

I slid one across the desk to her. "Don't let Hinson catch you with it."

She smiled very briefly again. "He won't. If I think of anything, I'll be in touch."

I thanked her and moved to the door. A quick peek showed the hallway empty. I ducked out of Rachel Heaton's office, exited to the outside, and wound my way around the building and back to my car.

At the office, T.J. and I had already discussed the events of the morning. I sipped coffee which had grown lukewarm as my cell phone rang. I didn't recognize the number. "Hello?"

"The police just arrested my dad." No greeting or lead-up.

"Gerald?"

"Yeah."

I set the phone down, put my finger over my lips in T.J.'s direction, and tapped to put the call on speaker. "Tell me what happened."

"Cops took my dad away."

I leaned back in my chair. "On what grounds?"

"Apparently, they found his prints on the burner phones from the hotel room." Gerald's voice held no emotion. He may as well have been discussing the very pleasant fall weather.

"Nothing else?" I asked. "Just some prints? No murder weapon?"

"It's enough for the detectives, I guess."

I rubbed my forehead. The police did nothing for over a week. Gonzalez sent me away with two boxes of printouts. Finally, whoever processed the phones finished working on them. Now, two days later, fingerprints turned up. Something changed. We would need to look over the case notes again. "Did your father call his lawyer?"

Gerald scoffed. "We can't afford one. Not after Dad lost his job."

"Get a public defender, then. At least for the arraignment."

"I guess," he said.

"You guess?" T.J. and I both frowned.

"I didn't want to think he could do it, but the cops found some reason to arrest him for my mom's murder. Maybe he really did it. Why would I help my dad now?"

I didn't have a good answer, so I waited for Gerald to say more. Or display any kind of emotion. Instead, he stayed quiet.

"This doesn't make sense," I said finally. "I can't believe your father would do it."

"I'm sure you know how it is. Cops have had the case for a while. Why else would you be working it?"

"I know the sergeant who's in charge of the case," I said. "I'll talk to him and see what's going on. Maybe I'll convince him he has the wrong man."

"I'm not sure it'll matter." Gerald sighed, and his voice sounded somber when he spoke. "They think they have their man."

"They've been wrong before."

"Well, maybe they're not this time. They told me the prints were solid."

"Gerald, I—"

"I was just letting you know," he said and broke the connection.

"Weird," I muttered.

"He's seemed strange the whole time."

"I know . . . and I remember I chalked it up to everyone grieving differently." T.J. grinned, but it faded quickly given the gravity of the situation. "This was an unusual call. He wanted to let us know, but it also sounded like he didn't want us involved anymore."

"Maybe he really thinks his father did it."

I shook my head. "He strikes me as aloof, and I don't think he cares about what's happening with his dad as much as he should. It's a big leap to think he's capable of murdering his wife."

"What are we going to do?" T.J. wanted to know.

"We're going to stay on this. Hinson is an asshole, and Gerald is a weirdo. Maybe it's nothing, but it could be one or both of them are involved somehow."

"You going to read Gonzalez the riot act?"

"Yes. I wish I had a couple boxes full of paper to give him for effect."

"I'm sure you'll manage fine without them. I'll check the report on those phones in the meantime. I don't remember seeing anything about prints."

"Me, either," I said as I stood and shrugged into my wind-breaker.

———

I parked near the BCPD precinct and stormed inside. Gonzalez sat at his desk talking to a much younger uniformed cop. He glanced up, saw me, and gave the fellow an excuse. When he left, I walked in and shut the door behind me. "Gotta train the next generation," Gonzalez said.

"You going to teach him how to arrest people based on flimsy evidence?"

"It's new evidence."

"Something's weird about those phones," I said. "They were getting processed initially, so they were in inventory but not analyzed. Then, you get them back, and the techs pull a pretty tame conversation off. Now, days later, someone suddenly thinks to dust for prints?"

He shrugged. "Investigations are fluid."

"So is shit, sometimes."

"All right, it's not a conventional order." Gonzalez waved a hand. "Yeah, I'd like it if all the work on the phones got done at the same time. Things don't always shake out the way we want. It's my job to put it all together however it comes in."

"He didn't do it," I said.

"Evidence strongly suggests he did," Gonzalez said. "You know the percentage of people killed by their intimate partners?"

"Yeah."

"It's always the husband." Gonzalez spread his hands. "We're charging him with two murders. If you can find evidence someone else did it, great. Maybe there's a better suspect out there. If so, you might want to find him soon. Mister Russell is about to be processed." He glanced at his watch. "For his sake, I hope it's soon, or he'll be in the clink all weekend."

"I've never seen something like this before," I said. "Can you double-check with the tech folks?"

"You think I haven't?" Gonzalez pointed at me. "You work for the Ellicotts anyway, right? I'm sure they'll be happy to hear an arrest was made. They might decide they don't need to keep paying you to prove the husband of the other victim didn't do it. Might want to tread lightly when you talk to them."

I shook my head. "Fine. You'd better listen when I bring you new evidence."

"I'll be all ears," Gonzalez said.

I turned and walked out of his office. As soon as I stepped into the hallway, I saw two brawny cops leading a handcuffed Edgar Russell down a corridor. He turned, and we locked eyes for an instant before he disappeared. It was only a brief glance, but his face was pale and his eyes conveyed the terror he felt. "You brought him here?" I asked Gonzalez.

"It's my case," he said. "He comes to me."

"At least it'll be faster when you have to let him go." Before Gonzalez could give me another lame reply, I headed for the exit. He was right—we didn't work for the Russells, and the Ellicott family might consider this arrest to be the resolution they'd been seeking.

I knew it was wrong, however. T.J. and I would keep digging even if the money dried up.

CHAPTER 16

"YOU SAW HIM?" T.J. said. "They really arrested poor Edgar?"

"They did. He looked as petrified as you might imagine."

"What the hell is his son doing?" She crossed her arms and stared at her screen.

"Fiddling while Rome burns as far as I can tell," I said.

"You're ready to admit something's off about him?"

"I think we can say his behavior isn't simply grief. There's something else going on."

"Let's find it," she said.

"I'm more interested in Marcy Russell," I said. "The Ellicott ladies might be willing to chalk all this up to a jealous husband who learned his wife was stepping out."

"You think so? It also means Raymond was an adulterer."

I shrugged. "People are weird. If they take the arrest to be the end of things, they're not going to pay us after this morning."

"What are you saying?"

"I'm saying we might be *pro bono* from here on out," I told her.

"And we'd be working for a man who's in a holding cell and hasn't officially hired us."

"Yep."

"I'm in," T.J. said. "Edgar's getting railroaded."

"I think he is, and we need to figure out who's driving the train."

"Hinson?"

"Maybe." I still wondered what investment opportunity he pitched at the country club. "The circumstances of Marcy's death gave him a convenient excuse to dig into the school rulebook and fire Edgar. It doesn't mean he killed her, but it certainly looks like someone trying to cover his own ass."

"What are we going to do about him?"

"I'd love to find a way to get you into the school," I said. "After my visit there, a few more people know me. I can't really be incognito, and we have to presume some of the folks I run into are going to rat me out to Hinson." I figured Rachel Heaton and the groundskeeper would not be included in this number. Lobdell the lacrosse coach was an unknown.

"You still have your disguise from the case in Frederick?" T.J. asked with an amused smile. "Maybe you could apply to be a music teacher."

To go undercover inside a shady company, I wore a long blond wig and colored contacts. The consensus was I looked like a failed rock singer who took to database administration when his career at the mic cratered. "It would work so long as no one asked me to play an instrument or sing," I said. "Both seem important for a music teacher."

"You didn't take piano lessons as a kid?"

"I did," I said, "but it's been ages since I played. If the *Jaws* theme or the pieces of a few songs I remember are good enough, then I have a chance."

T.J.'s amused expression faded, yielding to a serious stare. "We need a tactic in the meantime."

"Marcy's husband is on his way to jail. I don't think she was a random victim. We need to know why someone chose her to be in the hotel room."

"Are you saying this because the Ellicotts are likely to tell us our services are no longer needed?"

"It doesn't hurt," I said. "Looks like we'll be putting in some weekend hours. Let's get to work."

———

People always leave digital trails.

The careful among us can get pretty good at covering them up. Most either don't know or don't care, however, so what they do and where they go online is easier to uncover. We didn't have any physical asset belonging to Marcy Russell, of course. Her real phone was conspicuously absent from the crime scene, and the BCPD found "nothing of interest" on her home laptop. I wondered about her machine at Sterner and wished again we could get someone into the school.

For now, I would need to get creative.

In addition to her work email, Marcy Russell maintained addresses with Gmail and Yahoo. Recent search history on her laptop confirmed this. I went to both sites, entered her handle, and made a few guesses as to her password. A swing and a miss every time. I could try to reset it, but without access to her phone, I wouldn't receive the verification message. On a lark, I checked her cell carrier. Marcy could check and send texts online, but to reset the password, I would need to get a code from her email.

Vicious circles were not my friend today.

I tried the handle at other less prominent email providers. A hit returned from an older local company which was somehow still in business: crabmail. I couldn't remember the last time I heard someone mention it. Marcy probably stopped using it ages ago when the bigger companies came around. It meant I would be unlikely to find anything interesting or incriminating hanging around in her inbox.

It also meant she might still have an older, less secure password in place.

I tried EdgarGerald. Nothing. Next, GeraldEdgar.

Welcome, Marcy Russell, the splash screen said. "I got into one of her old accounts," I told T.J.

"Without her phone? Nice."

"Let's see if there's anything here." The inbox was barren. Ditto sent items. Bits of spam and junk flittered in, and they got sucked into whatever filter caught such messages. A folder called *Older Mail* showed promise, so I opened it. The newest message in here was at least five years past. The odds of finding something directly relevant to Marcy's recent murder were small. I scanned the subjects as I scrolled down the page. One caught my eye.

Thank you for registering on Bloghouse!

I presumed this to be another older site. It was, and despite the declining popularity of blogs over time, people still used it. Six years ago, Marcy chose the very clever handle Marcy for her writings. I tried the same password as on her email. Many people just didn't know better back then, and credential reuse was common.

Marcy apparently did know better.

After getting stymied twice, I chanced the link for resetting the password. If it still pointed to a phone number or email address I couldn't access, getting in would become exponentially harder. Not impossible, but part of the hacking calculus is the timeliness and value of information versus the level of effort it takes to get it. We were already dealing with old posts. They would need to be critical to the case to justify the time it might take to break in.

Thankfully, the system cooperated. Because Marcy hadn't updated her contact information in a long time, it prompted me for a phone number. I entered the one for the burner in my desk drawer. It vibrated a few seconds later, I read the code, and entered it. The site asked if I wanted to update my details now. I declined.

Based on the date range, Marcy started the blog over a decade ago. She posted often in the early days—and got quite a few comments on some of her entries—but the frequency tailed off over time. I wondered if her colleagues and bosses caught on. She mentioned where she taught and wrote under her own first name. If someone could make fog on a mirror held under their nose, they could connect those dots. A few entries caught my eye as I scanned them, including a post about a certain new arrival to The Sterner Academy.

The New Captain: Rough Seas Ahead?

I've been teaching at The Sterner Academy for years, and in that time, I've seen a few principals come and go. The newest arrival, Anthony Hinson, is an interesting specimen.

He's a man in a hurry; he left the classroom to jump straight into administration as soon as he could from what I heard. Now, I believe in the merits of ambition, but when your compass points only to the corner office, I have to wonder. Will he have our backs when we're navigating the choppy waters of academia? After all, he wasn't a teacher for very long, and he's already been in an office longer than he spent in the classroom.

His initial email to the staff talked about fully evaluating all thirteen grades at Sterner to see if there were "efficiencies to be gained." I can't help but worry. Efficiency is a term best suited for assembly lines or Silicon Valley, not for nurturing young minds.

In the end, the captain sets the course, but the crew keeps the ship sailing. I just hope Principal Hinson remembers that when he's steering us through what looks to be a turbulent year ahead.

"Interesting," I muttered. "I got into a blog Marcy used to write."

"You're doing better than me." T.J. frowned. "I'm not making much progress over here."

"Don't worry about it. Her writing tells me she's never been a fan of Hinson."

"Smart woman."

Another post from two years ago jumped out at me.

Iceberg Dead Ahead?

We're knee-deep into the new school year, and I've got to say that something's off. I don't mean the lingering scent of sanitizer that has become a classroom norm; I'm talking about the curriculum changes.

This year's academic roadmap feels like it was sketched on the back of a napkin, somewhere between a cocktail party and a board meeting. We have new materials . . . sometimes, at least. For a school with a lot of money, I'd think we could have actually ordered all the books and manuals we needed. Sure, students can find some stuff online, but we've never punted to a vendor's website before. Where did these new materials come from?

I also have to wonder who decided some of this stuff would be a good idea. It's like people heard the complaints about Common Core and ran to something which seems to be its opposite. Who decided that "market-driven ethics" is something we should be teaching in high school?

It feels as though we're building a house of cards on a shaky table. Our students deserve a firm foundation, not a curriculum that leaves everyone wondering where the hell all this came from.

I remembered Rachel Heaton's words from earlier: "Curriculum development is a multi-billion dollar business if you do it right."

The final entry talked about Marcy's decision to run for the school board—something I think her husband didn't yet know before she died.

Course Change

It's taken a while and considerable reflection.

I've made a tough decision. I've decided to resign from my position at The Sterner Academy after this school year. I can no longer stay quiet while Sterner rolls out more curriculum changes. A smattering of parents have complained, but nothing ever happens. A few have even pulled their kids out of the school. No matter. We have a waiting list.

While I can't dive into the specifics of what's going on—suffice it to say there's a bigger puppet master at play—I can take action before this spreads.

I'm running for a seat on the Baltimore County School Board. Our education system needs voices that came up in the classroom, not just in administrative theory or worse, some undisclosed agenda. It's time to stop watching things change and instead make people prove their new ideas are better than the ones we know work.

My husband doesn't know I've decided to do this. I didn't even tell him I was thinking about it. I'll have to one day soon, but for now, I don't want him to question me or let something slip at work. I've told a few colleagues but no one else.

This is all new territory for me, and I'm scared. I hope no one finds out. I really think I can do good things. School boards have been a little crazy the last few years, but cooler heads will prevail. We need stability when it comes to the curriculum and more teachers to implement it. I think mine should be one of them.

I wished Marcy had gotten the chance to run.

I also wondered who the puppet master was. Hinson? Someone else? A private school didn't have to follow the county curriculum if it used its own. There must have been a plan in place to expand the experiment beyond the hallowed halls of Sterner.

If someone found this post, it could have made Marcy Russell a target. Maybe even a bigger one than a county councilman.

————

We continued down the Marcy Russell rabbit hole.

T.J. managed to sweet talk someone pulling later hours on a Friday at the University of Baltimore into sending us Marcy's transcript and some newspaper articles she wrote which had never been digitized. Despite their age, they painted a picture similar to the one we already had. Even then, Marcy knew she wanted to be a teacher and wrote from this perspective. She went after courses, curricula, and even professors she felt weren't upholding the university's standards.

"It's kind of surprising she lasted anywhere," T.J. observed.

"True," I said. "This line of thinking would often lead to someone wearing out her welcome."

"And her blog was under her own name?"

"First only, but yes. How many Marcys could there have been at Sterner? Either the administration didn't know about her blog or didn't care."

"Maybe they found out late in the game."

I nodded. "Maybe. Ellicott established his position over time. It seems like they had a lot of overlap even though we don't have anything suggesting they knew each other."

Before T.J. could answer, the door opened. Rachel Heaton walked in and closed up shop behind herself. "I hope you don't mind me coming by," she said. "I guess I'm lucky you're still here. Your address is on the card, and I didn't want to discuss this over the phone."

"No problem," I said. I briefly introduced Rachel and T.J. as the former took a seat in one of my guest chairs.

"I suppose news travels slowly at Sterner," Rachel said. "Some at least. The kind the administration might not want anyone to know."

"What do you mean?" I asked.

"Perhaps you knew this already, but I just learned Principal Hinson fired Edgar Russell. He used the morals clause because of Marcy's . . . circumstances when she died."

"We knew. The police recently arrested Edgar, in fact."

"What?" She paled. "Impossible. There's no way she would have an affair, and he wouldn't kill her even if she did."

"The other family hired us," I said. "Considering what's happened today, however, we're going to try and get Edgar Russell off the hook."

"Good for you," Rachel said. "When you came to my office, you told me you needed a way into the school."

"Do you have one?"

She nodded. "But not for you." Her cool eyes flicked to T.J. "I have the budget and authorization to hire a secretary, a position which has been vacant for some time. Perhaps it's time I filled it."

"I'm in," T.J. offered.

"What would it entail?" I wanted to know.

"T.J. would work for me. I could probably hold off on the official paperwork for a day or two to make things less complicated. She would have the same access to the school any other secretary does."

"Is everything on the same network?"

"The PTA isn't segregated," Rachel said.

"That could make things easier," T.J. said. "I could poke around and see if Hinson is trying to hide anything."

"You could." Rachel nodded. "I will say that I have some actual work you could do, also, and you would need to so no one got suspicious. If the principal is involved, he'll be on alert."

"What would my hours be?"

"I know you have a real job, so I'd be flexible. Come in at eight-thirty Monday, and you can leave when the school day is over if you need to get back here."

"I guess I'll need to make my own coffee in the mornings," I said.

Rachel smiled. "I get the feeling you'll survive. This is the way in you need."

I nodded. "T.J.'s in. Let's do it."

CHAPTER 17

SHORTLY AFTER RACHEL HEATON LEFT, the door opened again, and the Ellicott women walked in. When they first came to see us, Susan and Paula had puffy red eyes. Not today. Both ladies fixed T.J. and me with determined gazes. "You heard the news?" Susan said. They stood near the guest chairs but didn't sit. Paula looked at the swath of empty space in the middle of the floor. With T.J.'s desk near the rear wall and mine off to the left, we had room for a small meeting table.

"We did," I said.

"Were you going to tell us things had been wrapped up?"

"No."

"Why not?"

"The county police and I differ on the issue of the case being concluded."

"You don't think he did it," Paula said. It wasn't a question.

"No, I don't."

"Neither do I," T.J. added. "We think there are much better suspects."

"What if we're happy with the way things are now?" Susan asked.

I shrugged. "Then you tell us you want to wrap things up

here. We tell you how many hours we worked, and you settle the bill."

"It's not like you found who killed my father," Paula said.

"I don't think the police have, either," I said. She frowned, so I explained. "We've been unable to establish any link between your father and Marcy Russell. They didn't know each other at all . . . certainly not well enough to be in a hotel bed together."

"What's your point, Mister Ferguson?" Susan demanded.

"My point is simple. If they didn't know each other, there's nothing for Edgar Russell to discover. There's nothing for him to act on. Sergeant Gonzalez likes to cite facts about intimate partner violence and tell me stuff like, 'it's always the husband,' but it's not. Edgar is a convenient scapegoat. I think the cops have the wrong man, and I'm going to keep trying to prove it with or without your continued involvement."

"Well, we're satisfied with the investigation now. Let's settle our bill." Susan walked to T.J.'s desk and sat. Paula didn't join her. Instead, she dropped onto one of my guest chairs.

"You really think they have the wrong guy?" she said.

"I do."

"Can you prove it?"

"Legally?" I said. "Not yet. While we're speaking of the judicial system, the cops have no murder weapon, and I think they're going to struggle to put a good motive together. Edgar will get arraigned, but I think the case is going to fall apart unless they come up with something big."

"Which you don't think exists."

"Correct."

Paula crossed her arms. "Who do you think did it?"

"I'm not sure yet, but we're running down a couple of angles. One of them is likely to be right."

"Why?"

"Because we've done an investigation, and we're following what we've learned."

She glanced at her mother and then back to me. "Mom just wants to put this behind her. I understand . . . but I also want to see the right man caught."

"You told me you talked with the Russells." She nodded. "What did you think?"

"I don't think the husband is a killer. He was grieving at least as hard as we were." Her brows knitted when she continued. "The son is a little weird, though. He didn't seem very broken up about the whole thing. Mom told me everybody has to grieve in their own way, but I found it kind of off-putting."

"We did, too," I said.

Paula leaned closer and whispered. "Is he one of the people you're looking into?"

"I can neither confirm nor deny the targets of our ongoing investigation." I added a slight bob of my head. "This is a sensitive matter. I'm sure you understand."

A small smile played on her lips. "Totally."

"Let's go, Paula," Susan said as she strode toward the door. "I'm happy to have this behind us."

Paula stood, thanked me for my time, and followed her mother out the door.

"I hate to speak badly of a widow," T.J. said, "but I really don't like her very much."

"From her perspective, we didn't find anything." I shrugged. "The cops say they arrested the right man, and she's going to believe them. People want closure especially in times like this."

"Even when it's wrong?"

"Sometimes, it's part of the appeal," I said.

T.J. glanced at her watch. "Don't you need to wrap up the evening, boss?"

I looked at the time. It was a couple hours after I usually left, but I didn't think anything else of it. Then, I remembered. "Gloria's interview," I said. "Fucking hell."

"I don't think they can quote you on that."

"Let's talk more about Sterner over the weekend. Try to keep your head down at first. Let me know if you can get to things like your personal email."

"I will." T.J. shoved me toward the door. "Go play willing interview participant for your wife."

"It'll take all my acting ability," I said.

"When's the last time you were on stage?"

I thought about it. No one would have ever called me a budding Pacino or Denzel, but once I started getting serious about lacrosse, other school activities took a backseat. "Fifth grade, I guess. Maybe sixth."

"Wow." T.J. chuckled. "Good luck."

I knew I would need it.

———

When I arrived at Gloria's house, I found my wife a blur of motion.

She flittered from one room to the next, adjusting her hair, tugging her dress at the shoulders, and generally trying to get herself and the place ready in about a hundred different ways all at once. She would ask a question and leave the room so I never heard more than a word or two before her voice faded. "You look great," I said, both because she did, and I figured it covered the bases.

Gloria wore a very nice blue dress. Her earrings matched the shade perfectly. The dress was a little more modest than she normally went for, but this was an interview—and photo op—designed to sell her as a serious and philanthropic business-woman. Low necklines and short hems were not the order of the day. Without a wealth of time to change, I quickly doffed my jeans for a nice pair of chinos and swapped my black quarter-zip for a more conventional light cyan cashmere sweater.

"I wasn't asking you how I looked," she said, managing to stay in one room long enough for me to hear her. "But thanks."

"Anything I can do?"

The doorbell rang downstairs. Gloria groaned. "If it's the reporter, you'll need to stall her. It should be a charcuterie tray I ordered."

"I won't tell her about the lasagna, either," I said, smoothing my sweater as I hustled down the stairs. Sure enough, a college kid stood on the other side of the door. He handed me a wrapped plastic tray with an impressive selection of meats and cheeses. I knew Gloria had her choice of wooden boards to set it all on. The amount of food could probably feed a dozen people. I tipped the guy a five and carried the fancy snack inside. "You have a preference for which board to use?" I called up the stairs.

"Not really," Gloria said as she moved around upstairs. Before I could walk away, she added, "Actually, the darkest one. It'll go best with the coffee table."

"Exactly what I was thinking." I had no opinion on the matter, of course, and Gloria would know this. I got the dark wooden board out of a cabinet and left the plastic tray on the counter. Gloria would want to arrange it. We had about ten minutes until the reporter was slated to arrive.

Six minutes later, Gloria came downstairs. She looked great and smelled good. I couldn't identify the perfume. She owned an absurd selection of bottles and had a fragrance for every occasion. By contrast, I owned three bottles of cologne, one of which was a spare of my favorite and sat in the medicine cabinet in Gloria's *en suite* bathroom. I spritzed a little on when I got ready, but Gloria still smelled better than I did. She moved rows of sliced meat and cheese from the restaurant's plastic tray to her board with surprising speed.

"There's a sleeve of crackers in the pantry," she said. I got them. She pointed to the cabinet holding the plates. I had enough presence of mind to get down a medium white ceramic model for the crackers and three small ones for snacks. "It's like you've done this before." She grinned at me.

"My parents set a lot of these out when they were still called meat and cheese trays. We millennials and our fancy terms."

A few minutes later, we waited in the living room. Gloria made sure she had bottles of water—both plain and sparkling—a few varieties of soda, iced tea, and her usual healthy wine selection. I figured coffee might be the drink of the day. I could certainly use six cups spiked with whiskey to make it through the next hour or so.

The doorbell rang again. The witching hour had arrived.

———

Claire Stevenson looked to be about the same age as Gloria or me —with my wife having crested thirty over the summer, her discussions of the two-and-a-half-year gap between us ceased. She was a petite and pretty redhead who wore a sharp gray pantsuit under a North Face jacket. I took her coat and hung it in the foyer while Gloria facilitated the introductions. After a round of handshakes and how-do-you-dos, we adjourned to the living room.

Gloria and I sat beside one another on the full-sized couch. Claire dropped onto the matching loveseat. The room also featured a recliner, coffee table currently holding the charcuterie board and accessories, a keyboard on a stand, and two bookcases. Claire's eyes scanned the tomes before she took out her phone. "You mind if I record?"

"Not at all," Gloria said.

"Great." Claire set her phone on the coffee table. She added a notebook with a bunch of scrawled questions beside it. I could see her recorder app before the screen faded. "This is Claire Stevenson with the *Baltimore Sun*. I'm here with Gloria Reading Ferguson and her husband C.T. It's the evening of October seventh." Claire smiled. She had a good one. "Everyone's seen a bunch of superhero movies by now. Let's talk about your origin story. What motivated you to start a fundraising business?"

"A few things, really. I'm lucky in that my parents have money, and they've always been interested in helping others. They have a foundation. So do C.T.'s parents. When I finished college, I wasn't really sure what I wanted to do. I started getting involved with the foundations and some of the charities they work with. Before he became the mayor, Vincent Davenport trusted me to help him put on a couple of events. I loved doing it. The organizing, making sure everything ran smoothly, the giving back . . . all of it. Davenport was probably my biggest backer, so once he became the mayor, I looked into starting a business in order to keep doing the same work."

"Some people would consider your parents to be one percenters. Do you think having access to their money and connections gave you an advantage?"

"Sure. I tried not to lean on them once I struck out on my own, though. My parents are doing their thing, and I'm doing mine. If our interests align, and we end up putting on an event together, so be it."

Claire glanced at her notepad. I munched on some salty ham and tried to stay inconspicuous. "Can you describe the core mission of your company and what you hope to do?"

"The mission statement was hard," Gloria admitted. "It's simple to say, 'I want to raise money for other people.' How much money? Which other people? What's the criteria? How do you make sure they benefit from it? There are numerous things to consider beyond just the funds. In the end, I went with 'Supporting people and doing the most good.' I have some part-time help, but I do most of this myself, so I'm really picky about the causes and companies I get involved with."

"I guess having a husband who's a private investigator can help you there." Claire's eyes shifted to me for a second. "Have you ever asked C.T. to look into a prospective business partner?"

"No." Gloria shook her head. "I vet them myself. We'll inevitably talk about things, and he would tell me if I'd be doing business with someone I shouldn't." I offered a thumbs up but remained quiet. This was Gloria's moment, and I hoped Claire's questions didn't wrangle me into it any more than they needed to—which should have been not at all.

"You mentioned numerous factors beyond just the money," Claire said. "How do you measure success, then?"

"It's in two parts. First, how much did we raise by the end of the event or the end of the window? Whatever organization we're helping has a goal. Second, in the weeks after, did the money get to where it was supposed to go and help whoever it was supposed to help?"

"You keep track of this?"

"I feel like I have to," Gloria said. "There are some very good charities out there that pay considerable administrative salaries and fees. People need to earn a wage, sure, but it means some groups are doing less than they could. Most of that information is easy enough to find because legitimate charities need to declare it."

Claire nodded as if Gloria had passed some secret test. "You talked about Mayor Davenport. Obviously, he's stepped back from his business since he won the election. If he asked you to put on a fundraiser for his reelection, would you do it?"

I sat as still and expressionless as I could. Gloria always got along with Vincent Davenport, and I never did. I would grudgingly admit he'd done a good job as mayor, and if dragged to some function by my wife, I would put on my best alcohol-aided smile. "I don't know," Gloria said. "All the things I did with him before were for his charitable foundation. It's still running, but I haven't been involved in anything he's done since he took office. I'd need to think about it. It would have to be more than just raising money for the campaign coffers."

"Makes sense." Claire jotted a couple notes. "Where do you want to take the business in the next few years?"

"Bigger." Gloria smiled. "The goal is to help people. So far, I've done a few things locally. I'd like to venture outside of Baltimore and get more involved on the state level."

"Nothing national?"

"If a big national organization wants to work with me, I'll certainly take the call." Both women laughed. "It would be nice on some level, and I'm sure there would also be a few headaches involved. I might need to grow the business in that case."

Claire's head bobbed to a beat only she heard. "Does your husband help at all?"

Gloria glanced at me before answering. "It's not really something he's experienced with."

The reporter looked at me. I wanted to stay out of the story, but she seemed determined to bring me in. "C.T., you don't get involved?"

"It's Gloria's business," I said, "and it's really not my area of expertise. I'm happy to be a sounding board, but she's the one making the decisions."

"Does she serve as a sounding board for you, too?" Claire pressed.

"It's rare for her not to know at least something about what's going on with my cases . . . at least in terms of big picture stuff." I shrugged. "Partners should support one another."

Thankfully, Claire turned her attention back to Gloria. "Walk us through a typical day. What's it like to be a fundraiser?"

"I'm not sure I have a typical day," Gloria said. "I can spend huge amounts of time doing research, scouting venues, or putting out fires with some upcoming event. Some days, I have to do all of them. It really depends on what events I have coming up, how soon they're happening, and how often I've worked with the other entities involved."

"What other entities?"

"The venue management. If there's dinner, how experienced is the wait staff? Does the kitchen offer a full menu? Can the chef make changes if people ask for something different? Open bar or cash bar? Even if no one's eating, it's nice to work with people who have done this sort of thing before. Logistics aren't for every-one." She paused to breathe and chuckle. "It's a lot. More than you might think at first glance . . . and definitely more than you'd expect just from going to a few things."

"Fundraising can be a crowded field," Claire said. "What makes your company stand out?"

"When you're a small business," Gloria said, "on some level, you're selling yourself." She was absolutely correct. It was obvious in my case because my name was on the door, and I took some risks T.J. didn't. On a different scale, the same was true of Gloria. As much as I didn't like this interview, she was killing it. "I'm offering me, my experience, my connections, my ability to get things done."

"What if it's not enough for someone?"

"They'll go somewhere else . . . and probably have a worse experience." Gloria softened any sting from her caveat with a bright smile.

"You think your company can make a big difference?"

"I wouldn't be doing this if I didn't."

Claire took a couple notes and ended the interview in short

order. "Excellent. With the background we already have, I think this is going to be great. Thanks for inviting me into your home."

"Thank you for coming," Gloria said. She even sounded like she meant it. We both stood and shook hands with Claire, who headed out into the evening air a moment later. My wife breathed a sigh of relief. "It's over."

"You crushed it," I said.

"Really?" She leaned in and hugged me, and I was happy to return the favor.

"Definitely. I want to hire you after hearing your answers."

"Well." She undid the top button of my shirt. "My rates are high but negotiable." She planted a lingering kiss on me. "If you want a discount, though, you'll have to earn it."

"I plan to," I said as we made for the stairs.

CHAPTER 18

"IT SOUNDS like you're bait again."

T.J. rolled her eyes. She loved Melinda, but the woman acted like an overprotective grandmother at times. T.J. thought of her Gran. She died young—62—and the effect on ten-year-old Tamera had been profound. If Gran had made it another ten years, T.J. figured her life would have turned out very differently. She was happy now, at least, for the first time in quite a while. Gran would be pleased. "Melinda, I'll be working in a school. A fancy private school, at that. They have their own security team."

"Who work for the principal, I presume?" Melinda said. "A man who might be a suspect in the investigation."

"Maybe he is. We're looking at a couple of different people right now. The police arrested the husband because they think it's always the husband. Case closed."

"There's evidence, right?"

"We think it might be dubious," T.J. said. "There are some inconsistencies in the timeline compared to how these things normally go." T.J. understood things like chain of custody and chain of evidence in broad terms. C.T. would understand them better. A couple things seemed fishy to her even with her more limited experience. Why were the texts from the phones not included initially? It seemed like shoddy work to produce one report and then go back to make a major revision. Then, there was the matter of the prints suddenly cropping up. Another "discovery" which should have been there all along if the BCPD did things right.

This was how it worked on *Law & Order*, after all.

T.J. remembered watching reruns with other girls in Weasel Boy's stable during their downtime. They used to hope some of the fictional TV detectives would roll up, bust their pimp in the mouth, and set all the women—a decent percentage of whom were under eighteen—free. It was one of the reasons she jumped at the chance to work for C.T.

"You take your share of risks," Melinda said.

T.J. shrugged even though they weren't on a video call. "It's my life."

"And you've only lived twenty-one years of it."

"This guy doesn't know me. He's only ever met C.T. As far as he knows, I'll be the new secretary for the PTA president. Maybe he's shady, and maybe he's not, but I'll be able to tell from up close. Once I'm inside on Monday, watching him gets easier."

"You mean in person or electronically?"

"Some of both," T.J. said.

Melinda chuckled. "I can't believe a PTA president has an office in the school let alone the budget to hire a full-time assistant."

"Sterner's big on partnership . . . according to their website at least. At forty thousand a student, I think they can afford to carve out an office and an employee for this lady. They probably see it as a small cost in making the parents feel empowered."

"Even if they're really not," Melinda said. "Look, I know I can't stop you from taking risks, and I probably sound like your grandmother."

"You kind of do," T.J. said.

"Still, I worry about you. Be careful."

"I will. How much trouble could I get into at the ritziest school in the city?"

Melinda didn't answer. T.J. figured it was for the best.

———

After a quiet weekend, T.J. was up early Monday morning. Even though her job at The Sterner Academy was a setup, she decided to treat it like the first day of a new gig. She needed to take it seriously. Hopefully, Rachel Heaton wouldn't have too much work for her, but the woman needed a secretary for a reason. The day wouldn't be all spying on Principal Hinson. T.J. dug out the heavy bag and affixed it in place. She strapped on her gloves, picked an upbeat playlist to stream through her earbuds, and got down to business.

She moved through a warmup, single punches, combinations, elbow strikes, and kicks. When she finished, a nice sheen of sweat covered her skin. She dropped to the floor and did sixty pushups and crunches in sets of twenty each. Now breathing hard, she guzzled some water before killing the music and getting in the shower.

Thirty-five minutes later, T.J. was clean, professionally attired, and wore an appropriate amount of makeup. She put very little on for her normal job, but her boss didn't charge people forty grand. Might as well look a little nicer when showing up at a fancy school. It was a longer drive from her house, but she'd built in some time for traffic. Good thing, too. Despite leaving in plenty of time, she pulled into The Sterner Academy's long and elegant driveway with only a few minutes to spare.

Though not a teacher, she counted as staff, so she swung her Mustang onto the staff lot. No gate restricted access, but a burly man dressed in a typical security guard's uniform did. T.J.

explained who she was, her boss' name, and the fact that it was her first day. This all seemed satisfactory to the guard, and he waved her in. Luxury vehicles—mostly SUVs—of various makes filled the spaces. Land Rover. Porsche. Mercedes. Lexus. She thought again how a place like this wasn't part of her world.

T.J. left her car and reported to the administrative wing. It was an impressive lobby which could have been taken from any of a number of major corporations. All it needed was a fountain and a few statues. The woman behind the desk looked to be in her thirties. She wore her dark hair up and certainly dressed the part of private school secretary with a long and formless dress coming down to her ankles. She scrutinized T.J. before offering a polite, "May I help you, young lady?"

"Today's my first day. I'll be working for Rachel Heaton."

"Yes." The woman's severe expression softened a little. "She said she had a new person coming in today. About time, too. You must be Tamera."

"I go by T.J., but yes."

"Missus Heaton is already here. I'm sure she'll be expecting you. I just need to see your ID, and then I can give you your access card."

T.J. handed the woman her driver's license. As soon as she'd been eligible after turning twenty-one, she got her picture retaken. How she'd passed the test five years previously after a night of drinking and getting high remained a mystery. The toll of the prior evening showed in her former photo. In this one, she looked clear-eyed and composed. Like someone who had her life together versus a girl who was circling the drain.

The secretary plucked a plastic card about the same size as a license from her desk drawer. A metallic chip like the ones on credit cards sat in the center toward one end. The older woman entered a few things via keyboard, put the small card into another device that looked like a reader, and waited. After about ten seconds, she pulled it out and handed it to T.J. "You're all set. We'll get your picture taken in the next day or two, but this will let you access the building and login to a computer."

"Thanks," T.J. said. She noticed the other woman wore a lanyard around her neck. Of course, its strap carried the logo and name of The Sterner Academy. "You have one of those?"

"Sure." She grabbed one from the drawer, looking a little less happy about spending a few extra seconds on the interaction.

T.J. extended her stay with another question. "Is this the principal's office?"

"No, dear. Doctor Hinson is upstairs. This is reception. Do you know how to get to Ms. Heaton's office?" T.J. said she didn't, and the secretary gave her directions which seemed simple enough to follow. A minute and two turns later, T.J. found the door in question. The area was about the size of C.T.'s entire office—not bad for a PTA president. Rachel Heaton was dressed almost exactly like she'd been when she visited Friday evening.

"Good to see you," she said, and she shook T.J.'s hand. "Eager to get started?"

"I am."

"Good." Rachel shut the door before continuing the conversation in a quieter voice. "I know your boss sent you here for a certain reason, and I'm on board with that. Here's the reality . . . you're here as my secretary, and I have work I need you to do."

"I figured you might," T.J. said. "At least I'm not far from the main office."

"But you can't exactly keep an eye on things from your desk here. If I can create situations to get you in there, I will. Like I said, though, I have work to do, and undercover or not, you're supposed to be here to help me."

T.J. nodded and sat at the smaller desk. It was a little smaller than the one she used at her normal work space, but it would do nicely. An actual desktop computer sat on the floor, with a keyboard, mouse, and monitor on the surface. "Let's get started, then."

———

T.J. spent about three hours getting logged in, learning where things were on the network, discovering the shared printer a hundred feet away, and doing the actual work Rachel Heaton needed. In her school days, T.J. never paid attention to the PTA, mainly because she didn't have a parent who gave enough of a shit to get involved. The tuition bill alone at Sterner would keep most people interested. Rachel had many files to sort, complaints to sift through, emails to categorize, and responses to draft.

C.T. had mostly been quiet. He and T.J. agreed she wouldn't do too much on the first day. It would be easy to cast suspicion on a new employee, and with no one paying them at the moment, getting incriminating information quickly became less of a priority. They did enjoy a good chuckle at the network drive structure used by Sterner. "Who actually leaves people's home folders on the local hard drive?" C.T. wondered. "You're just asking for data loss."

She'd picked up enough in her time working for him to know enterprises should point the default save location to some network location. The tiny performance hit would barely be noticeable in modern networks, and regular backups would ensure information got preserved in a catastrophe. "Rachel said a script backs up everything when you log out,"

"Several dependencies there," he said. "Can you get to your personal email?"

"Yes."

"Okay. I'm going to send you something. They might block certain file types from getting downloaded, so I'll put it in the body of a message. If you dump it into a text file, you can turn it into an executable."

"Will do," T.J. said. She remembered how. It was one of the earlier things C.T. taught her after she showed an interest in the cyber dark arts.

"Remember," her boss said, "your first day is about blending in. You're the new girl. Not there to cause any trouble."

"I get it." A few minutes after the conversation, Racheal Heaton said she was going to lunch. She didn't invite T.J., who used the moment to ask a question. "Does everyone head out around now?"

"Teachers don't," Rachel said, "but staff often will. There's probably one person in the main office. Maybe she drew the short straw today."

When Rachel left, T.J. locked her workstation and checked the hallway. Minimal activity. She left the PTA office and headed for reception. The woman who got her situated this morning told her Hinson was upstairs, so she headed up the steps. Whoever designed the campus did a great job. Large windows enabled a terrific view of other buildings and athletic fields from virtually anywhere—even the landing on the way to the second floor.

As T.J. popped out into another hallway, a young woman hustled from the office muttering something about only having a few minutes into her phone. T.J. looked through the floor-to-ceiling windows and saw no one else. She ducked inside. Hinson's office was clearly marked on the left. The man wasn't there. No harm in ducking in for a moment. After a final glance over her shoulder, she moved into Hinson's very spacious sanctum.

The square footage jumped out at her first. This office was about the same size as her entire apartment. Bookshelves lined three of the walls. The one behind Hinson's massive desk remained unobstructed so he could enjoy a nice view of The

Sterner Academy's grounds. The rest of the area was wasted space. No circular table for collaborations. No couch. No coffee machine. Just carpet.

T.J. busied herself looking at the books. Most of them were treatises on education, history, language, and other subjects school administrators thought they should display. One shelf about halfway down the left wall caught her eye. A few volumes filled each side, but a pair of bookends and several tomes sitting apart from the rest occupied the middle. The largest was titled *THE REACH CURRICULUM MODEL*, with thinner spines showing titles of *RIGOR*, *EXCELLENCE*, *ACHIEVEMENT*, *CREATIVITY*, and *HABITS*. "Sounds boring," T.J. muttered as she used her phone to snap a few pictures.

She kept exploring the shelves but found nothing of interest. Sitting at Hinson's desk opened her up to a bunch of problems if someone happened to come back and see her. She tested the drawers as she passed by and found them all locked. As she scanned more books, footsteps approached. T.J. hurried to a guest chair and dropped in just before Anthony Hinson walked in. She recognized him from his website photo.

"Who are you?" he said. "You're not a student."

CHAPTER 19

I STILL WOKE up before eight on Monday. There were mornings I missed sleeping for another half-hour. This would be among them. As I stretched and headed downstairs, I realized I didn't need to hurry into the office. T.J. would soon start her first day as a spy at The Sterner Academy, and I had no reason to be at our workplace other than to start more coffee to perk.

With hot caffeine on my mind, I set a pot to brew. I'd never been good at going back to sleep once I'd been up and about, so I figured I would stay awake. While java dripped into the carafe, I stuck my head into Gloria's fridge. She had enough supplies for me to put something together. About ten minutes later, with the coffee finished and turkey bacon sizzling in a pan, Gloria came downstairs. "Morning," she said, giving me a minty kiss before filling a mug for each of us.

"I was hoping to bring you breakfast in bed."

"What's the occasion?"

"I'm married to the fundraising star of the city," I said.

"Claire's article is live already?" Gloria asked.

"I don't know. I haven't looked, but it seems at least a day early. She might have needed the weekend to recover from all the charcuterie"

Gloria chuckled. "I guess I'm just eager to see it."

"I would be, too."

"Is T.J. headed to Sterner?"

"She is." Toast popped up, and I set it on a plate to butter it. "She's probably on her way by now. Can't show up late on your first day . . . especially not there."

"You think she'll get in trouble?"

"I doubt it. We talked about not rocking the boat on day one. The new girl will be fresh in everyone's minds."

Gloria grinned. "Would you wait a day or two?"

"No."

"Do you expect her to?" my wife wanted to know.

"I expect her to use her judgment." I assembled two plates of sourdough toast, turkey bacon, and scrambled eggs and carried them to the table.

"You lean on her quite a bit. More than you expected to, I think."

I pondered the comment and bobbed my head. "She's been great. At first, I felt like it was doing a favor for Melinda. I would take on T.J., give her some of the work I don't like doing, and we'd both win in different ways. She's made herself more valuable."

"Maybe Melinda has some more people she can send my way."

"T.J.'s friend Amy is in the program now," I said. "I think she's learning social media management."

Gloria nibbled on a slice of bacon. "A useful skill to have. Maybe I'll look her up in a couple months."

We finished our breakfast, and I refilled our coffee mugs. After a few swigs, Gloria asked, "I guess you're not in a rush to get to the office?"

"Not really, no."

"What if a client is waiting for you?"

I shrugged. "They can slip a note under the door."

"I love your cavalier attitude sometimes." Gloria stood, slinked to my side of the table, and lowered herself onto my lap. "I'm not in a hurry this morning, either."

"You just like it when I call you the new fundraising star of Baltimore," I said. She answered by kissing me before we got up and hustled into the living room. Later, I reheated both our mugs and presented hers to Gloria.

"You know exactly what to give a girl after sex on the couch," she said.

I grinned. "It's an acquired skill." She finished her coffee and headed upstairs for a shower. I looked out the window, saw the rain, and dressed in workout clothes. The cheerfully polite streets of Brooklandville could wait. I availed myself of Gloria's weights and treadmill downstairs. After about forty-five minutes, I needed a shower, too. I left the house after ten-thirty and enjoyed a commute free of traffic.

As I pulled into the lot, T.J.'s yellow Mustang was conspicuous by its absence. I hoped no one towed it from the private spots at Sterner, and I also hoped she'd manage to steer clear of trouble on her first day there.

———

Because two cups of coffee are never enough, I set a half pot to brew after unlocking the office and setting my backpack down. No messages waited on the voicemail. If a prospective client stopped by, they didn't leave a note under the door. A quick check of my email showed nothing I needed to respond to with any haste. If the morning were going to be rainy and dreary, at least it was polite enough to also be slow.

I grabbed my favorite mug as the java neared completion. Footsteps came up the stairs. Heavy ones judging by the clatter they made on the metal, and more than one set. There was no time to get my pistol from the desk. As three large men bounded in, I finished pouring my mug. "You guys need a detective?" I asked.

"You know why we're here, asshole," one of them said. They all stood taller than me, with the shortest about six-three and the tallest maybe six-five. Each man outweighed me by a good fifty pounds, though their physiques suggested they partook of beer and cheeseburgers more often than workouts at the gym. The mouthy one was the lone blond of the group. The tallest guy shaved his head, and the other had hair almost the exact same shade of dark brown as me.

"I presume you're here to hire me," I said, "but calling me an asshole isn't helping your cause."

"You gonna play dumb?"

"I know . . . I should leave it to you." They all glared. "You could at least let me put some milk in my coffee before you threaten me. What happened to manners?"

The blond stepped forward. Maybe they voted him the mouthpiece on the drive here. "Listen here, you prick—aaaah!"

His empty threat dissolved into a scream when I threw hot coffee in his face.

He stumbled to the side, and I helped him find the floor by banging his head against my desk. The other two closed in. "You work for the principal?" I asked as I took a fighting stance. "Learning from your mistakes is a sign of education."

"The fuck you talking about?" Baldy demanded. His frown and puzzled expression told me he didn't know who I meant by the principal. Interesting. It didn't let Hinson off the hook completely, of course, but now I needed to consider who he might be using as an intermediary. First, however, I needed to get these three cretins out of the office.

My clean-shaven foe went for a big punch as the brown-haired man moved to flank me. Rather than turn it away, I shifted to the side, caught his wrist, put my left hand against the back of his arm, and shoved hard. Baldy collided with Brown Hair, and both grunted. Neither went down, but they bounced off each other. Chrome Dome stumbled farther away, so I focused on the guy whose hair matched mine. He was back on his heels, so I kicked him in the midsection. He continued his rearward trajectory until his butt bounced off T.J.'s desk.

As he stood up straight again, I led with my right elbow, slamming him flush in the mouth. He recoiled, and I punched him hard in the solar plexus. Footsteps approached from the rear. I put Brown Hair down with a hard right to the face and spun away just in time to avoid a haymaker from the bald guy. He followed with another. I blocked it, but my rapid dodge a second before meant I never got my balance, and his next punch took me in the face and knocked me over.

I fell into an open area. He advanced with a mean sneer on his face. I raised my fists, and his eyes followed my hands. This gave me a great opportunity to kick him in the knee, so I did. It wasn't hard enough to break the joint, but he bit off a curse and backed away favoring his left leg. I regained my feet quickly and made sure I took a balanced stance. My adversary shifted his feet so he could punch with his left hand.

It didn't go as well for him as he might have hoped. I blocked two jabs, then a cross, and then a hook. The technique wasn't bad, but most people aren't ambidextrous fighters, and this fellow proved to be much better with the right. After blunting the hook, I kicked him in the left leg again. He called me a bastard before throwing another punch. I responded in the same manner.

He lowered his hands, so I clobbered him.

To his credit, he didn't go down, but a solid kick to the chin sent him sprawling on top of the first guy who managed to stir before his teammate landed on him. I took out my phone and snapped pictures of all three men. "Time for you all to leave." I walked to my desk and grabbed the 9MM from my top drawer. Baldy was the first to see it. "You can walk out of here, I can toss you down the stairs, or the medical examiner can take you out on a slab. Your choice."

"This ain't over," the mouthy blond had the nerve to say as he stood up and rubbed his head.

"It will be if you don't get the fuck out."

They had some more curses for me, of course, but all three left on their own power. I moved to the doorway and watched them depart, then observed from the window as they piled into a drab van with a mud-covered rear plate and drove away. This time, at least, I managed to snap some pictures. Maybe Anthony Hinson didn't send this trio of goons, but soon, I would know who did.

———

A couple years ago, the Baltimore Police Department connected to the Maryland State Police system for facial recognition technology. The MSP system then reaches out to the FBI and other acronym-heavy national databases. On my first case, my cousin Rich—then a uniformed sergeant—left me unattended at his desk for a couple minutes. I snagged his PC's address information thanks to his glaring oversight, and ever since, I've been able to convince the BPD's systems to accept my computer as one of its own. Their recent ransomware issues made this dicey for a while, but with services restored, I was back in business.

Because he besmirched the good name of men with dark brown hair everywhere, I started with the guy whose shade matched mine. His name was Clement Eppler, and he did not have a criminal record. I ran a few scripts to scrape his social media, but as far as I could tell, he had no connection to Anthony Hinson or The Sterner Academy. The bald fellow—Abner Swan —likewise enjoyed no connection to Sterner or Hinson, but he'd gotten popped a couple times for simple assault. I wondered if taking a beatdown today would make him less likely to earn the third strike. Probably not. Prison would show him the delta between his estimated and real-world toughness.

The blond man's photo took the longest because I wasn't able to get a great straight-on shot. Still, the algorithms crunched away, the ones and zeroes reached a consensus, and the face of Willard Little stared back from my screen. "Why can't goons have normal names anymore?" I asked my empty office. I almost felt bad beating up on guys named Clement, Abner, and Willard. They'd probably gotten pummeled a lot as kids. Why couldn't three muscleheads named Tim, Bobby, and Sal walk through the door with malice in their eyes and evil in their hearts?

Willard's social media included no formal connection to Hinson, but I found an indirect one to Sterner—he was Facebook friends and LinkedIn contacts with Ronald Lobdell the lacrosse coach, as well as fellow goon Clement Eppler. I got the feeling Lobdell didn't like me when I met him on campus. He probably reported the incident to Hinson who then ordered him to take care of it. I wondered if the coach knew of his failure already.

Even without a direct tie to the principal, this meant someone at the school sent three men to my office this morning with bad intentions. What if I had been out somewhere, and they found T.J. here by herself? We'd texted earlier, but I wanted to stay off the comms today so she didn't draw any unnecessary attention. This was something she needed to know, however. I fired off a quick message.

Hey, three guys visited the office this morning. I sent them away. Turns out one of them is connected to the lacrosse coach, so I think you need to be careful there. Let me know you got this.

After a few minutes, she didn't respond, so I sent a brief follow-up. When my assistant again didn't respond, I called her.

No answer.

CHAPTER 20

T.J. SAT motionless in the chair as Hinson entered his office. "I asked you a question, miss." Hinson frowned at her. He almost looked distinguished with his hair graying at the edges. Somehow, being in his presence made him seem even more imperious and condescending than his picture and bio suggested. He was reasonably tall, probably about C.T.'s height, and he wore a slim-fit black suit. "You're too old to be a student, and a few years too young for one of our parents. Who are you?"

"I'm new," T.J. said. "Today's my first day. I'm working for Ms. Heaton, and I wanted to come up and introduce myself."

"And you decided you'd simply walk in when no one was around?"

"I just got here." She shrugged and tried to keep her breathing neutral. Getting caught on her first day might get her fired—possibly from both jobs for such a massive screw-up. "Figured I'd enjoy the view and wait for a moment."

Hinson came around the desk and scanned its surface. T.J. hadn't touched anything. He must have found everything to his liking because his frown eased, and he tried a smile which looked like the one a politician might deploy to a gullible voter. "Nice to meet you, then. I heard you'd be starting. It's Tamera, isn't it?"

"I go by T.J."

"Welcome to The Sterner Academy, T.J. I'm sure Ms. Heaton is relieved you're here."

"She is."

"Have you seen much of the campus?"

"I'm afraid not," she said. "Only the drive in and the view from the windows. I've been working since I got here this morning."

"Well, I'll make sure one of our students gives you a tour. We have ambassadors do the same for incoming families. This is a great campus. We're quite proud of it."

"I'm sure you are."

"I'm a bit surprised you stopped by," Hinson said. T.J. tried not to fidget, and it was about as difficult as trying not to think of an elephant. Hinson looked more at the ceiling than her, so he didn't seem to notice her moment of unease. "Miss Heaton runs the PTA . . . quite successfully, I might add. She's a huge asset to the parents of this school."

"She certainly seems to be."

"I won't say she and I are adversaries but . . . well, it's not her job to tend to the overall well-being of the school. She needs to make sure the parents are happy, which sometimes puts her at odds with teachers and the administration. Did she suggest you come and see me?"

"No," T.J. Said, adding a shrug. "I'm here on my own."

"Why?" Hinson wanted to know. "Have you introduced yourself to the assistant principals?"

"Not yet." T.J. wondered if she should have looked for them first. Going right to the top violated the chain of command principle, and a man like Hinson could be a stickler for it. She wondered if he did anything he could to make young women feel ill at ease. This time, she sat on her hands to avoid a fidget.

Hinson smiled, and it almost looked sincere. "You thought you'd start with the top dog?"

"The principal at my high school was something of a jerk," she said. "He was big and had a loud voice, and he used it every chance he could. An intimidating guy. When I was a freshman, I was terrified of him, and I don't think I ever really got over it." It was sort of true. The physical description of Mister Moore was accurate, at least. T.J. found him to be a loud clown, however. Even if she'd finished high school, her opinion would have stayed the same. "I didn't want to get off on that same uneasy foot here."

"I certainly hope I wasn't intimidating." Hinson added a laugh. The man possessed a skill for making people think he was being genuine. He really could have been a politician. Maybe he wanted Councilman Ellicott dead out of sheer jealousy. As her boss was fond of saying, people got killed for worse reasons every day.

"Well, it did feel a little like I was in the principal's office again there," T.J. said.

"All good now, I hope." She nodded. "Welcome to The Sterner Academy, T.J. I'll send someone around later to give you the campus tour." He waved a hand. "Miss Heaton won't mind." Hinson glanced back down to his desk, signifying the end of the conversation from his side.

"Thank you." T.J. stood and left the office. On her way out, she passed the young woman who'd left a few minutes prior, now carrying a white paper tray which trailed the smells of Chinese food. It was only when she made it back to the stairwell that she was able to breathe normally again.

———

A short while later, Rachel Heaton returned to the office. She set her bag down, placed a small container inside the dorm fridge, and took her seat. "Any issues come up while I was gone?"

"No," T.J. said. She made sure the door was mostly closed and lowered her voice. "The principal's area was empty, so I popped into Hinson's office." Rachel's eyes widened behind her glasses, but she remained quiet. "I got to look around for a couple minutes before he came back."

"He caught you in his office?"

"Yeah."

"You need to be smarter," Rachel said. "I admit I don't like Hinson very much. I don't know if he's involved in whatever you think he might be, but there's no love lost between us, and it's probably not just because our jobs bring us into conflict sometimes. He's far from an idiot, though, and he's been in education long enough to ferret out when young people are lying."

"Young people?" T.J. asked.

"You don't look too much older than many of our seniors."

"I guess I'm not." T.J. chuckled.

"How old are you?"

"I didn't think you were supposed to ask that."

Rachel smiled. "I'm not going to fire you. People can't ask those questions because of age discrimination." T.J. didn't say anything. "All right. I'll start. My son is a freshman. I'm thirty-eight."

"You don't look it," T.J. said.

"All credit to my mother. She still has great skin at sixty-two."

"I'm twenty-one."

"Wow," Rachel said. "If you stick around long enough, some senior is going to ask you to prom."

"Gross."

"Let's focus on happier things, then. I'm going to forward you a bunch of emails with documents attached. Those documents need to be printed out and filed. We do keep electronic records, but we also operate at the whim of the school. I don't want some administrator to cut off my access in a fit of pique. So we also have paper backups. You'll need to file them. If there's an existing record, just add it in the folder. If not, create one."

"All right."

"Do you do this kind of work for your boss?" Rachel asked.

"We use cloud backups for everything, but I also maintain printed copies." T.J. chuckled. "I think I basically saved him there when I started. He was terrible at it."

"Well, I can do it, but I've fallen behind. I haven't had a secretary since last school year."

"Why not?"

Rachel smirked. "The usual reasons. Some unspecified budget concern. Can't hire over the summer." She waved a hand. "They're all crap. I think Hinson didn't want me to have one. The administration talks a good game about parental involvement and the PTA, but ultimately, I'm a thorn in their side. I'm glad you're here, I absolutely have work for you, and I'll be very sorry when you go back to your real job."

T.J. wondered if Rachel would try to inhibit the investigation somehow. It would get her an extra day or two of a free assistant. This was a cynical thought—something C.T. might have come up with. Nothing about the woman suggested she'd be so underhanded. "Might as well put me to work, then."

Rachel did as she said and forwarded many emails along with links to resources on a shared drive. T.J. opened them one at a time and sent them to the closest printer. Simply opening the documents, hitting Control-P, and verifying they went to the right location each time took twenty-five minutes. Filing them— especially if Rachel wanted them sorted by something other than last name—would probably take at least twice as long. T.J. figured she'd have an armload of papers to carry back with her.

She walked to the closest printer. The hallway was empty of students and staff, and not many sounds and voices made it past the closed doors in the wing. An exit led to another building. No harm in exploring. T.J. walked through down a double wide corridor framed and covered in glass. After about a hundred yards, she emerged into another building. Signs told her it was the middle school wing.

As before, doors remained closed, and the area was largely empty with classes in session. Lockers lined the walls, their rows broken only by doorways. A mechanical *whirr* drew her attention. A camera mounted inside a clear dome on the ceiling looked down at her. T.J. spotted a few more along the hall. It made sense. The technology was different, and the smell was much better, but this building reminded T.J. of her high school. No matter the tuition, these places came down to classes and lockers.

T.J. left and headed back to the admin building. A few more cameras lined the ceiling, and she spotted still more in the main wing. It gave her an idea for when she finished her work for Rachel. T.J. found the printer in a small room that smelled like burned ink. High tuition couldn't mask the fact that most places used the same class of office machines. T.J. grabbed the healthy stack of papers and carried it back to her desk.

Rachel didn't ask why she'd been gone longer than necessary. T.J. first sorted the printouts by first letter of the last name—"letterbetical" as C.T. called it. She then went back and finished with a proper arrangement. Some students appeared twice for different reasons—usually bad grades, disciplinary issues in the classroom, or involvement in either end of a bullying incident. It seemed some kids were still dicks even in fancy schools.

Her temporary boss took a few phone calls, turning away for some semblance of privacy in the shared space. With the filing done, T.J. figured she'd do something for her real job. She and C.T. often got into camera systems. Many companies plugged the devices in and simply left the default credentials in place. T.J. poked around on the network until she found the make and model information in a security document whose access should have been more controlled.

Another Word file helpfully provided the URL, user ID, and password to access the control system. Sometimes, it really was this easy. Documentation provided consistency and allowed organizations to maintain continuity in the event of staffing changes. It also allowed curious people to learn information they shouldn't have access to.

T.J. opened a browser and keyed in the credentials. Her screen filled with small views of the campus camera system surrounding a window holding buttons to control the playback. These actions would get logged, but as her boss often told her, logs were worthless unless someone watched them close to real time. Nothing she'd seen at The Sterner Academy suggested they did this. They'd opted for marble and painted brick instead.

Rachel handed her a few more secretarial things to do, and T.J. did them while multitasking and figuring out the camera system. She deduced the naming system quickly enough—three numbers corresponding to the building, floor, and a final integer for the device identifier. It took a little time, but T.J. isolated the electric eyes closest to Hinson's office and the reception area on the first floor. She also noticed a camera which offered anyone looking a great shot of Rachel Heaton's door. "You're probably watching," she muttered, thinking of the principal.

"What?" Rachel said.

"Nothing. Just looking at something." T.J. knew Rachel was a smart woman. She would have seen the cameras, and she probably checked for hidden ones inside the office space. Spying on someone he saw as opposition sounded like a page out of Hinson's playbook.

T.J. did a few more filing-related things for Rachel as the

afternoon wore on. Around two o'clock, Hinson appeared on a camera leaving his office and heading for the stairs down to the first floor. He popped up in a new small window once he emerged. Where was he going? It was too early for him to leave. T.J. didn't think he was the type to work hard, but he would also want to be seen in his office—at least looking busy—as long as possible. Hinson moved down the hallway past Rachel's office. T.J. watched as he checked the corridor and then opened a side door.

Another man stepped in. T.J. couldn't get a good look at the newcomer as he kept his eyes pointed downward. The two chatted amiably as they moved back the way Hinson had come. When the duo passed a camera a little ways up the hall, the device got a good shot of the recent arrival.

He looked an awful lot like Gerald Russell.

———

"Oh, my gosh," T.J. whispered. What was Gerald doing here? By all reason, he should hate Anthony Hinson for firing his father over some ancient morals clause. However, the principal opened the door, and the young man happily walked in and engaged in conversation with a man he should have punched.

"Something interesting?" Rachel wanted to know.

T.J. didn't answer right away. Rachel seemed like she was on the right side of this, but she still worked inside The Sterner Academy. After a moment of thought, she said, "Here's a hypo-thetical. If your father's boss fired him because of something your mother did, what would your opinion of the boss be?"

"I'm pretty sure I'd hate his guts."

"Me, too."

Rachel's eyes widened. "Wait, you mean Edgar and Marcy's son is here?"

"He just walked in a few minutes ago and had a nice little chat with Hinson."

"How are you seeing this?"

"I got into the camera system," T.J. said in a lowered voice. "It wasn't difficult. I'm surprised a high schooler in computer science hasn't tried."

"I'm not sure I like that." Rachel frowned. "I didn't know you'd be hacking the school."

"It's the twenty-first century." T.J. shrugged. "My boss and I don't wear trench coats and hide in old doorways very often. We do a lot of our work online." Rachel's expression didn't change. "I got all the info I needed from a Word file. You said you wanted to help us catch whoever killed Marcy."

"I do," Rachel said with a sigh. "Maybe I just don't want to know the methods you're using."

"I'll stop telling you, then." T.J. picked up her phone. She'd turned off notifications when she went sneaking around, and now she saw C.T. had texted and called her a few times. She answered his message. *Three guys . . . not bad for an older man. I haven't met the lacrosse coach yet.*

A response came in a moment later.

> You're not missing anything. He has all the charm of one of the sticks his players use.

> I got into the camera system, btw. Really easy. All the information I needed was in the documentation.

> Great! Anything useful yet.

> Yeah. Someone came to visit Hinson. He brought the guy in a side door. They were chatting like old friends. I'm about 97% sure it was Gerald Russell.

Seriously??

T.J.'s phone buzzed with an incoming call from C.T. She wheeled her chair into the corner and turned to face the drywall before answering. "Hey, boss."

"What the hell is Gerald doing there? I wanted to throw Hinson out the window before I even met him."

"No idea." She realized C.T. wouldn't know of her visit to the principal's office earlier today. "I managed to get into his office briefly when no one was there."

"Tell me you didn't get caught on your first day."

"I did," T.J. admitted. "Hinson himself came back and found me. I heard him in time to sit in a guest chair. Told him I'd been waiting to introduce myself, the principal at my high school was a scary jerk, blah blah blah. Seems like he bought it."

"You flattered him," C.T. said. "Good play."

"It would work against you, too," she pointed out.

"If you compare me to Hinson again, you're fired."

T.J. chuckled. "Fine. I snapped a few pictures while I was in there. Not sure if it'll be anything we can use."

"Good. When you're done, swing by the office, and we can go over it all."

"You buying dinner?"

"Don't I always?" C.T. said.

"I guess you do. Or your credit card does at least." T.J. looked at her monitor and the many tiny security screens covering its real estate from her perch in the corner. "I'm not sure where Hinson and Gerald went after. I didn't see them pop back up on any of the cameras."

"It's a pretty big school. Four main buildings. If they're doing something shady together, Hinson is smart enough not to invite a co-conspirator into his office."

"True." T.J. said. "All right. I'll drop by when I'm done here."

"Be careful. Sounds like you've met a few people and made some good inroads today. Hopefully, it all went under the radar. Watch your back."

"I will." T.J. ended the call. She wheeled herself once again to her desk. Hinson and Gerald remained ghosts.

CHAPTER 21

I REMEMBERED the guy in the red glasses from Hinson's aborted fundraiser at the Roland Park Country Club. With a little time until T.J. finished at Sterner and arrived at her real office, I could busy myself with extra research. Other than Zeb, no one at the table stood out. Faceless potential investors. Sometimes, I recognized members of the Baltimore area elite because they came to my parents' events or Gloria's. I'd never seen any of those men before. Hinson wasn't exactly making an appearance on *Shark Tank*.

When I was busy making an ass out of Hinson—all too easy because he did most of the heavy lifting—I didn't get any photos of the others at the table. A quick check of past events on the Roland Park Country Club's website revealed a ton of pictures. They were designed to show off the space and demonstrate rich people having fun, but they often leaked information to people who cared about it.

I needed to go back eight months on the calendar, but I spotted my red-spectacled friend at an event in the first quarter of the year. I scrolled through the photos until I found the one which showed him best, downloaded it, and cropped it so he was the sole focus. Facial rec told me he was Rory McSwain, and he had no criminal record. Another search revealed McSwain was a venture capitalist and self-described "serial investor." I didn't think Baltimore housed a lot of VCs—a point in the city's favor—so McSwain might have been in demand for people getting things off the ground. Like whatever Hinson was there to drum up interest in. I still didn't know.

T.J. texted to tell me she was on her way. It seemed a little early for dinner. I've always been a firm believer pizza is appropriate in ninety percent of situations, so I ordered three pies to be delivered. My assistant and I would put a hurting on two. I'd give the third to whomever still worked in Manny's shop downstairs. From the clanks and curses which made it up through the floorboards, I guessed three or four men remained.

With dinner sorted, I went back to McSwain. He maintained a website, and it used far less flowery language than Hinson's official bio. Thank goodness for small mercies. One nugget jumped out at me. *I grew up poor and went to public school my whole life. Education is important, and parents should be able to get a good one for their kids even when the city or county lets them down. Thus, I've always tried to devote a percentage of my portfolio to scholarship, especially technology and innovations for the classroom.*

It sounded good, but "a percentage" could have been minuscule. A single investment at one-one-hundredth of McSwain's net worth would satisfy the statement if anyone bothered to look into it. Hinson obviously worked in education and thought he was some shining star in the sky according to his bullshit bio. Could he have come up with something to whet McSwain's appetite?

A short while later, T.J. arrived. I told her pizza would be coming soon, and the delivery driver pulled into the lot in short order. I tipped the fellow, took two boxes, and told him to deliver the third to the crew still toiling away on the first floor. T.J. had already set out plates and napkins. We each grabbed two slices.

"I'd love to know what the hell Gerald Russell was doing there," she said after an initial bite.

"You're sure it's him?" She showed me a picture on her phone. Hinson was clear on the security footage. The other man almost looked right into a camera like he didn't know it was there. "All right, it looks a lot like him. We'll presume it is. What's the connection?"

"No idea. Gerald should hate Hinson. Unless his body turns up on campus overnight, I think they're up to something."

"You're casting Hinson as the corpse, I presume?"

"Yeah, but I guess either one could take out the other."

"It would be awfully courteous of them," I said. "Maybe whoever dies will write out a long and detailed confession first."

"What are we going to do now?" my assistant wanted to know.

"You should eat your pizza and go home. You've been working two jobs today. I'm sure it hasn't been easy."

"What are you going to do?"

I shrugged. "See what I can uncover. You did a lot of the legwork. Now, I'll run with it. If I hit on anything, I'll let you know."

"Can I have the rest of the cheese pizza?"

"Help yourself," I said. "I'm hoping the pepperoni will give me inspiration."

"What about indigestion?" T.J. said. "You've been shoveling it into your mouth pretty quickly."

I grabbed a third slice. "If it's the price for an epiphany, I'll pay it."

———

T.J. sent me the rest of the photos she took after she got to her car. I transferred her pictures to my laptop so I could view them on the big monitor. She snapped some good ones of Hinson's absurdly large office. Any space so immense for a lone occupant is a vanity project. As a vain person, I felt confident in this assessment. I remembered his packed shelves from my prior visit. The idea anyone read so many books about any single topic was preposterous, but Hinson expected people who set foot in his sanctum to believe it.

I scrolled through several photos before something caught my eye, and I needed to go back and look again. Hinson dedicated a shelf to a few books in particular. I didn't notice them when I stopped by earlier, but T.J. did, and she had the picture to prove it. *THE REACH CURRICULUM MODEL*, the title of the first book, sounded like something important. Maybe a project Hinson would need investors like Rory McSwain to bring about. The individual books—*RIGOR, EXCELLENCE, ACHIEVEMENT, CREATIVITY*, and *HABITS*—sounded good, but I didn't trust Hinson to develop the curriculum for basic dog obedience.

At least then, one of his students might bite him.

None of this explained a possible connection to Gerald Russell, so I dug into the young man further. He'd mentioned earning his master's in education, which I confirmed in about thirty seconds. When T.J. and I visited the Russell men, I remembered wondering why someone who said he didn't care much about learning got a graduate degree in it. *There's a lot you can do with the theory. It doesn't mean I need to teach kids.*

He was right. It would open up avenues like curriculum development.

My deep dive continued. I found a blog Gerald never associated to himself by name, but he registered it under an email account he used elsewhere. Like mother, like son. He wrote it under the handle of Scholarum. Maybe he expected people to be impressed with his use of a first-semester Latin vocabulary word.

A few commenters chided him for his anonymity. None gave him any credit for the handle, which I have to admit amused me a little. Most of Gerald's missives were brief and aired a specific grievance about education—usually public even though his parents both taught at a ritzy private school. One entry in particular caught my attention.

American Education: Let's Reboot the Machine

I'm not going to sugarcoat the truth—our education system is a hot mess. Yep, I've got a master's in the field. Nope, I don't want to be a teacher. Not in this system, at least. Call me a pessimist, but I've seen the cogs in this machine, and let me tell you, they're rusted beyond repair.

My parents have been teachers for decades. Toiling away in the classroom trying to get through to other people's kids. They've tried to instill their love for learning in me. It didn't work. All I see is a system stuck in the 19th Century and in dire need of a major upgrade, not just a patch.

We're teaching kids to pass shitty standardized tests rather than think critically. What's the point of memorizing the Pythagorean theorem if you don't understand the "why" behind it? We're churning out robotic minds—which can't compete with countries we should be dominating—instead of fostering innovators and free thinkers. There's no factory for the next generation of leaders, but we seem to think we've made one.

Wrong.

Let's talk about the curriculum. Seriously, can someone tell me why we still teach cursive? I get it's "traditional," but so were horse-drawn carriages. Times have changed. Why are our kids still reading books written by people who died before the automobile hit the streets? It's not enough to just throw in a coding class and call it modern. We need a curriculum which is adaptable and can evolve with the world around us.

Kids need rigor to achieve excellence. We need to foster and teach creativity and lifelong habits. No one should give a shit about Jane Eyre anymore. Some teachers might already be going down this road, but they're few and far between. We need to do this bigger. This is our upgrade path.

The solution? Tear it down. Start from scratch. Build a new framework with the principles I mentioned. I'm talking about a curriculum that doesn't just ask, "What do you want to be when you grow up?" but also "What problems do you want to solve?" and "What creative solutions can you come up with?"

I know this will be easier said than done. Inertia takes time to overcome, especially at the institutional level. But unless we embrace radical change, we're just rearranging deck chairs on the Titanic. *And we all know how its journey ended.*

How interesting he worked in the book titles in Hinson's new model. I shifted my focus from Gerald to the REACH model. A website belonging to New Modern Curriculum showed a pretty generic splash page with only a sign-up form and contact link. I checked the Internet Archive and found an *About Us* page from almost two years ago. NMC stated a goal of starting regional but working up to nationwide implementation. The CEO showed as Melanie DeBerg, with Anthony Hinson having the flashy—and rather punny—title of Principal Consultant.

Another quick query told me Melanie DeBerg was the maiden name of Melanie Hinson.

"Bingo," I said to the empty office.

———

I called T.J. to fill her in on what I'd learned. "Jesus Christ," she said. "He's actually working with Hinson."

"Probably has been for a while."

"Which means . . . "

"Yeah," I said, "he must have known his mother was on the

hit list. She and the councilman could have beaten the drum against some new curriculum."

"You think Marcy knew Hinson was involved?"

"He wasn't exactly hiding those books in his office. I didn't notice them, but you did. We can presume any teacher has spent time in there on multiple occasions. Marcy could have seen them and done the same research I did."

"All this over how to teach children," my assistant lamented.

"Pearson is a multi-billion dollar company," I said. "Like Rachel said, even if you don't really do it right and go big, you can still make millions. Gerald's parents are private school teachers, so I'm sure he's not awash in cash. Hinson has enough money to swing a country club membership, but I'll bet he's leveraged to the max. It's all about image for people like him. They'll go up to their eyeballs in debt if it allows them to look rich and important in the right circles."

"You certainly travel in interesting company."

"I've met a lot of people like Hinson through my parents over the years. None of them are as special as they think they are."

"What's our next step, boss?" T.J. asked.

"We're going to proceed like everything is normal," I said. "You keep working at Sterner for now. Just remember Hinson might not be a killer, but he must have been involved in what went on. Don't seek him out. Try to avoid him if he's roaming the halls meeting the little people or whatever he thinks a CEO principal should be doing."

"All right. What are you going to do?"

"Given what we learned today, I'm going to talk to Gonzalez in the morning."

"You think it'll do anything?"

"I don't know." If this were a city matter, and I took what I knew to my cousin Rich, he would act on it. He'd grouse about everything, and he'd question my methods in at least two mildly insulting ways, but in the end, he wanted to put the right people away. I knew Gonzalez did, too, but I didn't work with him as often, so his actions were less predictable. "He's an honest cop. I presume he wants guilty people in jail and innocent people not."

"Is what we have enough?" T.J. wondered.

"It might create reasonable doubt," I said. "More a consideration for a prosecutor than a police sergeant. Gonzalez knows I have some issues regarding the evidence timeline, too. He's downplayed them with the usual police hand-waving, but maybe we can put both factors together and get a package deal."

"Here's hoping. Good luck tomorrow."

"You, too. Try to stay out of trouble. If you land yourself in it anyway, make sure you call me."

"I will." She ended the call.

So far, Hinson only knew I was investigating, and he'd already experienced me being a thorn in his side. None of the information I put online mentioned T.J. or offered a photo of her, so even if he dug into me, he'd really have to go deep to make a connection. I hoped he would continue to focus on me and not pay much attention to the new girl in the building.

CHAPTER 22

POLICE HAND-WAVING WAS in full effect.

"Let me get this straight," Gonzalez said when I called him at eight-thirty the next day. Even though sounds of driving came over his end of the connection, I could hear amusement in his voice. "You think the guy's son and the principal are in cahoots?"

"No one says 'cahoots' anymore," I pointed out.

"Fine. Working together. The principal is pushing some new curriculum for schools, the son is on board, and they decided to kill both mom and councilman because those two might have gotten in the way of this fledgling empire?"

"Pretty much."

"You know it sounds like bullshit, right?"

"Try it in a more serious tone next time. You'll get there."

"It's like bad *Shark Tank* fan fiction," Gonzalez said.

"There's no Mark Cuban in this," I told him. "I looked into a couple of the guys Hinson was making his pitch to. They're investors with a clear bias for educational products."

"Like some fancy new curriculum."

"Right." He didn't say anything, so I kept going. "The biggest player in the space is Pearson. Multi-billion dollar company. Even a moderately successful one can crank out millions, though.

You don't need me to tell you money is one of the oldest motives in the world."

"Yet you just did."

"I figured you might need me to tell you after all," I said.

A loud horn blared in my ear, and I winced and moved the phone away. "Sorry," Gonzalez said. "Some people are assholes when they get behind the wheel."

"If only you knew someone in the police force who could pull them over."

He chuckled. "I don't write tickets anymore. Instead, I get to deal with private eyes who think they know how to investigate murders better than I do."

"Sounds like you get to interact with some very smart people," I said. "Probably handsome, too."

Gonzalez sighed. "Look, millions of dollars will go a long way for motive. You don't have anything concrete, though. You've told me about some books on a shelf, a company set up in the principal's wife's name, the son having a degree and writing a blog . . . they're all interesting data points, but they don't add up to something I can take to a prosecutor or a judge."

"We know the councilman was big on education. Marcy Russell had talked about resigning and running for the school board. It's not unreasonable to think her principal knew about it. Somehow, he gets wind of it, realizes two people now stand to block him and his company from—"

"His wife's company," Gonzalez pointed out.

"Whatever. On paper, sure, but it's just to avoid a direct tie. Anyway, two people stand to block him and *his wife's company* from making millions, so he does what pricks with some money in his situation always do."

"I'm telling you it all sounds good. You gotta bring me concrete proof if you wanna get the husband out. Right now, we got his prints."

"I have some questions about the evidence and order of operations, too."

"Save 'em for later," Gonzalez said. "You only get to tell me how to do my job one way at a time." He broke the connection.

"Goddammit," I grumbled as I set my phone down. Gonzalez wouldn't consider the strange timeline of the evidence unless I brought him usable proof of ties between Hinson, the younger Russell, the nascent curriculum company, and the pair of murders committed. T.J. would have started her day at The Sterner Academy by now. She might be able to find some more intel, but she would need to do it around the work Rachel Heaton gave her.

I cracked my knuckles and got going.

———

After a couple hours, I'd found some decent data, but I knew it wouldn't be enough.

Councilman Ellicott went on record earlier in the year about education and changing curricula. "I've had enough of it," he said in a meeting whose minutes were available on the Baltimore County government's website. "What today's kids learn is already considerably different than what I learned. We joke about 'the new math,' but it's real. I had trouble helping my own daughter a few times. What good is all of this doing? We keep coming up with new standards and new tests, but more and more of what we're teaching is how to pass the damn tests. I want kids to learn real skills, but I don't want to bring in another new curriculum. We just installed this one two years ago for heaven's sake, and we spent tens of millions of dollars on it across the state. Let's focus on teaching our students the right things before we force everyone to start over so quickly."

I already heard Gonzalez telling me this was great but not something he could use by itself.

"Worst voice in my head ever," I muttered as I kept working.

A few more of Gerald's blog posts as Scholarum didn't tell me much. It was amazing how much differently he and his mother wrote about education, the curriculum, and school boards from within the same house. They may not have been aware of one another. Marcy's post indicated she knew there was a "puppet master" pulling the strings on programmatic changes within The Sterner Academy. With what I now knew, this had to be Anthony Hinson. Somehow, he must have learned she planned to resign at the end of the school year and run for the board, putting her in a position to shoot down any proposed changes to how county schools worked.

Again, the annoying Gonzalez voice in my head told me I needed more.

I'd swung and missed a couple times on going deeper when my phone rang. T.J.'s number showed on the caller ID. "Tired of filing already?" I said.

"I had my fill of it when I did it for you."

"How's it going today?"

"All right," she said. "Rachel has some real work for me, but I can still get into the camera system. I was hoping no one would discover what I did yesterday."

"They're probably not equipped for it," I said. "My guess is they have a few IT people onsite and they outsource a lot. Who's supposed to keep an eye on what, and how things get reported, often get lost."

"Whatever the reason, I can still access it. Trying to keep an eye on our favorite principal. So far, he's stayed in his office."

"Sounds like not much is going on."

"Not really. How about on your end? Did you talk to Gonzalez?"

"I did."

"Let me guess," T.J. said, "he's not playing ball yet."

"Nope. Tells me we have a few interesting facts but still no provable connections. We need more if we want to point the finger at anyone other than the man they've already arrested." *Point the finger.* "I still don't like the fingerprint timeline."

"You've done this more than I have, but it sounds like bullshit to me."

"How do we prove it, though?" I wondered. "The county crime lab ran the results. They pull from either the state or some federal upstream database. There's a super low chance some fakery or switching is going on."

"If it was Edgar's print, I'm not sure how." She fell silent. I was trying to think how we extracted our not-client from this predicament when my assistant came back with an idea. "Gerald was behaving kind of weirdly when we were at their house."

I thought back to it. Gerald's odd antics covered any occasion we met the young man, but the last time we were there, he kept trying to get his father to drink things. A glass of wine. A bottle of beer. Finally, the elder Russell accepted a glass of water. "The glass. Gerald wanted his father to drink something. He went oh-for-two before offering water."

"He might have been able to get the prints off the cup."

"A piece of packing tape would do it," I said. "Maybe he found another method. All he would need to do is hand it to someone in the BCPD or crime lab, and his dad becomes the prime suspect in his mother's murder. Police will accept it because so many people are killed by their partners."

"You need to talk to Gonzalez again," T.J. said.

"Lucky me. He's going to tell me I still don't have proof, and I'm accusing someone who works for the county of some pretty shady shit. This will be a terrific conversation."

T.J. offered a cheery, "Good luck, boss!" before ending the call.

———

I left the office, fired up the S4, and headed for the highway. When I made the left onto President Street to pick up I-83 North, I dialed Gonzalez. "Two calls in one day," he said. "What the hell did I do now?"

"If it's any consolation, I think it's what one of your cops or techs did."

"Not exactly consoling me much. Do you have some new theory with no evidence?"

"I resent the characterization," I said. "I have a new theory with some thin and speculative evidence."

"Good thing I'm sitting down," he said. "Can't wait to hear it."

I downshifted and zoomed around a box truck whose driver had no business occupying the left lane.

"Hear me out. The councilman was a proponent of education, but he generally wanted to keep things as they were. The dead teacher published a secret blog post. She was going to resign her position and run for the county school board because she didn't like the curriculum changes at Sterner and thought someone would try to institute them on a wider scale."

"The principal."

"Along with the younger Russell, yes."

"Right. They're in cahoots."

"My parents are both over sixty," I pointed out, "and I never hear them say 'cahoots.'"

"I'm an old soul," Gonzalez said. "Go on."

"The principal is a consultant for a curriculum development company his wife runs on paper."

"Pretty sexist of you to presume she doesn't do anything."

"She might do a great deal," I said. "In the end, it doesn't matter. His involvement does. He has the prototype books in his office at school, and Gerald Russell wrote a blog a while back mentioning them by name."

"The cahoots are deepening," Gonzalez said, sounding like an amused sports announcer calling a ludicrous sequence on the field.

"They're run deep enough for Gerald Russell to want his own mother dead so he could try and make millions with her boss. You had the case for a week and didn't get anywhere, which isn't a bad result for Hinson and Gerald. Once T.J. and I took an interest, he knew he needed a suspect."

"Is this where you come back to the prints?"

"It is," I said.

"I told you investigations are fluid."

"Yeah, yeah. Look, I know you'd prefer things to go in a particular order, but it's not like you're ticking things off a checklist. Not everything will happen in the desired sequence. Phones turning up in evidence days into the case, and then someone decides to dust for prints even later? It's fishy."

"I don't think so," Gonzalez said.

"It's so fucking fishy you could fry it and dip it in tartar sauce. Who had the epiphany to check for prints?"

"Why?"

"Because what if his motivations weren't as pure as the driven snow?" I said. "Gerald and Hinson stood to make millions if their new program caught on. Not hard to spread a little money to a rookie cop or young lab tech." When Gonzalez didn't say anything, I hit him with something else. "T.J. and I went to see the Russells. Gerald made three attempts to get his father to drink something. Finally, he got him to take a glass of water."

"You think he lifted the print from the glass." It wasn't a question.

"Anyone who's watched *CSI* reruns would probably know how."

I heard the clacking of keys over the connection. "There's a request to do another check for prints in the log. No reason given."

"Another?" I said. "The first didn't turn up anything?"

"I guess not."

"You want some fries and Old Bay with your cod?"

"All right," Gonzalez said. "You have my interest. It sounds like you're driving. Meet me at the crime lab. You know where it is?"

"Yes. When I help you solve the murder of a councilman and take down a dirty cop, make sure to mention me when you accept your commendation." He ended the call. I doubted he would honor my request.

———

The crime lab occupied the basement of the BCPD's main precinct. As a homicide sergeant, Gonzalez had a desk there. I parked in the usual garage, walked into the building, and headed below ground. I stepped out of the stairwell and stood in front of a pair of glass double doors. They allowed me a view inside, where computers, microscopes, and other forensic equipment covered long counters. It looked like I would expect a modern operation to look. Gonzalez saw me, moved to the wall, and pressed a button. The double doors slid back, and I walked in.

"Not a fan of you trying to implicate a cop," he said. His expression suggested he'd chugged a half-gallon of lemon juice while waiting for me to arrive.

"Hello to you, too."

"You heard me."

"I did," I said. "And I'm sure . . ." I gestured toward a middle-aged man with glasses in a white lab coat. " . . . your friend there would be salty if I said a lab technician did it."

"I probably would," the fellow added in a nasal tone.

"Meet Doctor Young," Gonzalez said.

"Medical?" I asked.

Young shook his head. "Forensic science Ph.D."

"I looked over everything after we talked," Gonzalez said.

"You mean after you rudely hung up on me."

He plastered a mock smile onto his face. "Yes. I checked all the logs. The additional request for prints came from Officer Josh Bradley."

"He on your team?" I said.

"No. He was one of the first to respond to the original nine-one-one call at the hotel."

I frowned. "So the luck of the draw means he can make case-altering requests?"

"Anyone whose name is on the record can ask the crime lab to perform certain tasks," Young said. "As an initial responder, Officer Bradley would have this ability."

"I'm not trying to tell you how to run your department," I said to Gonzalez, "but you might want to add an additional layer of supervisory approval on these things."

"Sounds like you're telling me how to run my department," he said.

"Yes, but I wasn't trying to."

"If I may," Young interjected. "Honoring the request or not is up to the personnel in the lab. We tend to act on the reasonable ones and kick any of the more interesting variety back for approval."

It made sense. The crime lab existed to help county police process evidence and solve crimes. They couldn't get in the way of their own mission. "No one thought it was unusual for an officer to request prints when someone already did the work?" I said.

Young shrugged. "It's possible for anyone to miss something."

"We're not talking about the grand parlor of a mansion, though. These were two burner phones. Pretty small surface area to dust for prints. I would think it's hard to miss any."

"It happens. When the request came in, whoever was here gathered the phones and found a new print."

"How convenient."

"C.T. here thinks the print got planted," Gonzalez said.

Young frowned, accentuating the worry lines in his forehead. "No one checked the phones out of evidence until a technician worked on what Officer Bradley asked."

"Do police have access to this room?"

"Yes. It's keycard based. Their IDs will let them in."

I glanced at Gonzalez who already moved toward the nearest computer. "I'll see if I can check from here," he said.

"I want to run a theory by you, Doctor," I said. I explained about the conduct T.J. and I witness at the Russell house. "If Gerald used tape or something to gather the print, could it then be planted on the phone?"

"It could be transferred, yes," he said. "You'd probably need someone with a basic understanding of how investigations work."

"Someone like a county police officer?"

He frowned again. "I suppose so, yes."

Gonzalez banged away at the keyboard. I looked around the room. It was a nice setup. The counters were long and wide enough to hold all the necessary equipment. Walkable aisles ran between them. Locked drawers, some of them refrigerated, held evidence. A wastebasket near my feet contained enough crumpled pieces of paper to make it almost full. An idea popped into my head. "How often are these emptied?"

"I think we have a contractor who does it twice a week," Young said. "Usually overnight."

I squatted and rooted through the can closest to me. It held only papers and a disposable coffee cup. I moved on to the next. "What the hell are you doing?" Gonzalez wanted to know.

"It's possible Bradley tossed the tape in the trash when he finished."

"He'd have to be pretty dumb."

"Not really." Having struck out, I walked to the wastebasket on the other side of the long counter. "He might have thought the trash gets taken out every night. He also probably figured no one would catch on to what he did in time." Another dud. I was now oh-for-three. At the bottom of the fourth can, I found a piece of packing tape hiding under several papers. "Here." Young rushed over. I pointed to the tape, and he grabbed it with the final millimeters of a pair of tweezers. A sheet of paper stuck to one of the side edges.

"I don't know what I can do with this," he admitted.

"Bradley accessed the crime lab," Gonzalez said. He pointed to the monitor even though Young and I couldn't read the text from where we stood. "It would give him enough time to transfer the print to a phone and make the request."

"There's no access control on the evidence lockers?" I asked.

"Not yet," Young said. "You're supposed to add an entry to the ledger whenever you open one. We're due for an upgrade."

"The honor system doesn't work for everybody." I turned to Gonzalez. "If there has to be an official request, you need to ask Doctor Young to process the tape."

"Already starting," Young said.

"Now, you need to figure out where the hell Officer Bradley might be. There's definitely a crime here, and one of yours is involved."

"Yeah, I know," Gonzalez grumbled.

CHAPTER 23

GLORIA WAS IN THE AREA, so we met at Fells Point's iteration of The Abbey for lunch. I preferred the Federal Hill location we'd gotten carryout from last week, but both made for a great meal. My wife was already seated when I arrived, looking terrific in a lavender cashmere sweater and dark blue jeans. She smiled as I slid onto the chair across from her, and I couldn't help offering one of my own. "Glad you could make it," she said.

"Me, too. I've already been to the BCPD crime lab and back."

"Doesn't sound too far."

"Driving on Eighty-three works up an appetite," I said.

A waiter of college age and with a blue stripe in his otherwise black hair approached our table. Gloria ordered an iced tea. As I usually did at The Abbey, I chose an imported beer the server recommended and left the pronunciation to him. As he left, I mulled what to get for lunch. This month's exotic meat was camel, and I had as much interest in trying it as I did a burger made of jelly.

When the young man returned with our drinks, Gloria and I each decided to build our own burgers. She opted for turkey with a salad on the side. Figuring only one of us needed to eat healthy, I got beef with pepper jack, jalapeños, and a basket of fries.

Gloria would need to take one. Her commitment to eating well was strong but not absolute.

"You're quiet," my wife said a couple minutes later after I'd sat in silence.

"Thinking about the case."

"Tell me about it."

I caught her up on the current theory regarding the fingerprint evidence, Gonzalez's renewed interest in listening to me, and the likelihood of a BCPD officer being on the take, even in a very limited way. "The crime lab is going to test the tape," I said in conclusion. "If they can find Edgar Russell's print on there, it proves my theory."

"And they'll release that poor man from jail," Gloria said.

"Yes." I wondered how his son would take the news. Edgar had no idea how—and by whom—he'd been framed for his wife's murder. He couldn't simply go home again. Even if Gerald didn't take direct action against him, the son could tell Hinson, and the goon squad would be on the case.

This made me recall the connection to lacrosse coach Ronald Lobdell as our burgers came out. Gloria added a little pepper to her salad and then took a tiny bite of her turkey burger. She'd probably have at least a third of it to take home. Like a proper Marylander, I sprinkled Old Bay on my fries and started on my burger with a man-sized chomp. "It seems like you want to get back to the office," Gloria said as she eyed my plate a couple minutes later. It was mostly empty.

"Yeah. Sorry I'm not the best lunch date today. I need to do a couple things."

"I get it." She smiled. "I'm married to the PI star of Baltimore, after all."

"We're a couple who both burn bright," I said. I finished my lunch a minute later, kissed Gloria goodbye, and left her my card to pay for the meal. She waved it off and wished me good luck.

Fuller in both appetite and spirit, I made the short drive back to the office. I texted T.J. and asked if she could send me some info on the coach including which bank received his direct deposit. She told me she couldn't get into things like HR and payroll, so I suggested we overcome this limitation.

> I'm going to send you an email. Copy the body of it, make it an executable, and run it. It'll let you pass the hash.

> Pass the what?

> A Windows login vulnerability Microsoft can never quite seem to fix, though most corporate networks don't help the cause. Let me know what you get.

A few minutes later, she replied with the info I needed and a promise to never doubt me again. I knew she wasn't good for the second part but thanked her for the data. Lobdell did his banking at Baltimore County Savings and Loan, which sounded like a place his grandparents used and he followed suit because he got lollipops there as a kid. On their site, I used the prompts for password recovery. Lobdell used a Gmail account to login.

It took several minutes, a few VPN resets, and some choice curse words, but I finally convinced Gmail to let me change the password on the account. From there, the banking account crumbled with surprising ease. Lobdell maintained a decent balance. Scrolling down, I found what I'd come for soon enough. Wire transfers of $3000 and $5000 corresponded to when a pair and a trio of goons visited my office.

Lobdell and his benefactor were not getting their money's worth.

I figured the coach would love to hear my thoughts on his financial acumen in person.

———

After heading down The Sterner Academy's long driveway, I nabbed the last visitor's spot. Dismissal would be happening soon, so if I caught the coach out on the fields somewhere, he would either have a final period gym class or the lacrosse team getting in a fall practice session. As before, I skirted the main building as much as possible. Sure enough, I found Lobdell with a group of boys in lacrosse gear. I stopped and watched him run the team through a few basic warmups and drills, remembering when I did them in high school and college.

Once players broke up into groups to work on keeping their skills sharp, I approached. Lobdell spotted me, and even from fifty yards away, his grimace was very clear. And satisfying to see. He moved toward me, and we came together near the edge of the grass. "Nice afternoon for practice, Coach."

"What are you doing here?" he demanded, trying to intimidate me with the combination of his size and a scowl.

"I know a couple board members," I said. "Wouldn't want them to be associated with a lousy lacrosse team and loser coach."

"We've made the playoffs every year I've been here!"

"Pfft." I stepped around him and moved closer to the action. He followed. "Half the teams in the conference get in. You want me to congratulate you on a coin flip?"

"I suppose you did better when you played?"

"We won it all when I was a junior," I said, projecting my voice a little so the players nearby could hear. "Lost by a goal going for the repeat in my senior year." A few lads stopped practicing and drifted nearer.

"You're here to compare your pedigree with mine?" Lobdell joined me in vocalizing for the audience. He added a needless and fake laugh. "I'm a successful lacrosse coach at one of the best schools in the country." By now, most of the team stood within earshot. The coach took the bait. "You're a private investigator." Lobdell addressed his team. "Boys, let this be a lesson for you. When you don't do the fundamentals well, you end up adrift. Mister Ferguson here works a pretty meaningless job. He wouldn't be Sterner material."

"Actually, 'Mister Ferguson here' was four and oh against Sterner in high school. JV and varsity. Then, 'Mister Ferguson here' got a lacrosse scholarship to Loyola."

"In Maryland?" one of the students asked.

"Yes."

"Were you . . . ?"

"I was there in twenty-twelve," I said. "My final year. We won the national championship." Wide eyes and smiles greeted me from behind helmets now. I turned to Lobdell. "Now, I'm sure someone who's a 'successful lacrosse coach at one of the best schools in the country' has done at least as well on the playing field, right?"

"Uh . . . well . . . I—"

"Did you even start in college?" I broke in.

Lobdell opened his mouth and snapped it shut before offering a quiet, "No."

"Damn. I guess forty grand for tuition doesn't buy top-level coaching these days."

"Listen here, you—"

"Anybody have questions they want to ask a former NCAA champion?"

"We're playing Curley as our first game of the spring," one of the boys said. "Any advice?"

He presumed I must be familiar with their style of play. Maybe I was. "They still have the same coach . . . long gray hair? I forget his name."

"Winke," Lobdell said.

"He was their coach when I played," I said. "They favor

defense. I don't think he knows how to put a modern offense together. Anyway, we beat them with a lot of motion and quick passes. No one should hold the ball for long." I turned to Lobdell. "You see it the same way?"

"Well, I . . . uh . . . I haven't installed a game plan yet. We're still a few months out." Lobdell frowned at his students paying attention to me and moved in to my space. "This is private property. You're trespassing."

"So were the five guys you sent after me, Coach." To his credit, Lobdell's expression didn't change. I raised the stakes. "At least two of them needed a hospital visit afterward. Probably three. Hope you weren't planning on exchanging Christmas gifts this year."

He put on another forced laugh. "I don't know what you're talking about."

"I guess eight thousand for hired muscle doesn't go as far it used to, either." His eyes got as big as plates. "Inflation and all. Still, based on the results, I would have asked for a refund."

"How did you get into my bank account? I'm going to report this to the police!"

"Oh, please do. I'm sure they'd love to hear how you came by the money, who sent it to you, and for what purposes. I snapped some pictures of your friends, by the way. It'd be easy to tie them back to you." I slipped my phone out of my pocket. "Want me to dial nine-one-one for you, Coach?"

"Fuck you," he muttered, and a few of his players laughed.

"There are two lessons here, boys," I said, making sure the team could hear me. "First, if you want something done right, you shouldn't pay cut-rate prices for it when you're too much of a coward to try it yourself. Second, working at an expensive private school doesn't make you smart. If anything, it's probably a daily reminder you're trying and failing to punch above your weight class." I turned to the dejected Lobdell who couldn't meet my gaze. "Boxing metaphor in case you didn't know."

He had nothing to say. My work here was done, so I hoofed it back to my car and left the campus.

———

After I'd returned to the comfort of my own office, Gonzalez called. "Good news. Edgar Russell is getting released."

"You finally decided to listen to me?"

"Young got something off the packing tape," Gonzalez said. "He was concerned it would probably only be a partial. Tape was folded onto itself and all. Anyway, he sent it to the state and asked them to rush it. They've added some fancy new AI processing to their system. Came back with a partial match to Edgar."

"And it was enough to get him out?" I asked.

"Prosecutor agreed, and a judge signed off. He should be getting processed as we speak."

"It's always nice when we can get reasonable doubt before the trial even starts."

"You and I might differ there," Gonzalez said. "You find anything else yet?"

"Look who's suddenly interested in what I might have."

"Hey, it wasn't the husband this time. I need a new suspect. You got something solid?"

"Would you settle for amorphous?" I said.

"At this point, maybe."

"All right. I'm looking into the principal of The Sterner Academy, Anthony Hinson. There's a coach at the school who's involved, too, but I think it's minimal on his end. He knows some of the wrong people."

"What's his name?"

"Ronald Lobdell. Five guys came to get me off the case. Two the first time and then three. I got some photos of the second crew, and there's a connection to him. Plus, a little birdie told me he got some unexplained wire transfers right before both incidents."

"Sounds like I'll need to do my own digging, then," Gonzalez said. "We want things to stand up in court."

His mention of court made me think of Officer Joshua Bradley. I wondered how he fit into all this. Someone could have slipped him an envelope of cash, I supposed, but it made more sense if he already knew someone. "Hang on, I want to check something."

"You're on the people's time now."

"They can afford to wait a minute." I'd recently used AI to refine my social media scraping scripts. The same results came with four fewer lines of code. I plugged in Bradley and waited for the results. It wouldn't take long. "Here we go. Your young officer was a college classmate of Gerald Russell."

"The son?"

"Yes. Have you found Bradley yet?"

"Seems he has the day off," Gonzalez said.

"So the man takes money from his criminal friend, shits all over your investigation, and now you don't know where he is?"

"We'll find him."

"I can go over my rates if you want some help." Gonzalez grunted and ended the call. He could find Bradley. We didn't always get along, but Gonzalez was a good cop well versed in doing things like finding people who wanted to remain under the radar. I only wondered where young officer Bradley would be and if Gerald Russell holed up somewhere with him.

CHAPTER 24

ON HER ROUNDS of the admin building, T.J. spotted a certain black Audi S4 in one of the visitor's spots.

When she retraced her steps a half-hour later, her boss' car was gone. She returned to her undercover office. Rachel walked the opposite direction up the hallway, her cell phone pressed to her ear. T.J. ducked inside and called C.T. "I saw your car here."

"I paid Coach Lobdell a visit," he said.

"You were keen to pass on some lacrosse tips?"

C.T. snorted. "He should be so lucky. You'd think a school which rakes in all this money could hire one of the top coaches in the area."

"What did you find on him?" T.J. wanted to know.

"He's involved somehow," C.T. said. "At this point, I think he's just a broker for the goons who visited the office twice. Probably not cut out for much more. Hinson doesn't seem like the type to have a broad circle of trust."

T.J. kept her voice low as footsteps moved up and down the corridor outside the office door. "Hinson paid him?"

"Someone did. Two wire transfers, so we can't trace them. Could have been anyone from pretty much anywhere. My guess is Gerald did it. Hinson probably doesn't want to be seen slumming with the commoners in a convenience store. Eight thousand dollars total . . . three the first time and five the second.”

“The local goons’ union must have a no refunds policy,” T.J. said with a chuckle. “I don’t remember them doing so well.”

“They didn’t. He clearly has a network of morally gray friends to call on, though. It makes him useful to someone like Hinson and dangerous to me and you . . . you especially because you’re there at the school.” T.J. didn’t say anything. “I can hear the gears turning in your head,” her boss continued. “You want to keep an eye on Lobdell.”

“I do,” she confirmed. “I basically have the run of the place. Might as well use it while I’m here.”

“He’s outside with the team now.” The sound of car chimes came through the connection, followed by a door opening and closing. C.T. must have gone back to their office. “It’s the offseason, so they’re probably not drilling and practicing every day. Tomorrow’s Wednesday. Edgar Russell is getting released. It would be nice if he could bury his wife before the end of the week.”

“I agree. He’s already had to delay it.”

“Be careful. If Lobdell catches you, you’re going to be on the spot. His hackles are probably up after talking to me today. I don’t think he’ll extend you the benefit of the doubt.”

“I’ll try and do my best sneaking,” T.J. said. “If something goes south, I’ll call you.”

“Make sure you, do.”

“Aye-aye, Captain.” T.J. ended the call. As she set her phone back down, Rachel walked in.

“Why do I get the feeling you’re not going to be working for me much longer?”

T.J. smiled. “I appreciate you giving me the chance to do this, but we’re going to try and wrap things up soon. A couple things went our way today.”

Rachel nodded as she dropped into her chair. "All right. I don't know what's happening, obviously, but this whole mess sounds dangerous. Two people are dead. I don't want to see you become the third."

"Neither do I," T.J. said.

———

The next morning, T.J. woke up in time to run two miles on the streets near her apartment before beating on the heavy bag. Today was Wednesday, and she wanted to put a bow on things today and avoid return trips to The Sterner Academy all week. She thought of Rachel Heaton who allowed her to work in the building and keep making a case. It felt a little silly, but T.J. thought she'd be letting Rachel down by concluding things today. The woman needed a proper secretary.

Hopefully, the next principal would let her hire one.

After a shower and quick breakfast, T.J. got to Sterner right on time. Rachel was already there, of course, and a stack of papers awaited T.J. on her desk. "Those are complaints against teachers placed by PTA members," Rachel said. "As president, I have to at least consider what's been said. Some of them are completely spurious, of course. I'd like you to take a pass through the pile and filter out the good ones."

"What about the bad ones?"

Rachel shrugged. "We're a big proponent of recycling."

T.J. snickered and got to work. The first printout she picked up was a doozy. A parent—whose name should have been Karen —complained because her son got a B in eighth-grade algebra. The reason she provided: *My son doesn't get B's. This must be a mistake.* "I take it unfounded complaining about grades allows the school to improve its environmental standing?"

"Wow." Rachel grinned. "First one, too. Those are my

favorite. Some parents think their little angels should never get anything less than an A."

"How do you deal with people like that?" T.J. wondered.

"By being a politician. I tell them I hear what they're saying and encourage them to schedule a short one-on-one with the teacher."

"And if they still gripe?"

"The school gets involved. So long as the teacher is doing even the basics of documentation, the complaint never goes anywhere. Some seethe and threaten to pull their precious child, and then they make the tuition payment a month later. Welcome to expensive private education."

T.J. went through the rest of the papers. In the end, she'd put about a quarter into the legitimate pile and consigned the rest to be recycled. "You want to check what I've done?" she asked Rachel.

The other woman shook her head. "I trust your judgment."

Again, T.J. felt a twinge of disappointment. It had only been a few days, but Rachel was a good boss. She deserved a capable secretary. It would need to be someone else, however. "Are gym classes outside this time of year?"

"Weather permitting, yes," Rachel said. "Why?"

"I . . . need to look into someone."

"Sounds like Coach Lobdell." T.J. remained quiet. "You'll find him outside, I'm sure, but he won't be up to much. Better to catch him in his office at the end of the day."

"Where's that?"

"All coaches have their spaces in the gym. The fifth building, if you will. Most of it is a basketball arena, but one side is a bunch of offices. He'll be in there after his last class."

"Thanks."

"Be careful," Rachel warned.

"I've already been told," T.J. said.

"Then, let me tell you again. Hopefully, it'll sink in."

T.J. nodded. She spent the day watching the cameras for Hinson—the man either stayed in his office or popped into classrooms—and doing the work Rachel set out for her. The latter was enough to make her promise she'd never become *that* kind of parent if she ever had children. The gall of some people was simply astounding. When the dismissal bell rang, T.J. waited about fifteen minutes for the hallways to empty. Then, she got up and made her way outside. It was still a nice fall day, and a paved path led to the gym, basketball arena, and athletic offices.

———

T.J. enjoyed the walk. As much as she disliked Hinson and The Sterner Academy, she had to admit the campus was beautiful. Not to the tune of forty grand a year, but it was still a nice place to be on a pleasant fall day. She thought about how she might approach the situation. It would depend on how crowded the building was. The basketball team could be practicing. The football team might be using the weight room. She couldn't presume the place would be empty except for a few coaches finishing out their days. The building—named for whomever donated the most money for the cause—was an imposing brick structure.

She pushed the door open and walked inside. Even the lobby was impressive. Marble floors and a very high ceiling were the most notable features. Tall windows let in natural light. Gold-plated signs on the walls indicated the gym and basketball court, locker rooms, weight facility, and athletic offices—the latter on the far side. T.J. looked through the window in the door, saw no one milling around, and pushed it open.

The hallway was spotless white tile. Doors lined both sides. T.J. crept along, glad she'd worn a pair of tennis shoes and not something like heels which would have announced her presence.

About two-thirds of the way down, she heard a voice. It came from behind a door marked *Ronald Lobdell, Varsity Lacrosse*. It was open about a quarter of the way. T.J. ducked past, took out her phone, and started recording. Lodbell apparently wasn't worried about his voice carrying. It meant no one remained nearby to overhear him.

"Look, we made two runs at him already. I don't know what we do for the third. I'm not comfortable using guns. Too much shit can go wrong. I don't care what he said. If he wants a more permanent solution, he can find someone else to provide it. I'm not getting my friends in more trouble."

He paused each time. She was only hearing one side of the conversation, but Lobdell did a nice job incriminating himself. The recording wouldn't be admissible in court, but it might induce him to confess to his role in everything that went down. T.J. wondered why the coach fell silent when the door swung in, and he filled the hallway. "Who the hell are you?" he demanded, glaring down at her.

"Uh . . . hi, Coach. I just started working here a couple days ago, and I'm checking out the place. Really nice facility."

Lobdell's expression didn't change. His eyes scanned up and down T.J.'s body. She got used to it in her days working the streets of Baltimore. Since, she'd grown to revile this reaction from men, but she remained quiet and tried to look like a non-threatening new employee. The coach's gaze scrutinized her face before dropping again to her waist. "Let me see your phone."

"What?"

"Your phone," he repeated. "If you're the new girl just checking out the place, there's no need to take it out of your pocket."

"I just want a couple of pictures," T.J. said.

"Great. Let me see them."

She stuffed the phone into the rear pocket of her jeans. "I don't think so."

"Did you think I was giving you a choice? Who are you . . . really? And what were you doing outside my office?"

"I'm a new employee," T.J. said. "This is my fourth day, and I've never been in this building before."

Lobdell crossed his arms, and T.J. noted their thickness. He looked more suited to coaching football than lacrosse. "Even if what you're saying is true, it doesn't explain why you were camped outside my door."

The hell with this guy. T.J. wasn't going to be intimidated by him. "Concerned I overheard something I shouldn't have? Maybe you shouldn't talk about killing people at work."

"Give me your goddamn phone." Lobdell reached out, but T.J. stepped back. "I'm not playing, you little bitch." He stuck his hand out again, so she kicked it. He pulled it back, rubbed it, and glowered at her. "You're dead." He started toward her, and T.J. took off at a run. She reached the door at the far end of the corridor, lowered herself, and shouldered the bar open without losing much in terms of pace. She could run faster than Lobdell, but he looked to be in good shape for his size, so she couldn't presume he'd tire quickly and break off pursuit.

Behind her, she heard his voice. "Yeah, I need some help. Got a runner on campus. Meet me outside the east gate. She knows too much."

T.J. didn't have many options for where to go. She could head toward one of the main buildings, but she would need to badge in after hours, and Lobdell might catch her in those seconds. Her car was clear across campus. The surrounding neighborhood wasn't far. T.J. could try to lose her pursuer in an alley or a yard somewhere. She thought about calling the cops, but years of negative interactions with the police didn't help her perception of them. She was the one running, after all, and they might side with Lobdell.

Instead, she called C.T. "Where are you?" she asked when he picked up.

"I left the office early and came to Gloria's. Why? Is everything all right?"

"Not really. Lobdell caught me outside his office. I got a recording, but now he's chasing me, and I think he might have called in some reinforcements."

"Where are you now?"

"Running across the campus. He mentioned the east gate, and I think I'm looking at it. It leads into the neighborhood."

"I'm on my way. Try to stay ahead of him."

"Hurry, boss," T.J. implored.

"Count on it," C.T. said.

CHAPTER 25

NEW MODERN CURRICULUM was definitely one out of three.

I'd never explored education enough to know if their ideas were new or modern, and none of it mattered now. Melanie DeBerg had a bachelor's in the field before moving on to an MBA a few years later. Since then, her professional life had been spent in business development, corporate leadership, and "executive coaching," which sounded like a lucrative way to part rich suckers from their money.

Basically, she was the ideal partner for Anthony Hinson.

Gerald Everett, in addition to his graduate degree in education, also earned a bachelor's in technical writing. The combination made him an ideal candidate to draft a series of stuffy curriculum books. Because the tomes had yet to be officially published, I couldn't look up author information. NMC's website was cagey about this fact and many others. I went back to his blog under the not-really-clever *nom de plume* of Scholarum. Sure enough, he'd written a post about how technical writers and private school principals would save the American education system from itself.

As our society progresses, so too must our methods of

educating the next generation. We can no longer rely on antiquated public school systems and teachers to properly prepare students for the modern world. Private curriculum development by experienced professionals is the superior approach. It probably has been for a while. Now, it's time to act.

Public school teachers are often overworked, underpaid, and have little say in actual curriculum design. They are simply told to follow standards handed down by bureaucrats. How can we expect dynamic, thoughtful instruction from such a system? On the other hand, the right company could bring together technical writers and seasoned private school principals to carefully craft a new modern curriculum which would allow our young people to reach their potential.

Technical writers provide essential skills for curriculum development. They understand how to organize and present information. They know how to write objectives, structure content for optimal learning, and design assessments. Any tech writer who's also earned a degree in education would be doubly good.

Experienced private school principals also offer invaluable expertise. They understand the administration and real-world implementation of curriculum, and they have to do it while staring down angry rich parents. They know how to motivate students and train teachers effectively. Together, these professionals can create curriculum that engages students and delivers the knowledge and skills needed for success.

Public schools change standards and textbooks constantly in an effort to improve, but it is reactive and disjointed. Ultimately, no matter the program they pick, laws and funding basically compel them to teach to a test. This tactic has been failing our students for a long time. When was the last time you saw a doctor who didn't come from China or India?

Private curriculum developers take a proactive, cohesive

approach. They control the full process from writing to implementation, allowing for consistent quality and refinement over time. We cannot cling to nostalgia and think public schools have all the answers. Our children deserve the best education possible, and that means embracing private curriculum development. The future starts today. Let's help them reach for the stars.

An awful lot rode on the authorities never unearthing his old blog.

Gerald made two references to "reach" and even worked in a shameless plug for someone who happened to earn degrees in tech writing and education. Considering how long his parents worked at The Sterner Academy, Gerald would have known Anthony Hinson when he wrote the post. The pair may not have hatched their plan yet, but considering the Easter eggs in his entry, I would bet they'd already had a few conversations about what they wanted to do.

Gloria joined a conference in the next room, so I got up and nudged the door shut. With nothing happening at the office, I drove to my wife's house early in the afternoon. She told me she would be busy until about five, so I settled in at the spare desk I used and kept working. I'd just brewed some coffee and started on a fresh cup when T.J. called. I barely got a greeting out when she said, "Where are you?"

This couldn't be good. "I left the office early and came to Gloria's. Why? Is everything all right?"

"Not really. Lobdell caught me outside his office." Her breathing came through louder than normal. Was she running? "I got a recording, but now he's chasing me, and I think he might have called in some reinforcements."

Definitely not good. I got up and headed downstairs. "Where are you now?"

"Running across the campus. He mentioned the east gate, and I think I'm looking at it. It leads into the neighborhood."

"I'm on my way," I said, mentally calculating how long it would take me to get there. The time of day would help. I'd be tearing up the streets ahead of rush hour. Still, even driving quickly and getting lucky with lights left me about fifteen minutes away. "Try to stay ahead of him."

"Hurry, boss," my assistant said.

"Count on it," I told her.

———

The car's GPS plotted the fastest route from Brooklandville to The Sterner Academy. It said the trip would take eighteen minutes. If Lobdell found reinforcements, T.J. wouldn't have eighteen minutes. I aimed to shave at least six off the time. While I sped onto Falls Road, I dialed Gonzalez and reached him on his cell. "My assistant is in a bind," I said when he answered.

"How does this land on my desk?"

I explained the situation in brief. "She's being chased by the lacrosse coach and maybe some of his friends. T.J.'s in shape, and I'm sure she can run, but they probably can, too. The numbers alone might get to her."

"Where did she say she was?"

"She left The Sterner Academy via the east gate. Said she was heading into the neighborhood streets."

"Nice area," Gonzalez said. "People there would notice a bunch of men chasing a girl."

"If they're home, and if they can be bothered to call the cops about it. I'm heading there now at speeds not recommended on the road signs. It would be nice if you could send a car or two."

"I'll get someone on it," he told me and broke the connection. A few seconds later, T.J. called.

"They have bats."

"Shit. How are you holding up?"

"I'm staying ahead so far," she said. "I thought I might lose them in the streets or in someone's yard, but there are too many big houses here. Not enough stuff to disappear behind. Too many tall fences and gates."

"Drop a pin," I said. "I'll keep track of your location."

"I can tell you're driving."

"Speeding my ass off."

"Gotta go." She ended the call. Less than a minute later, T.J. shared her location with me. She'd made it over a half-mile east of the campus. A quick look at a red light told me she'd been right about the neighborhood. Houses were large, spread out, and owned by people who valued their property values and privacy. In a less affluent area, she might have been able to hide behind a shed or even duck into an open basement. Not near Sterner.

I zoomed around a few cars moving at a pace I would have normally found acceptable. Honks greeted me as I became the asshole driver people posted TikTok videos about. In warmer weather with the windows down, I could have heard the curses flying in my direction. My GPS now said the school was ten minutes away. I'd done eight minutes' worth of driving in five and needed to continue the pace.

My phone's map showed T.J. still moving east, but she'd also ventured a block to the south. She called again a moment later. "I'm starting to slow down." Her breathing was fast. "Hurry."

"I am. I promise." A light ahead of me turned yellow. I fought the urge to brake and instead downshifted, blipped the throttle, and blasted through the intersection north of seventy. If I stayed straight, I'd be parallel with her position in another mile or so. Despite having to decelerate for some traffic, I made all the lights along the way.

The Sterner Academy lay due west about half-mile away. I gunned it through another yellow and kept an eye on my phone.

Three more blocks. At the third street, I swung a hard left with screeching tires. I tapped the phone to call T.J. back and tell her I was a minute out.

She didn't pick up.

CHAPTER 26

DESPITE THE SIZE of the properties, I drove on a network of side streets—or I might have used the term in the city or other parts of the county.

T.J.'s pin kept moving, so even though she couldn't answer her phone, she was all right. I swung a right and headed down a pretty steep hill. My assistant came into view, running from my left to right on the cross street at the bottom. Lobdell approached and tried to grab her, but she put her kickboxing training to good use and gave him a hard punt in the balls. He went down to all fours.

Another man waded in swinging a baseball bat.

Across the road at the bottom was the long driveway to another ritzy house. I accelerated. T.J.'s eyes found the S4. I could almost see her doing the math related to my speed and trajectory in her head. She made it across the driveway while the tall blond guy still menaced her with a Louisville Slugger. He whiffed again and stood in the center of the asphalt. I guided the car directly at him and pressed the gas.

He turned at the last moment, and his eyes went wide before my sedan plowed into him.

The impact put most of his body on the hood, and his head

damaged my windshield when he flopped forward. I hit the brakes once I was in the driveway, and he fell off the hood and landed with a thud. He was out of the fight—and maybe dead—so I needed to focus on the four other men. I got out, drew my .45 in one clean motion, and pointed it at the closest miscreant, a short and stocky fellow who also carried a bat. "Give me a reason," I said. The idiot looked between his weapon and mine, came to the only sensible conclusion, and let the bat clatter to the street.

"There's a saying about knives and gunfights," I told him. "Same thing applies to bats." I backed up a step so I could also keep an eye on T.J. "You all right?" I asked her.

She put her hands on her knees and took a few deep breaths. Her blonde ponytail flopped beside her face. "Yeah. Thanks for coming. I'm not sure how much longer I could have avoided them."

"If you want to get in on the action, there's a shotgun in the trunk." I felt in my pocket for the key fob and hit the button to open the rear compartment.

"Hell yes," she said. I focused on the pale-haired guy who surrendered the bat and Lobdell, who'd managed to make it up to wobbly knees. The others turned tail and ran. My trunk slammed, and T.J. appeared at my side a second later. She leveled the twelve-gauge at one of the men who'd been taking home run cuts at her a minute before.

"If I were you," I advised the fellow, "I'd stay put." I approached Lobdell. His face was red and screwed up in pain. T.J. must have given him quite the kick to the family jewels. "Do you advise your players to wear cups, Coach?" He grunted but didn't offer a coherent answer. I fished out my phone and called Gonzalez as sirens approached. "I got her. Two guys here will be thankful for a ride to the nearest police station."

"Cops should be a couple minutes out," he said. "I'm on my way, too, but it'll take me a little longer."

"Nice of you to put in an appearance."

"It's my case after all."

"True," I said. "We're gonna need an ambulance, too."

"What happened?"

"In a moment of heroism, someone hit one of the men with his car."

"Does this mystery driver have a name?"

"I didn't catch it," I said, "but in addition to being heroic, he was very handsome."

"Uh-huh. You know you can call nine-one-one, right?"

"And miss your cheery voice?" Gonzalez's answer came in the form of hanging up on me. Sirens grew closer. Lobdell looked at the barrel of my pistol and frowned.

"It wasn't supposed to go down like this," he said.

I shrugged. "It never is."

———

Three BCPD cruisers arrived a minute later. I wondered how many ever visited these streets before. It only took one to settle a dispute about the height of someone's sculpted hedges. Six officers got out. The first one to approach was a large black man who reminded me of Baltimore Captain Leon Sharpe. "You C.T. Ferguson?" he barked. I read the name bar above the badge on the left side of his chest—Harp.

"The one and only."

"Gonzalez said you'd be here."

"A couple guys ran when it became obvious things weren't going their way," I said. "Both white. Fairly tall. Jeans and dark hoodies."

Officer Harp turned and pointed at the three men and one woman who climbed out of the two other cars. "Go look for them. You heard the descriptions?" They all bobbed their heads, got back into their County-issued sedans, and sped away with the light bars flashing. Harp turned back to us. "Probably the most action this neighborhood has seen in a while." He stared down at Lobdell. "Why do I think this is your fault?"

The coach wisely remained silent. "He's involved," I said, "but he's not the ringmaster. If we extend the metaphor, he's the guy who trains the lions."

Another approaching siren heralded the arrival of the ambulance, which rolled onto the scene in short order. Two paramedics rushed out to tend to the man still lying in the driveway. I moved closer. "He's alive," one of them said. Between the car and the EMTs, I couldn't get a good look at the fallen fellow, but the angle of his right leg suggested he wouldn't be walking anywhere for a couple months. The older of the pair fetched the gurney while his partner tended to their patient. T.J. lowered the shotgun as Harp and his partner cuffed Lobdell and his friend.

Neither this guy nor the one receiving medical attention were among the five who came to my office. Lobdell must have had a lot of assholes in his contact list. "How much did you offer these guys?" I asked the coach. He again remained silent. "I figured your first two rounds of spending would have gotten the point across."

"They're my friends," he muttered.

"Doesn't really speak well for any of you."

Gonzalez arrived a few minutes later. "I hear we found one of the runners," he said as he walked to our position.

"Four out of five ain't bad," I said. "Isn't that how the song goes?"

"Not exactly." Gonzalez pointed at Lobdell. "He doesn't look like a principal."

"Good thing. It's not in his limited skill set. Neither is being a lacrosse coach, but we all need a job."

"Fuck you," Lobdell said.

I spread my hands. "QED."

Gonzalez leaned down and got in the larger Lobdell's face. "Where's your boss?"

"Go to hell."

"You don't need to go down for what he masterminded."

"I ain't saying shit without a lawyer."

Gonzalez shrugged. "Have it your way." He gestured to the other cops, and Harp led Lobdell to one of the BCPD cruisers.

"Any word on your missing friend?" I asked when the others were out of earshot.

"No," Gonzalez said. "Haven't located him."

"How about Gerald Russell?"

"He's in the wind, too."

"You consider the possibility they might be in the wind together?"

"Believe it or not, I can come up with ideas, too."

With the injured man now in the ambulance, I walked to my car. There was minor damage to the front end, including a couple dents on the hood. The windshield, however, was cracked in several places all extending out from where the goon's skull hit it. A little blood remained around the center. I could drive it for now, but I'd need to replace the glass soon. "Sorry about your car," T.J. said.

"It's fine. Cars and parts can be replaced. You can't."

"You're just saying that because I'm still holding a shotgun."

"It helps." I popped the trunk again, and she put it back. "Why don't you go home? You've had a hell of an afternoon."

"You going to keep working this?"

"Yeah," I said. "I think we're pretty close."

"Then, I want to be a part of it."

"Your hands are still shaking." She held one up and frowned when it trembled. "It's natural. You're coming off the adrenaline high. I think you should take it easy for a while. If we're still on the hunt tonight, and you want to rejoin us then, fine."

She nodded. "All right. I guess I could use some time to decompress." She leaned into me, and I put my arm around her shoulders. "Drop me off at my car, boss?"

"You bet."

———

With the miscreants in custody, I followed Gonzalez from the school to his precinct. "Make some coffee," he barked before walking into his office. I found the machine, added the magic beans and water, and got rewarded with the wonderful aroma of brewing java. When it finished, I grabbed a styrofoam cup and filled it. Gonzalez still sat behind his desk. He eyed my white cup warily. "Where's mine?"

"You told me to brew it," I said. "You didn't tell me to bring you one. I'm sure you have your own mug anyway."

He grunted, picked a chipped black mug off his desk, and left. A minute later, the aroma of the coffee announced his return. After sitting again, Gonzalez handed me a piece of paper. *WORK ORDER* was printed in large font at the top. "For your windshield. If someone pulls you over, you show 'em the paper."

"Thanks." I slipped it into my pocket.

"It's not enough yet," Gonzalez said, "but let's go over what we know."

"Does this involve cahoots?"

"You're coming around on it."

"I feel like I need to cash a Social Security check when I leave," I said, "but yeah. It's a pretty good word."

Gonzalez flashed a grin. "All right. So the lacrosse coach takes his orders from the principal . . . who's in cahoots with the dead teacher's son."

I nodded. "Yes. They targeted his mother and the councilman because of their views on education and the need for a new curriculum."

"And we don't know the wife's involvement," the sergeant said. "She might be a paper CEO for their company, or she could be the one directing the murders."

"It's possible."

"We're going to run down some leads. With the lacrosse teacher and his buddies in custody, maybe we can get one of them to crack and give up a location. What are you going to do?"

"Figure out how it all connects. They have to be somewhere. Maybe they fled the state, but assuming they did does us no good. Might as well figure we can pin them down and catch them."

"Don't forget Bradley," Gonzalez added with a sigh. "I don't like a cop being involved, but we can't ignore what he did. Even if he just took a bribe, he might know something."

"He went to school with Gerald. His involvement could be deeper."

"What do you mean?"

"In terms of direct actions," I said, "maybe planting a print on evidence and suggesting the crime lab run it all again is it. Even though he's new, he knows how the county runs investigations." Gonzalez frowned. "Maybe even how you do. Insider info could be very useful to Gerald and Hinson right now."

"Why is it the more I talk to you, the less I like what you have to say?"

I spread my hands. "Just one more service I offer. Clients pay pretty well for the full package."

"Why don't you go off and do whatever sorcery you do in your office?" Gonzalez said. "We'll talk to the men in custody and see what we can come up with." Lobdell had already lawyered up, and if the rest possessed a lick of sense, they'd follow suit. I doubted this would be a productive avenue. He checked his watch. "Almost four. Let's touch base at seven. Obviously, call earlier if you find something important."

"I will if you will."

Gonzalez grunted. I knew he might cut me out if the BCPD unearthed a key detail without me, but this was the best I would get.

CHAPTER 27

THANKS TO TRAFFIC, it took almost double the normal time to get back to the office. A few minutes after I'd settled into my chair with a fresh mug of coffee, my father called. "You at work?"

"Yes," I said. "What's going on?"

"I'm in the area. I'll stop by shortly."

He didn't tell me anything else. I unlocked my computer, but his call had me worried something was wrong with him or my mother. I'd drained about half my cup when footsteps came up the steps. My father walked in, dressed in pressed chinos with a white button-down peeking out above the top of his gray tweed coat. He sniffed the air and jerked his head toward the carafe. "Help yourself."

Pouring himself a cup and easing onto one of my guest chairs, he took a sip and blew out a deep breath. "I've thought about what you said about Hinson and the Sterner board."

"And?"

"We're going to resign."

"Good," I said. "You might want to put a rush on the fax. Hinson is going down as soon as we find him."

"You've made progress, then."

"Yes. He's in league with the son of the murdered teacher." I avoided the word "cahoots" even though a man of my father's age might appreciate it. "When we saw him making his big pitch at the country club, he was trying to get investors for a new curriculum project."

"All this for school books and teaching plans?" A sad shake of his head accompanied the question.

"There's probably more to it," I said. "Even getting a couple counties to sign up makes them a few million. Hinson probably figured he'd parlay his time at Sterner into getting the new curriculum installed in Baltimore County."

"And the councilman stood in his way." My father nodded, satisfied with his own conclusion.

"The teacher, too. She was going to leave her job after this year and run for the school board. Guess what her position on bringing in a whole new educational plan was going to be?"

"Hinson found out somehow."

"As long as he's been there, and as ambitious as he is, I'm sure he has spies who tell him interesting things."

"Jesus, what a mess." My dad ran a hand through his hair, which remained full even into his early sixties. "Your mother and I thought we were doing a good thing when we started working with The Sterner Academy years ago."

"You were," I said. "It's not your fault Hinson is an asshole. I just don't want your foundation to be associated with him when he's in handcuffs. You won't have any control of the story."

"We'll resign as soon as I leave." He sighed. "I'm sorry I didn't listen to you."

"Don't worry about it, Dad. There were a thousand times I didn't listen to you and Mom. I think you're allowed to return the favor."

My father chuckled. "I guess you're right."

"As usual," I pointed out.

He finished his coffee, we said our adieus, and my dad left.

Talking about control of the story made me wonder how Gloria's puff piece was coming along. I hoped it was as airy as expected. Alone in the office again, I got back to work. Gonzalez would need my help. The BCPD didn't exactly distinguish itself with the investigation.

I hadn't made much progress when my phone vibrated in my pocket. Gloria texted.

> Just read a draft of Claire's piece. It's terrific! I think this is really going to be good for the business.

> Congratulations! I knew you were a star.

> You're shining, too. This going to be a late night?

> Probably. Rain check on a proper celebration?

> You got it. Love you.

> Love you, too.

Because enough people hadn't stopped by or messaged me in the last hour, footsteps rushed up the stairs a short while later. T.J. walked through the door. "I was hoping to find you here," she said. She'd changed her clothes, now wearing leggings and a black Orioles hoodie.

"I thought you went home."

"I did. Got a little rest and a shower. Now, I'm ready to work again." When I didn't answer, she added, "I need this."

"All right," I said. "Let's get back to work."

———

"What about properties?" T.J. wanted to know. We were only a few minutes into our search. "Not in Hinson's name. Maybe his wife's or some other family member."

"Gonzalez can check all those," I said. "I'm sure somebody's uncle has a house out in the sticks. Pretty easy to ask deputies in another county to stop by and check on things. We're not adding any value there."

She nodded. "The country club, too, then. He might be a member, but it's not a place he could hole up long term . . . and even if he could, the cops would already be on it."

"Right. The cops can take care of the obvious. People hire us because we can do more."

"You know we've been fired, right?" my assistant pointed out.

"I remember. I still want to close this out and make Hinson pay even if we're not going to earn another dime in the process."

"Me, too."

I checked the website for Hinson and wife's curriculum business. The *About Us* page showed an email address and phone number. I dialed it, but no one picked up, and there was no voice-mail prompt. Earlier, I'd used an archived version to deduce the CEO of the company was Melanie DeBerg. I found the same page again, but it also lacked any physical address. Returning to the live site, I poked around in developer mode but still didn't see anything of use.

Back on *About Us*, one of the links proclaimed, "Stay current on our curriculum efforts—join our mailing list today!" One more bit of spam getting consigned to the bin wouldn't hurt, so I clicked and entered an email I only use for situations like this. If Hinson and wife were compliant with current US law, they would need to include some form of physical address in the footer of the message. This could be something like a mailbox in a shipping store, but it would be a start.

A moment later, the email arrived. I opened it and scrolled to the bottom. Sure enough, they included an address, and it looked like a real one. I punched it into Google Maps. It sat at the end of a strip mall in east Baltimore. The street view showed the entire complex to be in disrepair with a few vacancies. The Hinsons' alleged location looked unoccupied, but even if they didn't use it regularly, the principal could be hiding out there now.

I called my cousin Rich and told him what I'd uncovered. "You know I work in homicide, right?"

"This involved two murders. Is there a double homicide division? Baltimore might need one. I could try them instead."

He sighed, barked, "Text me the address," and ended the call. I sent it to him. Once I did, I apprised Gonzalez of what we found.

"Holy shit," he said. "They might be the first people to get caught because they're actually following the law."

"We'll see what happens when we get there," I said. "No guarantees anyone's even set foot in there for months."

"Your cousin going to be there?"

"Someone will. I texted him the address."

"Let me know when we're going in."

I told him I would. A short while later, Rich sent a message. *Thirty minutes.* I passed the info on to Gonzalez who promptly complained about the drive time from the county.

You have a light bar, siren, and a V8. Figure it out.

His response was uncharitable, but I knew he'd be there in time.

———

Despite her objections, I left T.J. at the office. "You've already been chased by men with bats today," I told her. "If we run into people at this place, they could have guns."

"I've been shot at before."

"I know. I was with you. Here I thought you'd want to avoid repeating it."

"Yes, sir," she said in a sarcastic tone. "The dainty little flower will stay here while the manly menfolk handle everything."

"You want to come along in the future?" I said. "Put in time at the range. I had to. Rich still didn't want me there a few times, but I've proven I'm a good shot." She still grumbled, but I grabbed my bullet-resistant vest and left. My office was already in the eastern half of the city, so it wasn't a bad drive. Friday night traffic clustered in the predictable spots. A few minutes before the appointed hour, I pulled into the lot. The businesses which remained open were a sub shop, Chinese restaurant, cell phone store, and a hobby shop. The latter was the most crowded. Based on the outlines of letters remaining on facades, I identified one of the defunct stores as an electronics repair place. It stood to the immediate right of the Hinson property, sharing an adjoining interior wall.

The Hinsons' address looked like no one had trod inside in quite some time. Long dirty windows covered most of the interior, and the door was more glass than metal. Other than the lack of cleanliness, it was a typical setup for a place like this. The interior remained completely dark, and two of the three lights on the overhang near the door no longer worked. Rich and a couple of uniforms walked out of the hobby shop. "They have a few games going on," he said. "The owner told me he's been here three years and never seen anyone go in or out of the end unit."

"Not conclusive," I said as I slipped the vest over my head. "I doubt anyone's in there, but they could get into the place at odd hours. I'm sure it has a back door."

"It does. We've apprised all the other businesses there could be gunfire. None of them chose to evacuate."

Another car rolled up. Gonzalez and a uniformed BCPD officer got out. After a round of pleasantries, Rich brought everyone up to speed. "Uniforms will enter via the rear door. The rest of us will go in through the front. It's unoccupied as far as we can tell, but we don't know for certain. It's possible there's a lower level where someone could hide out and not draw attention."

"Weapons check," Gonzalez said. I'd brought my 9MM—a little more accurate for me plus greater capacity than the .45, both qualities I valued in a potential firefight—and confirmed all was in good working order. Gonzalez, Rich, and I flattened ourselves against the front of the defunct repair shop next door. The three men in different shades of blue ran around to the rear. One of them carried a battering ram.

Rich's radio crackled to life. "We're in position, Lieutenant."

"We'll break the glass and go in," Rich told us. Into his comms, he said, "Roger. Prepare to breach."

CHAPTER 28

THE TALLER of the two officers shattered the glass with a quick swat from his baton. He used the stick to brush any lingering shards away, then reached inside and unlocked the door. Guns drawn, we all crept inside. No alarm shrieked at our presence despite a window sticker proclaiming the place to be monitored. Rich found a switch to the right of the door, and light sort of filled the room. Three rows of long fluorescent bulbs in the ceiling were supposed to provide the candlepower, but about a third of them remained dark.

The illumination the tubes offered was enough to see no one hid here. A few shelves held nothing but dust and cobwebs. A couple cardboard boxes formed a short pile against the left wall. Other than these, there was not a person in sight and nothing of note. The uniforms who breached the rear scrutinized the area and soon lowered their guns. "Clear," one of them said, apparently needing to make the official pronouncement.

I remembered entering a similar building with Rich over three years ago. Like this one, it had been a retail space, but its previous tenant converted it to a church. While the space appeared empty, a trapdoor in the floor led to a small basement where two men hid. Two area rugs covered portions of bare concrete. "Let's look under those," I said, pointing to a blue and red-striped number which even Ikea would have been too embarrassed to sell. "Make sure there's no lower level."

Two men pulled rugs while four stood with guns ready. As the originator of the idea, I opted not to do the minor manual labor. It didn't matter. The covered portions of the floor were as bare as the rest. Rich replaced his weapon with his phone and fired off a text. "I've passed on all their information," he said. "Every jurisdiction in the state has it now. They won't be able to get on a plane, train, or bus." I found this unlikely—especially the part about the bus—but kept quiet. "The state police will share it with our neighbors to the north and south. Someone will find these people."

"It should be us," Gonzalez said. "One of us," he added when Rich crossed his arms.

"How did you find this address, anyway?" my cousin asked.

"I signed up for Hinson's company's emails," I said. "Federal law requires an address at the bottom. Working in education, I'm sure he's very familiar with regulatory compliance."

Rich snickered. "First time your explanation has been so mundane."

"Glad I could accommodate you. I'm more concerned with where Hinson is now."

"We put people on properties," Gonzalez said. "Any in his name, his wife's, or anyone in their families. It's probably long odds, but they could still turn up at one of those spots."

The way this played out probably did not fit T.J.'s sarcastic description of the manly menfolk handling things. I still didn't want her involved in potential shootouts, but maybe she could contribute in other ways. "I'm going to head back to the office," I said. "You all clearly need a brilliant epiphany to bring this home, and I'm the best candidate."

"Thanks for gracing us with your presence," Rich said, performing a mock bow.

"You got a secretary now, right?" Gonzalez said. I nodded. "Must mean it's her turn to think of something smart."

"We charge the same rate no matter who has the good ideas," I said.

———

"So you didn't end up saving the day?" T.J. said.

"Not exactly," I admitted.

"And now the manly menfolk need another perspective."

"You don't have to sound like you're enjoying this so much."

T.J. grinned. "Why don't you make us some coffee, and we can strategize?"

"You're fired," I said as I plucked the old filter out of the machine and dropped it into the nearby wastebasket. A couple minutes later, glorious brown liquid gurgled into the waiting pot. "Rich said every police agency in the state is going to be looking for the Hinsons. They shouldn't be able to flee, but he's more confident there than I am."

"All the houses are covered?"

"Gonzalez said they were."

My assistant frowned in thought. While she pondered the present predicament, I logged back into my computer. None of my Google alerts got tripped. I couldn't find an obvious electronic trail for the Hinsons. With time, I could probably get into their phones, but they were smart enough to switch to burners. "Hinson brought Gerald into the school," T.J. said after the coffee finished brewing.

"You mentioned it."

"And they disappeared."

"Or at least went somewhere the cameras couldn't follow," I

said. "I'm sure Hinson knows the dead zones in the coverage."

"There can't be many," T.J. grumbled. "I've popped into every building. It's hard to go anywhere unseen."

I poured us each a cup. T.J. glanced at her steaming java, but I could tell she was stumped. "Could they have gone outside? The fields wouldn't necessarily be part of the system."

She shook her head, and her blonde ponytail wagged. "I never saw them leave. All the entrance and exit doors are covered . . . often by more than one camera. They couldn't have headed out for a walk without me seeing them."

"We need to go back to the school," I said. It would be closed now, and all the staff and workers either already home or on their ways. I thought about the groundskeeper I'd talked to during my first extended excursion to the Sterner campus. He seemed to have fond memories of Marcy Russell and not much love in his heart for Anthony Hinson. "I met a groundskeeper or landscaper while I was there. He let me in and told me how to get to Rachel Heaton's office without anyone seeing me."

"Let's not wait for tomorrow," T.J. said, perking up when I mentioned her temporary boss. "Maybe Rachel knows. She's been in her post a while, and she definitely thinks Hinson is a prick." T.J. took out her phone and dialed a number. Rachel must have answered quickly. "Hi, it's T.J. Question . . . is there some place on campus a person might go to hole up? It would need to be in a dead zone for the cameras, I guess." She paused periodically to listen to Rachel's responses. I could make out a voice but no words. "You've been a help this far, so I'll tell you. We think Hinson is hiding somewhere, and it's no place obvious enough for the police to know about and check. Really?" Her brows arched. "And how would we find it? Hang on." She covered the mouthpiece with her hand. "Rachel has an idea, and she offered to show us."

"She can't just tell us where it is?"

"Maybe she wants to watch Hinson go down."

"I'd prefer she did it without getting shot," I said. "We don't even know if he's there, but if he is, he might have multiple people and guns with him."

"C.T. is concerned for your safety," she said into the phone. A grin came over her face a few seconds later. "She wants you to know she doesn't need your protection. The patriarchy isn't a shield."

"Tell her to print the goddamn bumper stickers." T.J. sat in silence. I rolled my eyes. There was no way my assistant—or her temporary boss, apparently—would sit this one out. I hoped I could get them to stay out of the way once we actually got into wherever the hell Hinson was supposed to be. "Fine. I'll tell Gonzalez. It'll probably take him a little while to assemble a team."

"Can you meet us there in an hour?" T.J. asked Rachel. She gave me a thumbs up before thanking the other woman and ending the call. "See? The manly menfolk just needed the women to come in and sort things out for them."

"You want to do what I do? Sort out getting yourself a vest and a gun."

"You'd still be protective of me."

"I would," I admitted, "but at least you'd have a chance to shoot back."

"For now, let's just find Hinson, Gerald, and anyone else hiding out at that damn school."

"Yes. Let's."

———

I found an older bullet-resistant vest for T.J. to put on. "The best strategy is try not to get hit," I said as we drove toward The Sterner Academy. The major crack in the S4's windshield was slightly toward the passenger's side of center. It didn't really affect my view of the road.

"Wow. You should teach this shit."

I grinned. "I meant I've had the vest for a while. Kevlar has a shelf life. It won't be as durable as a new model."

"I don't think anyone is going to shoot at me," she said.

"I'd rather not see any bullets fly at all."

We hit the long driveway a few minutes ahead of schedule. Despite being a bit early, six BCPD cruisers and one obvious unmarked car waited in the main loop near the visitor's spots. Since the cops did it, I, too, eschewed the lined spaces and left the S4 in the middle of the road. T.J. slipped the vest on and cinched the Velcro as tight as it would go. Another car approached after we got out. "She's with us," I told Gonzalez. "An escort."

"You couldn't talk her out of coming?" he said. "She coulda told you where the room is."

"I tried. Something something patriarchy."

The sergeant grinned. "I always knew you were a chauvinist pig."

"Oink oink," I said. Several of the cops nearby—men comprised the entire contingent—enjoyed a chuckle at the exchange. T.J. held her tongue and broke off from the pack to meet Rachel Heaton as she approached. The exterior lights of the school gave off enough glow for everyone to notice Rachel's yoga pants. Gonzalez leaned over and checked her out as she walked past. "Who's rolling in the mud now?" I whispered to him.

He shrugged and grinned as Rachel opened the front door, held up a hand to keep us outside, and deactivated the alarm. While the police getting summoned wouldn't be a big deal, we still didn't need the system going off and potentially attracting the attention of the neighbors. So far, the cover of darkness and the absence of red and blue police lights made for a nondescript evening. I hoped it remained one.

"The janitorial staff has a room where they keep supplies," Rachel said. "It's half a converted classroom, so it's not too big. There's a way into the basement from there. If our esteemed principal is here, my guess is that's where he'll be." Her tone strongly suggested she viewed Hinson with the opposite of esteem.

"A basement?" Gonzalez asked.

"The main building is the oldest. I think it was used as a fallout shelter decades ago. Since then, it's been repurposed. The newer buildings sit on top of slabs."

"Can you get us into the janitors' room?"

"No," Rachel said. "I have keys for the primary buildings and my office but nothing else."

"I can get us past it quietly," I said. A burly uniformed officer looked disappointed he wouldn't get to swing his battering ram and smash down a door tonight.

"Let's go, then," Gonzalez said. We all followed Rachel Heaton—some of the officers expressing unabashed interest in her Spandex-covered bottom—to the far side of the admin building.

"Cameras stop here," she said, pointing overhead to a smoky plastic half-cylinder mounted into the ceiling. "That one captures the next classroom but nothing beyond."

"What does it miss?"

"Nothing that's usually important. I don't know how many people are aware of it, but I would bet Anthony Hinson is."

We passed a door to the outside. It was labeled *Fire Exit*, but someone could come in, appear briefly on a single camera, and disappear. It would be a convenient way to sneak in a buddy or two for a weekend of hiding underground. Bring your own snacks. Entertainment not provided. "There," Rachel said, pointing to the last door on the right. I owned a special keyring— burglar's tools—which I learned to use during my time in Hong Kong. They can take a bit of time bypassing good locks, however, so I invested in a snap gun. It doesn't have the precision of my illicit implements, but it's faster if a bit louder.

I opened the main lock quickly and stepped aside. Gonzalez led the way as six armed officers went in with guns drawn. "Clear," one of them whispered almost immediately. "Nothing but shelves, supplies, and another door."

"That will take you downstairs," Rachel said. "The steps are wooden, so they might squeak. I'd appreciate if you'd let me leave before you go any further." Her eyes fell on me. "I'd prefer not to be around if there's going to be any shooting."

"Thank you," I said.

She smiled and stopped in front of T.J. "I guess I won't be seeing you again. You're a damn good secretary. Make sure he pays you like one."

"I will," she said, and even though I paid her well, I kept my mouth shut. Rachel left. T.J. rolled her eyes as a few cops ogled the older woman's departing form.

I moved into the custodial room. Shelves of supplies lined the left wall. Boxes were stacked neatly near the back. Mop buckets made it hard to navigate all the way to the rear. The door was at the end of the wall on the right. I again popped the lock quickly and flattened myself out so the cops could pass me. This time, I replaced my snap gun and drew the one which would serve me better in a firefight.

"You're not coming," Gonzalez whispered to T.J. She frowned but possessed the good sense not to protest. The sergeant pointed to a uniform who looked to be the youngest of the bunch. "Stay here with her. If all hell breaks loose, you're up." The officer nodded.

"Let's try to be quiet," Gonzalez continued. "We may have lost the element of surprise, but I'd like to take any assholes down here alive. Now, let's go."

We went.

GONZALEZ and most of his men led the way down the steps. I was second from the rear, the youngest remaining officer of the bunch trailing me. The stairs emptied to a long and wide basement. Rachel Heaton mentioned it served as a fallout shelter decades ago. This made sense. The area was certainly big enough to fit hundreds of teachers, staff, and students in the event of an emergency.

It wasn't nearly so crowded, however.

About a hundred feet from the steps, three cots sat in the middle of the room. A door—probably to a restroom—split the wall on the left. Anthony Hinson and Gerald Russell stared at our contingent with surprise. A third man stood near them and held a pistol. "Drop it, Bradley," Gonzalez ordered. Joshua Bradley froze. His presence here made sense—he'd played a significant role in getting Edgar Russell wrongfully imprisoned for Marcy's murder.

Bradley was about my height, a little broader in the shoulders, and wore his blond hair short. His blue eyes darted around as the cops with me fanned out into a semicircle. A scowl twisted his face. For all I knew, it was his default expression. "I'm not letting you take me, Sergeant," he said.

"I surrender," Hinson said. He raised his hands. Somehow, he managed to look down his nose at everyone. "None of you need to brutalize me. I have a very good lawyer."

"You rich assholes always do," I said.

"Mister Ferguson. You're a persistent pest."

"I don't think I'll be investing in your company after all, Tony. No need to diversify into the 'CEO is in jail for murder' market."

One of the officers put his gun away and approached Hinson. He barked an order, the disgraced principal lowered his arms, and the cuffs went on. The two headed to the stairs, Gonzalez's man keeping hold of Hinson's left arm as they moved. "I surrender, too," Gerald declared, raising his hands.

"Your own mother," I said, and he lowered his gaze. "I hope you get the treatment you deserve in prison."

Gerald soon joined Hinson in cuffs, and another officer led him toward the steps. This left four of Baltimore County's finest and me to stand off against Joshua Bradley, whose expression didn't change even as his compatriots abandoned him. "Looks like you're alone now," Gonzalez said. "Make it easy on yourself. You didn't kill anyone."

"Cops don't do well in prison," he said.

"They do even worse in the morgue," I pointed out. As much as I didn't like Bradley for what he helped his friend Gerald Russell do, I also didn't want him to take the suicide by cop route.

"He's right," Gonzalez said. "Look, we have the mastermind and the son. Your role was pretty minor. You fudged some evidence and sent the wrong man to jail. Yeah, you'll have to pay for it, but we're not talking life in prison. You've been a solid officer since you joined the force. I'm sure you can get a deal."

Bradley spent several seconds looking between his own gun and the ones pointed at him. His weapon remained pointed at the floor. If he raised it, everyone would fire on him—me included.

His face twitched, and his free hand shook. Even the one holding the pistol trembled a little. "Don't do it," Gonzalez said. "Put the gun down, and we can all walk out of here."

"I'll go to jail." Bradley continued to hang onto the gun. I stood on the far right of the semicircle. I jerked my head to the open space, and Gonzalez offered a fractional nod in reply.

"I told you," the sergeant said, "you're not looking at serious charges like they are." I slowly moved away. Bradley, focused on Gonzalez, didn't seem to notice me. Once I was more than ninety degrees past him, I slipped my 9MM away and stalked to his rear. "You probably have some good intel to share on what happened."

"Great," Bradley said. "I'll be a cop *and* a rat in jail."

Talking him down wasn't going well. So far, he hadn't noticed me. Enough light came from in front of him so I wouldn't cast a shadow. I was four steps away. Three.

"Let's just talk about it," Gonzalez said.

One step.

I closed the remaining distance, grabbed Bradley's wrist, and barred his arm. When he struggled, I kicked him in the back of the leg, driving him to one knee. His pistol remained pointed at the concrete. Gonzalez and a uniform rushed in to subdue him. Once he was under control, we all filed back out the same way we came in. When our contingent rejoined T.J. and the remaining officer on the main level, I got in Hinson's face. He tried to look me in the eye but averted his gaze. "You fired Edgar Russell for some 'conduct unbecoming' bullshit." He offered no reaction. "How would you rate your own fucking conduct, you prick?" Again, silence was the only reply.

I didn't expect anything different.

From The Sterner Academy, we followed the expansive BCPD convoy back to Towson. It would take a little time to get everyone situated, so T.J. and I drove several minutes past the precinct, bought a box of donuts, and headed back. "Aren't you kind of leaning into a stereotype?" she asked.

I shrugged as I parked the S4 and cut the engine. "If a donut makes Gonzalez a little more positively disposed toward us, our excursion was worth it." We headed inside to find things still in motion. Bradley was nowhere to be seen—they probably did his intake separately in the basement—while Hinson and Gerald Russell sat frowning near interview rooms. Gonzalez was not in his office. Hinson crowed for his lawyer a few times, and he kept it up even when the desk sergeant told him they'd already made the call.

Leaving T.J. in charge of the baked goods, I investigated the coffee situation, found it dreadful, and made a fresh pot. When it was finished, I filled two styrofoam cups and handed one to my assistant. "At this hour?" she said. Despite her mild objection, she accepted the cup and soon took a sip. Because Gonzalez and crew were still tied up, T.J. and I got dibs on the donuts of our choice—glazed for her and a French cruller for me.

A few minutes later, Gonzalez stormed back to his office. "Miserable prick," he muttered.

"This is how you talk to someone who brought donuts?" I said. "I even made coffee."

He rolled his eyes. "I meant Hinson and his goddamn lawyer." He jerked his chin at the box. "You buy those to bribe me into letting you watch what happens?"

"For as much as they cost now, I certainly hope so."

"You can see it on a monitor. Can't let you in."

"Rich sometimes lets me sit in," I pointed out.

"Your cousin is a fucking softie, then," Gonzalez said. "Defense lawyers love irregularities. No matter what role you played, you're not getting a seat at the table." He opened the box and plucked a chocolate glazed. "If watching in another room isn't good enough, feel free to go home."

"We'll stay."

"Great. Too bad you didn't bring any popcorn."

After a short delay, a female officer in plain clothes wearing her badge like a pendant invited us into an unused office. The only furniture was two chairs and a desk. A twenty-seven-inch monitor stood atop a desktop computer which sat on its side. An HDMI cable ran from the wall into the monitor, and the screen showed the interior of an interview room. Anthony Hinson sat next to a man with an expensive suit and sour expression. Gonzalez popped in after T.J. and I sat. "Use the keyboard to switch rooms. This is number one. You want the other, hit two."

"Got it," I said.

"You computer guys catch on quick," he said before heading off. On the screen, he walked into the interview room with Hinson. Gonzalez fiddled with something on the desk. The resolution wasn't the best, but I figured it was a recorder. "This is Sergeant Gonzalez conducting an initial interview with Anthony Hinson. His attorney is present." Gonzalez rattled off the date and time before getting down to brass tacks. "How's the curriculum business?"

"My client is a consultant for his wife's company," the lawyer said in a voice suggesting he had a background in radio.

"What's the official corporate position on people who might stand in your way?" Neither man on the other side of the table offered a response. Gonzalez continued. "As far as I can tell, the policy seems to be murdering them. Councilman Ellicott and a teacher at your own school . . . who, might I add, was going to resign and run for the school board." Hinson frowned when Marcy Russell came up but otherwise offered no reaction.

"Is there a question in there?" the lawyer asked with a sneer.

"You goddamn well heard it." Accused and attorney leaned close and whispered back and forth. "My client is prepared to offer you certain information in exchange for charge and specific sentence agreements."

"This should be good." Gonzalez crossed his arms and leaned back as much as the chair would allow. "What's he want?"

"Full immunity for himself and his wife," the lawyer said. "In exchange, he'll tell you everything about the scheme, Mister Russell's involvement, and the role investors played."

I wondered where Melanie DeBerg went. If Gonzalez knew her whereabouts, he didn't offer anything. "Full immunity?" he said. "Go jump in a fucking lake."

The attorney spread his hands. "I'm afraid my client has nothing to say, then. I'd like to know what charges are going to be brought."

"You know it's not up to me. I'll be recommending murder, conspiracy to commit murder, several financial crimes, obstruction of justice . . . they'll be enough to put your client away for the rest of his life."

"I'm not hearing any evidence."

"We have your co-conspirator Gerald Russell," Gonzalez said, turning to address Hinson directly. "We also have the man he used to help get his father arrested. I'm pretty sure they're going to sing like canaries. Who do you think they're going to tell me masterminded all this?"

"My wife is the company CEO," Hinson said.

"Jesus, what a prick," I said. "Throwing his wife under the bus."

T.J. nodded. "She's probably involved . . . but still. What a snake. Sounds like they deserve each other."

A few minutes of fruitless exchanges followed. Despite the grim situation Hinson faced, his attorney wouldn't budge. Someone rapped on the interview room door. The woman in plain clothes entered, whispered something to Gonzalez, and then left. "I'll reiterate my earlier question," the sergeant said. "This time, I'll be more direct. Did you and/or your wife orchestrate a plan to murder Councilman Ellicott and Marcy Russell?"

"I believe we've covered this already," his lawyer said.

"All right. Have it your way." Gonzalez stood. "By the way, New York State Police arrested Melanie DeBerg. She's being extradited back to Maryland." Hinson's head dropped, and he put his hands over his face. Being in the room would have made his defeated reaction much more enjoyable. It was still nice to see on the monitor, but I felt a little removed from what went on nearby. I understood Gonzalez's reasoning, though. "My understanding is she's willing to cooperate with the investigation. I guess you lose."

"Wait just a minute," the attorney demanded, but Gonzalez walked out of the room.

CHAPTER 30

T.J. DROVE BACK to her apartment once C.T. dropped her off at the office.

Watching Hinson and his attorney come to their senses and confess to what happened was satisfying. He offered up the person who did the actual killings—someone recommended by an investor who used the same man to murder a mistress the prior year. Gonzalez was pleased to solve a third crime. Still, T.J. felt tired. This had been a long day of working both jobs around being chased by angry men with bats. She pulled into her lot, parked her Mustang, and went inside. It felt great to sink into her couch. She let out a sigh and closed her eyes. The events of the day—and amount of caffeine consumed—left her wired enough that her foot bobbed even while lying down.

Despite the late hour, she called Edgar Russell. When he answered, he didn't sound like he'd been sleeping. "Mister Russell, this is T.J. I work with C.T. Ferguson." Her boss would have noticed her choice of prepositions.

"Yes. What can I do for you?"

"First, I'm glad to hear you got released. We're sorry that happened to you."

"It did feel like adding insult to injury," he said. "At least I was able to reschedule Marcy's memorial under the circumstances."

"I have some good news."

"I'm certainly in need of some." While Edgar didn't sound tired, not a single iota of happiness came over the connection. His voice was beaten down and depressed—for obvious reasons, but T.J. hoped he'd be able to move on with time.

"We caught Anthony Hinson tonight," she said. "Police also arrested an officer who was involved in the scheme, along with Hinson's wife, and . . . I'm sorry to say . . . your son."

Edgar sighed and didn't say anything for several seconds. When he did, T.J. struggled to hear him. "What did Gerald do?"

"He didn't want to be in the classroom like you or Marcy, so he ended up working on curriculum development. Anthony Hinson had similar ideas, and he and his wife owned a company trying to get something in place in the county and then across Maryland."

"Hmm." Another pause. "Killing the councilman makes sense, I guess. If you're a bastard, of course. Why my wife?" Tears broke his voice. "Why my Marcy?"

T.J. now wondered if her call did more harm than good to the grieving man, but she'd started down the road already. She needed to bring it home. "I'm not sure if she told you. If she didn't, I hate the fact that I'm doing it now. Your wife wanted to resign and run for the school board. A big item on her agenda would be blocking a new curriculum in the county."

"I had no idea," Edgar said, his voice a breathy whisper.

"My boss and I found a blog she maintained. A few of her coworkers confirmed it. If people in the building knew, Hinson must have learned about it."

"He and my son then decided to take out two threats and discredit them at the same time." He fell silent for a few seconds again. "Do you know if my wife ever even met the councilman?"

"Not as far as we can tell," T.J. said.

"Some comfort at least." Edgar sighed again. "I've lost my wife and now my son. I'm not sure I can keep working at Sterner after what Hinson did. None of this is on you, of course. I'm glad you were in my corner even though I never hired you."

"We don't like seeing assholes get away with things."

"Fortunate for me, certainly," Edgar said. "Thank you for calling. I . . . don't know how much sleep I'll get tonight. It's been pretty sparse since everything happened. Knowing you caught everyone might help me a little."

"I hope it does." T.J. ended the call. She still didn't know if she did the right thing, but the man needed to know. Even with the involvement of his son, hopefully Edgar could move on from the horrible events of the past couple weeks.

———

The next morning, T.J. woke up early. The events of yesterday afternoon and evening—plus her late-night chat with Edgar Russell—made for a fitful night. Around 7:45, she stopped trying to fall back asleep. A quick trip to her balcony told her it was a chilly morning, so she changed into athletic clothes and headed to the fitness center.

Only one other person—a girl T.J. knew to be a college student—used the place at this hour. The two smiled at each other, and then the other young woman resumed her work on the lat pulldown machine. T.J. stepped onto a treadmill, warmed up with a moderate walk for five minutes, and ramped up the speed to a nice running pace. She'd never had to worry about fitness as a teen—so long as she looked pretty, men would pick her—but in her current job, it mattered more.

T.J. flashed back to yesterday. Men chasing her with bats. Avoiding a few strikes which came too close for comfort. She was able to outrun them for a while, but she got tired before they did. Building her stamina was the next thing. After about ten minutes at six miles per hour, T.J. cut the speed in half for a few minutes, caught her breath, and went back to the faster pace. When she finished with a cooldown after a second ten-minute session, a nice sheen of sweat covered her skin.

Back in her apartment, T.J. dug out the heavy bag and set it up. She slipped her gloves on and fired off some jabs to loosen her arms up. Her phone buzzed. Melinda called. T.J. put in earbuds and answered while continuing to throw punches. "I saw the news reports online this morning," her mentor said. "Another successful case."

"This one was tough." T.J. worked in crosses with her jabs, alternating between the two. "I survived my first undercover gig."

Melinda sighed. "You know I don't like it when you put yourself in danger like that."

"I was the PTA president's secretary for a few days," T.J. said. "It's not a high-stress position. The access it gave me to the school ended up being really important." She deliberately omitted the men pursuing her through the neighborhood. Melinda's big heart made her a worrier, and even though T.J. no longer received any services from the Nightlight Foundation, she knew Melinda would always be protective of her.

"That's good to hear," Melinda said.

"I talked to the husband of the murdered teacher last night. Poor man. He buries his wife, and then, it turns out his son was involved the whole time. I wanted to tell him we caught everyone, but I don't think it helped him to hear it."

"It probably did. I'm sure he's going through difficulties we can't imagine, so even if he didn't sound grateful, I think he'll get there eventually. It might be a long road, and he may need some help along the way."

"I hope he gets it, then," T.J. said. She added a hook to her punching sequence now.

"Are you exercising?"

"Hitting the bag."

"Sounds like it," Melinda said. "You know I'm fond of saying people are only ready when they're ready. The man you talked to is in that boat. What you told him will matter a great deal even though his son was involved."

"I hope so," T.J. said.

"I'll let you get back to your workout. I just wanted to congratulate you."

"Thanks, Melinda." T.J. ended the call. She didn't feel like receiving congratulations at the moment, and she took this frustration out on the bag.

CHAPTER 31

I WOKE up the next morning to an empty bed.

This was unusual. My phone told me it was 9:18. I rarely got to sleep past about eight-thirty these days. Regardless of what day it was, I couldn't recall the last time Gloria got up before I did. After tending to my morning duties, I headed downstairs to find my wife sitting at the dining room table. The smell of coffee greeted me as I walked through the kitchen.

Armed with a steaming mug, I joined Gloria. She pushed a newspaper toward me and smiled. "It ran today."

"What is this relic?" I held the copy of the *Sun* up by the corner like it might bite me.

"I went out and bought a copy this morning," she said. "Got bagels, too. You should check the kitchen again."

"You're out of bed before me," I said, "and you bought a newspaper." I rubbed my chin. "If this is a mirror universe, shouldn't I have an evil goatee?"

My wife grinned. "You know you can't grow facial hair in any reality."

"You're probably right." I opened the paper and found Claire's article in the local section. *A NEW FORCE IN FUNDRAISING* ran along with a picture of Gloria standing in front of a building I couldn't place. She crossed her arms and put on her best don't-fuck-with-me expression. "Hashtag girlboss."

"We took so many photos," Gloria said. "I was a little surprised she ran that one."

"Maybe you'll pick up some clients because they're afraid of you."

"I'll take it."

I read the article. Claire did a good job profiling Gloria, going into her background, listing her money-raising accomplishments, and adding very little about her husband. For once, I was happy to settle into the background. This was her moment. "Excellent. I'm proud of you. Part of me wishes she'd called you the fundraising star of the city."

"That's your phrase," Gloria said.

"We could've worked out a licensing deal."

She chuckled. "Go eat a bagel."

I found a multigrain one, toasted it, and added butter and strawberry preserves. Four more remained in the bag. As I ate, my phone rang. I got up from the table to take the call, which came as a surprise. "Who was that?" Gloria wanted to know when I walked back in.

"Paula Ellicott. They heard what happened and want to stop by the office."

"I guess you should go in since you're late. When are they stopping by?"

"They're going to come in around eleven."

"Shouldn't you make sure T.J.'s there, too?"

"I hope she got some rest after yesterday." I dialed her number, and she answered quickly. "The Ellicotts want to stop by and thank us. Are you in the office?"

"Are they thanking us with a check?" she said.

"We'll see," I said. "I didn't ask."

"I was about to head in anyway."

"I'll bring breakfast." She didn't say anything. "Yesterday was rough. You good?"

"I'll be all right," she said, and I wasn't sure I believed her. "See you at eleven." She ended the call. I finished my coffee, showered, and got dressed. With a former client possibly bringing money, I opted for pressed chinos over jeans, combining a tan pair with a French blue sweater. After kissing Gloria goodbye, I bagged up two bagels and drove to the office, arriving about fifteen minutes before the appointed hour. No sign of T.J.'s Mustang yet. I headed upstairs and opened the office.

T.J. arrived while the coffee still brewed. She looked at my clothes and smirked. "Gloria take you shopping at J. Crew?"

"Tommy Hilfiger," I said, "and I bought these myself."

She found the bag of bagels on her desk, opened it, and took out a plain one. I probably should have made sure we had something to put on it. T.J. dropped it into the small toaster, found some butter in the fridge, and ate the bagel with her coffee a few minutes later. "Thanks."

"Sure. What's got you salty today?"

"I talked to Edgar Russell last night. Wanted to tell him what happened."

"Sounds like he didn't take it well," I said.

"I'm not sure how he could." She sighed. "I don't know what I expected, really."

"He's been through a lot. He'll come around. It'll take him some time, and he'll probably need help along the way, but he'll get there."

"I hope so." I glanced at my watch. Eleven on the dot. "They're due any minute."

T.J. shoved the enormous remaining piece of bagel in her mouth. She managed to avoid choking on it. "Ready to go," she said after sipping some coffee and wiping her mouth.

A moment later, footsteps rang on the metal steps.

Susan and Paula Ellicott opened the door. Last time, they dealt with the BCPD not doing much with Raymond's recent death, so they wore black. This time, both came clad in brighter colors. Susan opted for a red sweater and jeans, while Paula paired her dark denim with a gray shirt bearing a picture of a large pumpkin. It made me wonder when T.J. would start decorating for Halloween. I left her in charge of making the office look seasonal, and she always did a great job.

"Welcome back," my assistant said.

"Nice to be here again," Susan said.

"And this time under happier circumstances," Paula added. "We really weren't expecting much once the police arrested someone."

"It usually helps when they put the right person in cuffs," I said. We'd informed the women how we seriously doubted Edgar, and while I didn't come out and say, "I told you so," Susan's frown told me she inferred it in my tone. Correctly, I might add.

"We appreciate you sticking with it," Susan said as she and Paula sat in my guest chairs. T.J. grabbed hers and wheeled it toward our little group.

"Did the police tell you?" I asked.

"Yes. I think his name was Gonzalez. Same fellow who was working on the case before. I asked him if he was positive they'd arrested the right people this time." She chuckled. "He insisted they were. I asked if he got any help. He was squirrely about it, but when I mentioned you by name, he told me you found some important information."

"I don't think those guys even knew my dad," Paula said. "All this over some new curriculum they wanted to put in schools?"

"It could have made them millions," I said. "People get killed for far less every day."

"What information did you uncover?" Susan wanted to know.

"We were sure we knew the people involved. Once I convinced Gonzalez he'd put the wrong man behind bars, we kept digging. I found an address which turned out to be a dead end, but then we thought Hinson might choose to hide at the school somewhere."

"I'd been there undercover for a few days," T.J. said, taking over when I paused. She'd done the legwork on this part, so telling the tale fell to her. "The PTA president put me to work as her secretary. When I asked her if there was some place no one knew about to hide on campus, she pointed us right to it."

"Hinson's wife had already fled," I added. "Last I heard, she was being extradited back to Maryland from New York. He should have joined her. She was the only one in the group with any sense."

"The poor man they arrested." Susan frowned again and shook her head. "He lost his wife, got accused of killing her, and then had to find out his son was involved."

"The son was always weird," T.J. said. "Bad vibes all around."

I thought about the time we called him after his father was arrested. It had been an odd conversation. One of his phrases popped into my head. *Maybe they're not this time. They told me the prints were solid.* "I think he was gloating . . . in his own unusual way."

"He could be on the spectrum," Paula said.

"Now, he can be on the spectrum in prison." I shrugged. "What he did and what he let happen erases any sympathy I might have for him."

Susan opened her brown purse and pulled out a small blue folio. I wondered if Paula and T.J. knew what it was. I couldn't recall the last time I'd written a check. Susan found a pen and dashed off a check to the business for a thousand dollars. "You don't need to," I said.

"We should have listened to you," Susan said. She signed it, tore it off, and handed it to me.

While her mother recorded the transaction on the ledger, Paula said, "I guess we were a little quick to let you go. Once we got the news of an arrest, we just wanted to put this whole mess behind us." Her eyes welled.

T.J. nudged a box of tissues closer. "We understand. Thank you."

"Thank *you*," Susan said. Mother and daughter stood. "You're doing really good work for people. Keep it up." She smiled. "Enjoy the weekend. We will . . . for the first time in a while."

After they left, T.J. looked at the check. "This was a nice surprise."

"Here's another one." I flipped it over, grabbed a pen, and signed it over to her. "For you. A bonus."

"Really?"

"Really."

"Is it just because I got chased by men with bats?"

"Maybe," I said. "If they had knives, I'd need to pay you fifteen hundred. There's a hazard pay scale online somewhere."

She grinned and took the small piece of paper, folding it and slipping it into her pocket. "Thanks, boss."

"Don't mention it."

"You know I'm going to buy some Halloween decorations with it, right?"

"Please do. You're in charge of all festivities."

"Maybe I need a raise to go along with all this responsibility," she suggested.

"Maybe you should stop while you're ahead." I leaned back

in my chair. "I'll do one more thing for you, though. Because I'm such a nice boss, I'll let you take the upcoming weekend off."

"I normally have Saturdays and Sundays off," T.J. said.

"Don't ruin the moment by being an ingrate," I said.

END of novel #15.

C.T.'s next case leaves him as cold as the weather. When the snow falls across Baltimore, the bodies of women fall with it, and no one knows who's responsible. Can C.T. figure it out before T.J. involves herself to a dangerous degree? Preorder *Bleeding into Winter* today!

THE END

AFTERWORD

Thanks for checking out this novel! I hope you enjoyed reading the book as much as I enjoyed writing it.

I write mysteries and thrillers with action, snark, and flawed heroes. If this sounds like something you like, you can check out my catalog below.

The C.T. Ferguson Crime Novels:

1. The Reluctant Detective
2. The Unknown Devil
3. The Workers of Iniquity
4. Already Guilty
5. Daughters and Sons
6. A March from Innocence
7. Inside Cut
8. The Next Girl
9. In the Blood
10. Right as Rain
11. Dead Cat Bounce
12. Don't Say Her Name

13. Night Comes Down
14. Concrete Angels
15. Conduct Unbecoming
16. Bleeding into Winter (Summer 2024)

The John Tyler Action Thrillers

1. The Mechanic
2. White Lines
3. Lost Highway
4. Four on the Floor
5. Forced Induction
6. The Low Road
7. Backfire (Spring 2024)

I release 3-4 new novels per year. For the most current list of books, please visit:

- https://tomfowlerbooks.com - Direct sales
- www.tomfowlerwrites.com
- https://books2read.com/tomfowler

(**Note**: C.T. Ferguson appears in *White Lines*. John Tyler appears in *Don't Say Her Name*.)

While the suggested reading sequences appear above, each novel is a standalone mystery or thriller, and the books can be enjoyed in whatever order you happen upon them.

Connect with me:

For the many ways of finding and reaching me online, please visit https://tomfowlerwrites.com/contact. I'm always happy to talk to readers.

This is a work of fiction. Characters and places are either fictitious or used in a fictitious manner.

"Self-publishing" is something of a misnomer. This book would not have been possible without the contributions of many people.

- The great cover design team at 100 Covers.
- My editor extraordinaire, Chase Nottingham.
- My wonderful advance reader team, the Fell Street Irregulars.